THE YEAR OF THE FOX

A GOOD LIFE NOVEL

MERREN TAIT

LOLA PUBLICATIONS

Copyright 2019 Merren Tait.

Lola Publications. Raglan, New Zealand.

Print ISBN: 978-0-473-47626-7

Large print ISBN: 978-0-473-55522-1

Cover design by Bailey McGinn.

Author photo by Eleanor Gee.

www.merrentait.com

ONE
INTO THE BIG GREEN

I'M NANCY – mostly Nance, sometimes Nan, and when I'm unbearably endearing, Nancy Pants.

I'm not normally a contemplative person, but lately I've found myself ruminating on fences. A lot. Here's what I know: from where I stand (literally in front of my lounge window, metaphorically as an aggrieved neighbour) a good fence is a necessary comfort. It imposes order on the landscape. It offers a sense of protection. It separates.

My fence, or as I affectionately call it, The Line of Demarcation, is not a thing of beauty. It is constructed of wooden posts, rammed into the earth and joined by a series of wires. Simple, inelegant. And yet I have grown to appreciate it. I love the way the wires stretch into the distance in each direction, tapering off to a single point. I love their twang when my sheep rub up against the posts. And I love the fact that it says, without any need for verbalisation or habitual scent marking, *Back off. This is mine. That is yours.*

JANUARY.

It was on a sticky New Zealand mid-summer evening that I found myself crossing three fence lines (only one of which belonged to me) and courting a whole lot of over-the-fence trouble.

I had entered a patch of thick bush, full of tree ferns and leafy kawakawa, and could hear the babble of water running over rocks. I stepped through a screen of fern fronds to discover a stream running through a glade. The water was clear and tumbled over moss-covered rocks.

It was so picturesque in the soft evening light that I stood for several minutes drinking it in. A few metres downstream, the rocks had formed a partial dam, creating a pool, and I, uncomfortable from the day's dried sweat, felt there was little choice but to accept the water's invitation.

I removed my gumboots and clothes, peeled off my damp socks, and stepped tentatively into the water. It was gasp-inducingly cold, but boy was it good. Diving under, I swam the few strokes to the other side where the bank afforded a place to sit in the water. I set to work scrubbing the day's grime off, giving particular attention to the sourness of my armpits, then leaned back and closed my eyes, listening to the water's chatter.

"Ah, can I help you?" said a voice to my left.

"Fuck!" I replied and turned to see a man standing over my clothes and holding the ends of a towel draped around his neck. I covered my breasts with one arm and sat lower in the water. "Sorry. God, you gave me a fright."

"I gave *you* a fright? I come here every day after I've finished work, *on my farm*, and I don't expect to find anyone else." The light was behind him, so he was hard to make out, but I could see he was dressed in a singlet, shorts and gumboots, and that the top did a perfect job of showcasing his muscular arms. "You do know you're trespassing?"

"Yep. Sorry." The sibilance was lost among the din of cicada calls enveloping the clearing, so that it came out "orry".

He released his towel and shifted his hands to his hips.

Despite the cool of the water, heat pooled in my cheeks and my words tumbled out in a heap. "It's just I've been working on my land over a week now and I've never seen anybody around. Your existence hasn't really registered, sorry. And, ah, I've been taking some liberties exploring your farm in the evenings. That's how I found this place."

"Have you now?" He took a step forward.

"I'm building a house on that block of land next door to you" – I waved an arm in the general direction – "and I can't decide where the best place to put it is."

"Uh-huh." Another step.

My voice rose in pitch to match that of the sex-hungry cicadas. "So, I've been trying to get a sense of the lie of the land, you know, review all the different prospects, which requires doing some...reconnaissance on neighbouring hills."

"Right." He paused. "How's the prospect from my stream?"

I offered him my best smile. The one that turns my crow's feet into attractive laughter lines. "Gosh, it's gorgeous here." I made a point of looking around me. "You're very lucky to have this." I sank further under the water. "On your property."

The farmer stepped out of the shadow of the trees. He was somewhere in his thirties, with dark hair and darker eyes under a deep frown.

"Have you met Saffron yet?" the mouth under the frown said.

"Saffron?"

"Local eel. Has a name for making herself known by latching onto tender, dangly bits. I haven't swum naked in here since she nearly circumcised me when I was seven."

I sat upright. "Oh my God."

"She's much bigger now – prefers larger meat, calves mostly, the odd forearm."

I started edging my way back to the other side of the stream, searching the water for a long black shape.

"Doesn't hurt much, but once she clamps on you've got to allow her to let go in her own good time. Pull her off and her backwards-facing teeth'll tear the flesh."

Something brushed my leg. "Ngaaaaaarrrrrr," I shrieked, leaping to my feet to demurely scrabble, arse out, up the bank. I stood panting, facing The Frown's hastily turned back, and as my panicked brain jumped from *Eel!* to *Where are my clothes?*, my focus shifted to the back of his head.

It was turned slightly, the cheek rounded in a smile.

I pivoted towards the water and peered into its depths. Nothing. Not a ripple, not a shadow. "Oh, ha bloody ha. Good joke." I put a hand to my chest in a futile effort to calm my heart.

The head tilted down and chuckled into its gumboots.

"Yeah, alright." I took a deep breath and said more gently, "Could you at least pass my clothes? The sooner I'm dressed, the sooner I'm gone."

I was delicately handed my undies between two fingers.

I stepped into them and tried to pull them over my wet thighs, but only succeeded in rolling them into a tight band. With a grunt, I forced them to crotch level and attempted to peel them over my damp buttocks. When I finally succeeded in separating fabric from skin, I lifted my head and got a face full of sweat-laced sports bra. I jerked my head backwards and snatched it from his fingers. Offering an ungracious "cheers", I worked to turn it through the right way.

Now, the problem with sports bras is that because they're designed to hold all the soft parts in place so that they don't so much as jiggle, they are rather tight. I managed to get the thick elastic at the bottom of the bra as far as my armpits, and there, thanks to the firmness of the fabric and the clamminess of my skin, it refused to move.

"Fuck," I muttered under my breath. I couldn't get my arms into a position to effectively pull it down. I moved my arms uselessly from front to back then gave up, leaving them propped up like antennae and my face buried in boob-binding polyester.

I turned to face the stream. "Uh...could you just...?"

A snort and the bottom of my bra was yanked down.

"Thanks." I swung back around and was presented with my t-shirt and shorts. "Forget it. I'm sure you've seen a woman in her underwear before." I grabbed the clothes from his outstretched hand, marched around him and stepped into my gumboots. I walked on without looking back. "Enjoy your swim. Neighbour."

"Thank you, I most certainly will."

TRUDGING back across the paddocks to my property, I sunk into an ever-darkening mood. Being humiliated at the hands of a male made me think of Derek. I didn't like to think of Derek, but I was finding him increasingly hard to exorcise from my head. He was the reason I was here, after all.

Six months ago, Derek dropped the "met someone else" bomb and just to make sure I was really down and bleeding, strafed my forty-year-old pride by implying she was much younger.

There was only one course of action: retreat to the happy place of my childhood summers and nurse the pulpy mess of the Derek-shaped hole in my chest. That place was Pukeroa, a two-horse town nestled in the foothills of the Southern Alps. It was also the home of Margot, the mother I sometimes wish I'd had. When I'd arrived, she drew me to her ample bosom and offered a double gin and tonic when I came up for air. I asked for a triple.

It was in the window of the Pukeroa General Store that I saw the advertisement for the land. Three hectares of rolling, retired farmland with a magnificent view of the mountains for a price I really needed to negotiate, but didn't have the energy to. A few months later, with paltry change from the exchange of inner-city villa for lifestyle block, but still riding the high of resignation from a job I found little satisfaction in, I rolled back into town determined to forge a new life. One that was fulfilling and gave me purpose and on no account featured men of the falling-in-love-with variety. However, it wasn't long before I realised Derek had hitched a ride and shedding him would be a herculean task.

WHEN I NEGOTIATED the third fence, the one that did belong to me, I headed for my car and the phone that was nestled in the front console. I rang my oldest and closest friend, Hanita, and relayed the stream encounter with as much indignation as I could muster in the energy-sapping heat.

"I've named him The Frown. With capitals."

"*Farmer* Frown."

"Weak," I said, laughing despite myself.

"But look, Nance, to be fair you actually were trespassing, and he might have had a very good reason to scare you off. Like, a large and lucrative plot of marijuana, or he might be the leader of some over-sexed religious cult. He was probably keen to get you out of the water so he could view your potential as one of his wives."

"No, I think I'm safe there. Hemp sandals may

have been a giveaway, but he looked pretty plain Old McDonald in his gumboots."

"Was he hot? Or was he one of those crusty types that look like they're about to keel over from skin cancer at any moment?"

"No, he displayed a fine representation of all the major muscle groups. But that doesn't make him less of a dick!"

"It definitely makes him less of a dick. He could have just told you to 'fuck off', but instead he thought of an ingenious way to get you out of the water that would also entertain me. I like him."

TWO
WHO NEEDS A PLAN WHEN YOU HAVE A MULTI-TOOL?

MARGOT, the mother I sometimes wished I had, was an old family friend. Although younger by some fifteen years, my parents had developed a close relationship with her and her husband, Keith. Margot and Keith had a river running at the back of their large property that was made turquoise by the snow melt and we would camp in their backyard most summers. My brother, Will, and I were given unlimited freedom, despite the obvious danger of the river, while the adults talked politics or literature or religion, and smoked the odd joint. Our independence – while not rare, given our very liberal parenting – felt precious, and Will and I spent hours adventuring in Pukeroa's "wilds".

Now in her eightieth year, Margot was widowed and only semi-retired from her accountancy profession. She was small and round with extraordinarily pale skin, and while she might look diminutive, underneath that creased, cherubic exterior was a warp-speed mind fronted by a rapier tongue that was capable of sudden and surprising vulgarity. I loved her very much. Margot didn't take any prisoners, which worked for me. My New Life was by far the biggest and most important project I'd ever taken on and I knew she would keep me on an even keel. She'd make one hell of a project manager.

So, I shouldn't have been surprised that when I got back from my day of weed control and fence hopping and sat down at Margot's table with a cold beer, she announced that a week of tip-toeing around me was long enough and it was time to formulate A Plan.

With pursed lips, she slid a coaster under my sweating beer, then asked, "How carefully have you thought through the entire process of establishing a homestead on a large bit of land? The infrastructure needed, the cost, the timeframe?"

There wasn't a lot I could say. I hadn't thought it through, carefully or otherwise. When I announced I was going to survive on my finely-honed ability to make stuff up as I went along and the battery life of my cordless drill, she poked me in the bicep with a bony finger.

"Ow."

"My girl, this is no time for flippancy. You have a static income, which means, in case you haven't grasped the reality of your situation, no income at all. That very modest sum in your bank account isn't going to get you very far without a firm budget based on sound research."

A low rumble issued from the direction of the fridge. Derek leaned against it, shaking with laughter, one foot cocked. *I hope you brought your waders, Nancy, because you are out of your depth and treading shit. Do they make a full body variety?*

"Yes, I know." I eyed Derek through narrowed lids, then turned back to Margot. "It would have been helpful if the housing market hadn't taken a dive when we sold and I then had to split the shitty profits with the D-bag." I sighed. "But that's the way of things, so I have to accept it and move on." I toyed with the label on my beer bottle. "I know where I want to get to, I just don't know how to get there."

"And where's that?"

"Have a small house, be as self-sufficient as possible, and not owe any money to any bank."

Margot gripped my wrist before giving it two pats. "Excellent. Those are admirable goals." She paused, then said, "However, the last one's going to be tough. You'll have to be very resourceful."

I absolutely would. I just didn't know if I had it in me. A block of concrete rose in my stomach and rotated painfully. "Oh God, Margot, have I done the right thing? I know nothing about the process of getting a house built. I haven't even got a driveway to *get* to my future house."

Hey, Nancy. Derek crossed his arms and smirked at me. *I've got a snorkel you can borrow.*

"This may surprise you, my girl, but you –" she raised her gin and tonic glass and pointed a finger at me "– are not the first person to build a house. Start asking around. You'll find most people are very happy to share their experience and offer advice."

"But I don't know anyone who's built a house," I whined. "All the people I know either rent because the housing market's too inflated, or they've bought existing houses because to build means living a half day's commute to work, or they're still battling insurance companies after the earthquake."

"Well then, I'll introduce you to Stuart. He built a house a couple of years ago and project managed it himself. I'm sure he'll be happy to help you. He has a heart of gold that man. Lord knows how he keeps so chipper with that sphincter of a wife, but love works in mystifying ways."

MARGOT DIDN'T WASTE any time. She had Stuart around the next day for coffee and her special orange drizzle cake.

Stu, as he insisted I call him, was a gentle soul with a rugged exterior, his skin leathery from a life outdoors. He clearly adored Margot and because of that was only too willing to help. When he asked what my budget was, my answer was met with knitted brows.

"Hmm. That amount's not going to get you a lot. What skills can you bring to the table?"

"Nancy's renovated several houses all by herself," Margot announced proudly. "You should see the set-up she brought with her. My garage is full of power tool porn."

"That right?" Stu eased the knot out of his brows and raised them.

It was right. On both accounts. I had knocked a handful of houses into shape, and I had commandeered all available space in Margot's garage with my shit.

"Good on you, girl. That should bring your costs down if we can find a builder who's willing to have you help."

I sat up straighter. I was totally up for that challenge. Because I was a liberated woman living in the twenty-first century and I could do anything.

"It's not going to be enough, though." He rubbed his chin. "Look, if you're not fussed about having new fixtures, you could source second-hand stuff. I bet you'll be able to find some good quality gear that'll do the job just fine. Look good, too, if you clean them up."

That was fine by me. The "R" for my middle

name could have stood for "rustic", if "Robyn" hadn't got there first.

"Will you be paying rent during the build?"

"Nancy has a free room here for as long as she needs," said Margot, which was extremely generous, except...

"Actually, I kind of want to be up there? You know, understand the place, get a good feel for it so I can picture exactly what I want? I've...been looking at cheap buses I can convert and I think I've found one." I woke my phone and showed them the slideshow of pictures from the sales site. "Bit of a heap, but if I do a good job on it, I reckon it'll be a good investment. I could turn it into glamping accommodation further down the track. Or something. *If* I could get it to the site. You know anything about driveways, Stu?"

Stu looked at me over the top of his coffee cup. "Tell you what. I've got a small digger on the farm. You buy in the gravel and we'll have you a driveway in no time."

When his generosity was met with a tumble of thank-you words, he gave a single nod. "I like Steinlager."

WITH THE DRIVEWAY SORTED, the land was bus ready. It wasn't, however, Nancy ready. There was a clear priority that needed to be met for any kind of housing situation, even the temporary ones –

finding a mode of conducting one's business. So to speak.

Stu insisted that humanure, if handled right, would be great fertiliser for my future garden. I wrinkled my nose, then pulled up my big girl panties and set to work. It took me a day to build a set of pallet compost bins and a toilet out of a director's chair, toilet seat and paint bucket. All I had to do was christen it in both name and usage. With the director's chair having arms and a back, I'd made the most comfortable loo on earth. I could set up my open-air toilet in the perfect spot to afford a poo with a view, then recline and ponder how good life was.

I named it The Office.

I set up my tent and spent a long time watching the night sky. It was rich with stars, the black rendered insignificant by the Milky Way's mass of fine, silvery lights. It was something I could never hope to experience in Christchurch, the city I'd called home for most of my life.

Then I kept myself warm by stoking the fire of my broken-hearted rage. Derek lay next to me smoothly redirecting my pot shots into the sparkling heavens.

I'd say: "God, you're such a cliché – making yourself feel younger by dating someone half your age. It's pretty hard to disappoint someone with little experience and low expectations, isn't it, Derek?"

He'd reply: *And that one there,* he pointed to a

cluster of stars low on the horizon, *is Matariki –
Pleiades, the Seven Sisters, to the ancient Greeks.*

Then I'd say: "I 'spose her flexibility's half the attraction. And I don't mean in the bedroom, Derek.
You can mould her to fit the habits of your lifestyle. Is
that what turned you off me? Was I a bit too happy in
my own groove?"

He'd say: *See that shooting star over there?
Chances are it's more dust than rock, which is probably why so few meteors survive being burned up in
the earth's atmosphere. Thank the stars.*

Eventually, I tired of the parallel discourse and
retreated, falling asleep to the haunting hoot of ruru.

In the morning, I woke to the warbling of mag-
pies and the urge to do my business.

Given that the majority of my land was completely bare, the only choice for toileting privacy was
a patch of mature bush in one corner of the section.
The bush had been grazed before I bought the land,
so the area beneath the trees was clear of new growth
and offered a pleasant, business-doing outlook towards the alps.

I headed in its direction with increasing urgency.

I had just sat down and got underway when I
heard a car approaching on the road that bordered
one side of my land, and I realised with growing
horror that when I placed The Office in the bush for
privacy I hadn't considered where the road was. For
most of the property, the land was higher than the

road, but here it dropped away to lie below it. Any moment now the car would come around the corner and have a perfect view down into the bush.

There was nothing I could do. I was mid-stride. I simply had to accept the inevitability of the situation and try to make the best of it.

Derek sat beneath a tree, plucking grass. *How do you do it, Nancy? How are you so spectacularly adept at humiliating yourself? It really is deliciously painful to watch.*

The car gradually revealed itself. I had hoped it was a low-slung sedan with a solitary driver too busy concentrating on the road to pay attention to a woman sitting with her pants down in the neighbouring field. Unfortunately for me, it turned out to be a high-suspension utility vehicle carrying not just a driver, but an entire family. Also unfortunate: the road was gravel and the driver a responsible parent, which meant the ute was travelling at a reasonably slow pace. One of the kids in the back peered out the window, pointed at me and shouted something excitedly.

Five heads swivelled my way.

A single report of laughter pierced the air as the driver rolled down his window to give me a lazy wave. "Morning," he called out, "lovely day for it."

"Yep, she's a beauty alright," I called back as if pooing in public were a perfectly normal and pleasant way to pass the time.

THE BUS ARRIVED the following weekend, driven from Christchurch by my eighteen-year-old niece, Skye, with Will, her father, following in the car behind. I arranged to meet them in Pukeroa township so that I could direct them to the land.

It wouldn't be hard to spot me. Pukeroa, or "Puke" as the locals call it, boasted a total of eleven shops to service a several hundred-strong community and the peak tourist seasons of summer and winter.

I nursed a cup of peppermint tea outside the town's only café and intermittently watched the road. The main street reached out to the mountains, so as you drove into town, Rakiariki, the main peak in this area of the alps, seemed to balance itself precariously on top of the buildings' facades. It was the stuff of postcards, and so of course, every shop sold a postcard version of that exact panorama.

I heard the bus before I saw it. The graunch of a high gear being inexpertly shifted into a low one echoed between the two lines of buildings. I pulled my attention away from the couple quietly arguing next to me and looked up to see a large metal grub bearing down on the town's shops, the divided front windows like large, bulbous eyes.

"Mushroom pink" had been a generous description on the sales website. I had hoped the photos were over-exposed, but the bus rumbling its way towards me was more on the hot side of fuchsia.

"Oh Lord," I muttered into my teacup and stood up to wave at it.

It pulled over two shops down and I walked quickly towards the opening doors.

Skye's grinning face emerged first, then she turned to make her way gingerly onto the pavement where she reached up into a stretch. "Oh my God, Aunty Nan, I can't believe you just made me drive that beast all the way from Christchurch."

I pulled her into a hug. "Hello, my darling girl." I kissed her apple-scented hair. "Well done. It doesn't look easy to drive."

"No, it's an absolute dog. What vintage did you say it was? 1873?"

I gave her a squeeze. "1973."

My brother, Will, emerged from a car parked behind the bus. "Hey, Nan." He bent down to give me a kiss and said, "You are one brave woman taking this thing on." He slapped the bus' side. "Great colour. We've named it The Yam."

I turned my mouth down in distaste and he added quickly, "Out of affection, obviously."

I affected the sigh of the long suffering. "I'm guessing I'm not going to hear the end of it until I paint it."

"And gut it," said Skye. "It's going to take a whole

lot of pimping wizardry to turn this into a thing of beauty."

Will squeezed my shoulder. "And luckily you have what it takes, Nancy Pants. We have full faith in you."

Did they? I didn't. Now that the bus dream was a hot pink reality, the task of making it a liveable space seemed gargantuan, my house renovation skills inadequate. "C'mon, you guys must be exhausted. I'll buy you a coffee. Then we can test out the camber and gradient of my new driveway."

"And cake." Skye grinned up at me.

"And cake."

We turned towards the café to find a young woman taking my half-drunk tea away.

I ran to intercept her. "Wait, I haven't finished. Sorry, I had to leave the table for a minute."

She shrugged. "No worries." Placing the cup and pot back down, she looked up as Skye and Will scraped chairs out from the table. Glancing at Skye, she focused on Will. "You guys want anything?"

"Two very long, strong blacks, I think."

"And cake," Skye added. "What do you recommend?"

The waitress looked at her and blushed. "Um, our hummingbird cake is pretty good, I guess."

Skye smiled broadly at her, her single dimple denting her left cheek. "Great. One large piece of hummingbird cake, please."

The waitress left with a nod and a faint smile at the corners of her mouth.

"So, Aunty Nan" – Skye gestured towards the bus – "this really is it. You're leaving us for a glamorous life in a pink tin can."

My laugh came out a little high pitched for true mirth. "Yep, you all smell too much like petrol fumes and urban sprawl. You're going to be pleading sanctuary when the zombie apocalypse comes."

"Hey, I'm all for exploiting my relationship with you and making the most of your land. If I wasn't going overseas, I'd be camped up there now, planting trees and re-establishing eco systems and being an all-round fabulous eco-warrior."

I squeezed her hand. "I would love you to stay and help me out. Extend your gap year. Leave this all behind and come with me now." I tried to make my tone light and playful and not full of the desperation currently rising above the cheer.

"Thanks, Aunty Nan, but I have a plan and I'm going to see it through even if I have to cut my own leg off to do it." She rubbed at the spot of a running injury in her right knee.

"It's still giving you trouble?"

"Yes," Skye said resignedly. "I'm getting physio, but it's not helping much. I'm too young to be falling apart." She gave her father a gentle nudge in the ribs. "That's your and Dad's job."

"I'm not falling apart," Will retorted. "I can't afford to. Someone has to be a stalwart, provide the solid rock under the shaky ground of your aunty's mid-life crisis." He reached across the table and gave my hand a squeeze. "Just joking, Nance. I love what you're doing and am immensely, ridiculously envious."

THREE
PURE SCHIST

I SPENT three days cleaning the bus and getting it set up enough for me to move into, and then the full force of summer arrived.

It was impossible to escape the heat. I'd open up all the windows and the front and rear doors of the bus to tempt a breeze, but the most effective way of making bus life bearable was closing all the curtains to keep the sun out and living in a seedy half-light. If the solar panels I'd installed were capable of producing more power I would have stood permanently in front of the open refrigerator, preferably with my head inside.

I rang Hanita to whinge, knowing full well her sympathy would be contrived in the smug comfort of an air-conditioned house. Putting her on speakerphone, I stood in the middle of the bus in my underwear, my arms and legs spread so they wouldn't touch any skin.

"Oh my God, Hanita, it's so hot here. My heart arrhythmia's intensified ten-fold and I'm sweating in places I didn't know you could sweat. Even my *knuckles* are sweating and the beads on my upper lip are doing little to cool my face, but are doing a beautiful job of magnifying my moustache."

Hanita clucked her tongue. "You don't have a moustache."

"I bloody well do. I turned forty and it's like I passed through a magic portal to Hirsutelandia. I have to pluck the hair on my nipples, for goodness sake. When I was teleported into the age of knee wrinkles and greying pubes, couldn't they have thrown in some complimentary hair removal into the laser beam?"

"It could be worse. You could be a man. The hair on your head could fall out and get trapped on its descent by follicles in your back."

I stifled a chuckle. "Don't make me laugh. I can't afford to expend energy that might produce heat."

Hanita "Hmm"ed and said, "You know, at some point you're going to have to accept that middle age brings stuff with it we'd prefer didn't happen. But that's okay. Everyone gets older."

My "Hanita Kapur!" emerged breathy, scandalised. I wasn't middle-aged. I wasn't remotely middle-aged.

Ignoring Derek's scoff behind me, I said, "I intend to live to a hundred. That gives me another decade 'til I'm the 'm' word, thank you very much."

Mummified? Derek ventured. *Man-proof?*

I rounded on him.

He leant against the driver's seat, a finger pressed to pursed lips.

"Yeah? I *want* to be man-proof. I don't want a bloke sniffing around me until at least the next millennium."

"Nance," Hanita said gently, "at some point you've got to let it go. Not all men are Dereks."

"I'm not willing to give them the chance to prove that. I can't be humiliated again if I don't make an emotional investment. The shop is shut."

TO: nancypants@getwired.co.nz
    From: nightskye@webmail.com
    Subject: Bugger!
    Dear Aunty Nan, thought I'd update you on the latest developments. I've been referred to an orthopaedic surgeon as the damage is in the cartilage, apparently. Sigh. It's on Accident Compensation so it won't cost anything, and they tell me the waiting list isn't too long. Yeah right! I won't hold my breath on that one. The recovery will delay my travel plans significantly, though. I have been very good and not

shed any tears, but we'll see what the expert has to say before I commit to composure.

I got a book out of the library on France and I've decided I'll head there before going to Ireland. I particularly like the look of The Loire Valley and Brittany. The book has double spreads of chateau and villages in those provinces. It's sooooooo gorgeous, I'm sure God got sick of saying, "What?" at every page turn.

I've had two days of consecutive work filling in at a holiday programme, which is fantastic for the travel fund. I have eight children in my care and today they didn't want their usual person back, so I must be doing something right, or it's novelty value, or I'm better looking.

I thought I'd attach a jpeg so you could have an opportunity to roll your eyes at me, as I'm sure you're poised, waiting for one. This is my boyfriend. He's the bassist in a band called The Vents, which I presume you've never heard of because you're so old. I really like his style. It's a sort of an understated, sophisticated ruggedness. I don't know his name, so he's just my Friday night boyfriend.

Anyway, that's me. I miss you,

Skye

Xx

TO: nightskye@webmail.com
    From: nancypants@getwired.co.nz

Subject: Re. Bugger!

My darling, darling girl. I am so sorry that your knee problem looks like a serious one. I have my fingers crossed that the operation is straight forward (keyhole surgery isn't very invasive, be assured) and that it won't take you long to be back up and running again. I know it must be disappointing, but it will make your trip all the more sweet when you finally get there. You are very welcome to convalesce at my place.

Thank you for reminding me of my decrepitude. I'll have you know that this old lady has erected a shed for toileting privacy, plumbed in a claw-footed bath for my future sheep (because who wants to look at an ugly concrete trough?), set up a chicken run, and started stripping and relining the bus (not easy to manage when you're living in it), which is not too bad for someone who's just entered their fifth decade! It's hot work. Thank goodness Margot allows me to collect drinking water and un-stench myself at her place.

I had a listen to The Vents on Spotify. See, I'm not that antiquated – I can do digital. They're a bit angry electronica, aren't they? Oh dear. How easily you've forced me to show my age.

I've got all fingers and toes crossed for your appointment.

XX

Aunty Nan

ON A PARTICULARLY HOT and testing day, I had chosen to spend the morning doing paperwork – paying bills for materials for the bus and evaluating quotes for the house build.

After half an hour, a chin was placed on my shoulder and a series of tuts issued from the mouth above it.

When I started to balance up what I had spent and what I was likely to spend against the amount of money in my bank account, the block of concrete that had settled in my stomach on my arrival in Pukeroa tried to force itself up my esophagus.

I was going to run out of money a lot sooner than I thought.

I shrugged my shoulder violently and stood up from the table. Wielding a skill saw was suddenly a much more appealing prospect than staring at spreadsheets and willing new figures into existence.

An hour into the unsavoury task of installing insulation into the bus' ceiling, I heard a knock on the door.

"Hi-i," said a blonde, French-rolled head peering up the bus steps. "Sorry to disturb."

The body of the head revealed itself as it climbed the steps to the bus' interior. It was clad in a black chiffon singlet, skinny jeans and gold sandals with coral nails.

"You must be Nancy. I'm Mona, Stuart's wife."

She started to put out a hand to shake mine, then with a "Oooh goodness, look at you. You're a sweaty mess", withdrew it before I could taint her with essence of liberated woman.

"Well." Mona clapped her hands and pivoted to view her surroundings. "You are making this into something, alright."

In the dim interior of the bus it was difficult to tell if she said this with a smile or a grimace.

"Stuart said you were working on a glamping project and I just wanted to be nosy." She paused. Her "You don't mind, do you, babe?" was said as a statement, rather than a question. "I'm liking what you've done on the inside, but the outside – rather visually challenging, isn't it? You'll be painting it, no doubt?"

When I paused to draw breath to answer, she launched on. "You must go for Pure Schist. It's a kind of chic, muddy grey. I love colours on that spectrum. Grey communicates a level of sophistication that's very..." I could see her brain rummaging for a polysyllabic adjective. "Classy," she eventually said, "and why wouldn't you want to be surrounded by that?"

"Yes," I finally managed to get a word in. "Such a cheery colour."

"Isn't it? And as we can *just* see the bus from the corner of our deck, it would be great for you to choose something that blends in, babe. I'm sure someone like you would want to be at one with the landscape."

Before I could stop myself, my tongue ran ahead of me. "You know, I'm actually thinking of adding turquoise and yellow accents. The more colours on the rainbow spectrum, the better, I say."

Mona opened and closed her mouth twice before adjusting her tone to match the slightly aggressive posture she'd adopted on arrival. "Fine. Paint it whatever. Just make sure you don't let the neighbours talk you into agreeing to an easement through your land."

An easement? What did that mean?

With a clink of an oversized Pandora bracelet, the blonde head disappeared back down the steps.

As soon as she was out the door, I grabbed the biggest glass I could find and filled it to the top with wine. There was only one thing to do to expunge the acrid taste of that interaction.

A leisurely soak in the sheep trough.

Draining the bath, I carefully swished out the odd bits of algae that had started to accumulate and refilled it, before throwing all my clothes off and sinking into the coolness of the water with a groan.

It didn't take me long to work my way through most of my tumbler, and I was starting to regret that I hadn't brought the whole bottle with me when a voice from over the fence said, "Good afternoon, neighbour. Perfect weather for a dip."

"Jesus!" I spun myself over in the bath, miraculously managing to retain the remainder of my chardonnay. "Where did you come from? I didn't hear you."

The Frown pointed to his motorbike. "Electric. It's a bit of a stealth machine. I've startled many a beast with it, admittedly in less compromising situations." His eyes flicked over my naked backside.

"They make electric farm bikes?"

"Even the farming industry has been dragged kicking and screaming into the future that is the green revolution."

I didn't particularly want to show I was impressed, but "That's...very cool," slipped out anyway.

"Yep." There was an awkward pause, while I looked expectantly at him for an explanation for not only the very different behaviour he was showing me today, but the reason for his presence.

He looked out across my land appearing to survey the work I had done.

At last, he spoke. "Look, sorry about the other evening. I'd had an arse of a day and was really looking forward to some peace and calm in the pool. You know, shuck the shit off and get some perspective."

I let him stew in the discomfort of not knowing if I'd accept his apology or not for the length of a sip of chardonnay, before saying, "I can appreciate your protectiveness of that place. It's pretty special."

"You're actually welcome to wander the farm, just

take care of the electric fences and don't go into paddocks with stock in them. Some of them can get pretty feisty."

Stock? I'd never seen any animals apart from the odd rabbit.

"Okay, thanks very much."

"And, ah, you forgot these." He held up a balled pair of socks. "They're clean." They were presented to me, then The Frown thought better of it. "I'll just..." He dropped them on top of my pile of clothes.

"Thanks."

"No problem." A bleat from one of my sheep drew his gaze, then he shifted his attention back to me. "Why are you drinking wine in your sheep trough?" He leaned against the fence with a foot cocked on one of the wires, and the leg of his shorts had ridden up to reveal a tanned and nicely toned thigh.

Derek blew bubbles from where he was submerged in the bath beside me. Then he raised himself up and turned over, hooking his arms over the side as I had done. He whistled. *That is one hell of a vastus medialis. Ask him if his sartorius goes all the way up.*

I elbowed him back under the water.

"Because I was hot, and thirsty, and the water is surprisingly clear for having sheep saliva in it. Comes from the stream, don't you know?"

"Yes, I do know. I'm the one that pumps it up the hill for your bathing pleasure. Thank you for the courtesy of asking me if you could tap into my water pipe."

"Stu didn't ask you?"

"No, Stu didn't ask me." He shook his head, then let out a single bark of laughter. "Stuart, a bloody nice bloke who can't say 'no', especially to an attractive woman."

I looked at him sharply, but his gaze was aimed in the direction of Stu's farm.

"I think he'll be buying the beer after the next Twilight tournament."

"Rugby?"

"Bowls."

"You play *lawn bowls*?"

"Yeah. It's actually a really great game. Don't let the grey hair and starched whites fool you into thinking it's a tedious, formal game for geriatrics. It has this addictive level of intensity, I guess because it needs a lot of concentration and precision. And it's fun and very social. You should come try your hand at the next tourney."

"Okay. I probably won't to be honest, but I appreciate your effort in trying to convince me lawn bowls is cool."

A smile. "Your loss."

The two over-sized lambs I'd recently acquired as lawn mowers ambled over to investigate the newcomer, who raised his chin at them. "Who are these little fullas?"

"My newest babies. They're Sprocket."

"They're both called Sprocket?"

"No, that's the collective noun for them. This tubby one here is Sprout and this one with the black ear is Rocket."

"Ha! Nice. Very efficient." The Frown shot me a grin and, buoyed by the win, I involuntarily returned it.

"And that naked one over there, looking embarrassed," I said, pointing to a large, freshly shorn wether attempting to hide behind the trunk of a spindly tree, "is Woolly Wonka."

The Frown snorted. "Not really living up to his name, is he?"

"No, he's looking highly pissed off. It's a shame you weren't able to see him in all his woolly glory. When he had a full fleece, he did actually bear an uncanny resemblance to Gene Wilder."

I received a grin in reply and his eyes flicked again to my backside, which I thought probably merited being met by some degree of indignation rather than the smugness currently edging my lips towards a smirk.

"Do you have to keep looking at my arse?"

"Yes. It's very difficult not to look when it's presented so readily."

"You know, anyone would think you deliberately seek opportunities to see me naked."

"Anyone would think you deliberately *create* opportunities for me to see you naked." The Frown climbed back on his bike and started it. As he rode off, he shouted over his shoulder, "Did you put sunscreen on your bum? Your buttocks are on the pale side of white. Could make sitting difficult tomorrow."

I rolled over and sank under the water, wine glass hand in the air and let out a long groan.

When I re-emerged, Derek raised his glass in a toast from the other end of the bath. *Nicely done, Nancy. I must say, I am surprised to see you back on the wagon so quickly.*

"I wasn't flirting with him, Derek."

He looked thoughtfully towards the fence. *He seemed like a nice young man.* His eyes slid back to me. *How old are you again, Nancy? Ah yes, that's right.* He took a sip from his glass. *You know, it doesn't sound any better the more you say "fifth decade", does it? It still produces the same degree of wincing, one eye slightly squintier than the other. Much like sucking lemons.*

THAT NIGHT I rang Hanita to relay the second instalment in *Naked Encounters with My Neighbour.*

"How did you let him see you in the buff for a second time?" she asked, as if I were seriously moronic, rather than just the minor one I felt.

"He snuck up on me. He might look like a farmer, but I think he's actually a ninja."

"Was he wearing gumboots?"

"Of course."

"Not very ninja-like. All that flapping rubber would give you away pretty quickly. Maybe you're going deaf in your old age, or blind, or deliberately displaying yourself in the hope that he might see you."

"That's what he accused me of."

"Suffering from old age?"

At the dining table, Derek "hawed" into one of the pages of my *Home Design* magazine.

"No, Hanita. Purposefully flaunting myself for his benefit."

"And are you?" she asked after a pause.

Flick went the page.

"No! Can't a woman enjoy a bit of nudity in the privacy of her own land without being made to feel like she's parading herself?"

"The problem is, you live on a bare block on the top of a hill. Anything you do is going to be on parade. And you have managed to make a spectacle of yourself, how many times now? I make it three in under a month. That's a pretty impressive record."

I was quiet for a moment.

Flick.

"He's got really sexy knees. Is that possible?"

Hanita laughed. "If you're into joints. Most women go for biceps or buttocks, but if that's what blows your hair back, then I'm sure he'll be very flattered to have you perve at his knees. I thought you'd sworn off men, though?"

"I'm just looking. There's no harm in looking."

"Okay. Just be careful, won't you? You can't keep running away when things go south."

I "Fffft" a dismissal. "There will be no 'thing' to run away from. I can window shop, can't I?"

Derek looked up from the magazine, *I presume your metaphorical shop has one-way glass, because, Nancy, there's no way that boy's returning your gaze.*

I'D MADE an arrangement to meet with Margot the following morning to discuss my financial freak out. She had a pot of tea and a plate of homemade biscuits already on the table by the time I arrived.

I opened the discussion as any mature 40-year-old would by whining out an "Oh God" and following it up with unnecessary hyperbole. "I feel like I'm haemorrhaging money and the build hasn't even started yet."

"Yes," Margot agreed. "It feels like it's coming from every orifice, I bet. You're what we call in the industry, a financial haemophiliac. At some point you've got to staunch the flow before you bleed out."

I groaned dramatically and tossed my bag on a chair in a show of despair.

"Alright," she said in a conciliatory tone, "we'll see

what good we can make of the situation. Have a seat, my dear, and we'll get started."

"No thanks, I'm okay standing."

"We are going to be having a lengthy discussion about the drastic state of your finances, Nancy. It could take an hour or more for us to pick things apart and formulate a plan. For goodness sake, please have a seat."

"No."

"No? What's going on with you, Nancy? Sit down!"

"Look," I said with a sigh, "I'm not wearing any undies, okay? If I sit down you'll get a short, but intensive course in gynaecology. Plus, it's more comfortable. To stand, I mean, not necessarily the not wearing undies. Though actually that is quite nice, too. I had no idea how pleasant it is to feel the breeze through your pubes."

"Nancy," Margot said sharply. "Why aren't you wearing any underpants?"

I let out another sigh. "I, somewhat misguidedly, took on the sun in a battle of wills. It kicked my arse. Quite literally."

"And why would you want to expose the delicate flesh of your bottom to such a carcinogenic monster?"

"Because," I replied as if it were obvious, "I was attempting to protect the dignity of my lady parts from that farmer. The next-door neighbour one."

"Good Lord. Dare I ask...?"

"I was having a lovely naked time drinking wine in my outdoor bath when he turned up and accused me of stealing his water. I had to lie on my stomach to keep most of me hidden, while I defended my right to access bath water by tapping into his reticulation system."

Margot exhaled slowly. "My girl, it might be a sensible idea to try to get on the good side of your neighbours, especially as you're brand new to this community. It can be very insular, so you need to make an effort to be part of it. Common courtesy is such a simple thing. Yes?"

"Yes, I know. I thought Stu had squared it with him."

She eyed me and released a slow breath.

I took that as my cue to get ready for the dissection of my finances and turned around to get my reading glasses out of my bag.

"Dear God, Nancy, the back of your dress is clinging to your buttocks like a second skin. I can almost count the hairs around your arsehole!"

I twisted around awkwardly to get a view of my bottom and noticed, to my utter dismay, that I hadn't fully thought through the idea of smearing my bum cheeks with aloe vera gel, then choosing a thin floaty skirt to wear in a bid to keep fabric away from sensitive skin.

Margot laughed throatily in delight. "Ah, my girl, you are fabulous." She leaned forward to kiss me on the cheek and behind her back I offered my middle finger to a smirking Derek.

He'd just sat down with a sigh in the chair I'd left vacant and crossed his legs. I received a wink in return. He rubbed his hands together and murmured, *This should be fun.*

MARGOT WASN'T PARTICULARLY IMPRESSED with what she saw when she delved into the history of my bank account.

"Nancy, what's this thirteen-thousand-dollar transfer to a travel card eight months ago?"

"Um, my trip with Derek to The States for a month?"

She raised an eyebrow.

"What?" I said in petulant defence. "I was about to turn forty. I had to celebrate somehow."

"Couldn't you have just thrown a party like a normal person?"

"Margot, my twenties were alright but a bit shit in places, and my thirties improved on an upward trend towards almost happiness. I was determined to start this decade with a vibrant joie de vivre that was meant," I laughed humourlessly, "to go from strength to strength. A road trip in America was what I really wanted to do, so I did it. And I happened to have a bloody fabulous time." I took a bite of my biscuit. "I just didn't foresee that a couple of months after that I'd be dumped and voluntarily unemployed."

Margot peered at my online bank statement. "Did you foresee spending another four thousand near the end of the trip? What on earth was that for?"

"Ah, yes. That would have been our extended stopover in Hawai'i."

"And you spent *four thousand dollars?*"

"They have really good scuba diving there," I said weakly. "Margot, I saw manta rays! I saw one so close that if I'd stuck my tongue out I would have licked it. That, alone, is worth four grand."

A sigh escaped.

"Look, at the time, I was in a great financial space and happily coupled-up. It might look reckless now that things have changed, but I have absolutely no regrets about spending that money. Mostly."

Derek shifted in his seat, looking around behind his back and moving his weight forward. From underneath his buttocks he pulled out a mask and snorkel. *Aha! I knew I'd left them somewhere.*

Grinning, he presented them to me and asked if my legs were tired yet. *The thing about trying to keep your head above the shit is that sooner or later it soaks through your clothes, it oozes into your shoes and fills your pockets and then,* he shrugged, *it drags you under.*

Margot took a long drink of her tea and a still grinning Derek leaned forward in his chair, watching her closely. "Okay, here's what we'll do. I know you don't want to borrow money, so in order to make sure you don't have to, I'm going to set you a weekly budget for your day-to-day living costs and we'll meet twice a week to go through your invoices. You'll get at least three quotes for every job and we'll go through them together. You're also going to have to beg, borrow and steal favours from others. You could exchange odd jobs or do something like cook meals in payment."

She closed the lid of my laptop. "I know you've been taking time out for yourself after the rough few months you've had, but now, my girl, it really is time you got a job."

FOUR
SILVER FOX

JUST AS I'D finished tidying up my resumé, Will announced he was going to make the most of the last few days of the school holidays by bringing the rest of the family to my place for a camping trip. The job hunt immediately went on the back burner. They arrived on a fine, windless day and set up a large tent on the site I'd decided the house should go.

"Nan, this place is incredible," Will's second wife, Tava'esina, enthused. "What a find!"

"You know, Sina, I think that every day. When another invoice comes in and I watch my money drop another thousand on its descent to zero, I remind myself how lucky I am to be here, to have this. That it's all worth it."

We stood outside my chicken coop watching my recently acquired hens bathe themselves in dirt, and admiring the view I had generously given them when I positioned my homemade hen house. I wasn't entirely convinced they'd appreciate their sweeping vista of the mountains, but I thought I'd give them the benefit of the doubt.

"Are they boys or girls?" asked Ben, my four-year-old nephew.

"All girls."

"Why?"

"Because only the girls lay eggs."

"Out their bum?"

"Yes, out their bum."

"It's called a cloaca," my niece, Maia, added a little too helpfully.

My jaw dropped. "How do you know that?" I didn't know that. "Are you sure you're just six and not some twenty-eight-year-old genius dwarf?"

"Yes. We learnt about it at school."

I looked at my brother. "They teach chicken reproductive anatomy to six-year-olds?"

Will shrugged. "That knowledge has just been perfectly applied to a concrete situation. Who am I to judge what's relevant in the curriculum these days?"

"Aunty Nan, does it hurt?" Ben piped up.

"Does what hurt, darling?" I answered.

"Making an egg."

"It probably feels like doing a big poo. Does it hurt when you do a poo?"

"No."

"Then I'm sure it doesn't hurt the chickens either."

"Okay," he said with easy four-year-old acceptance. "Can I name this one Hayden?"

"It already has a name, darling. Princess Layer."

"And it's a girl, dummy," Maia pointed out with the gentle condescension of an older sister. "It can't have a boy name."

I looked at Sina. "Who's Hayden?"

"His new best friend. Everything is Hayden. He has a Hayden dinosaur, a Hayden Lego Batman." She chuckled. "Even his toothbrush is called Hayden."

"Well, Ben, sounds like Hayden is very lucky to have you as a friend." I bent down to give him a kiss on the top of his head and he put his arms up for a cuddle. I lifted him up and pointed out a couple of chickens with particularly beautiful plumage. "See that one there? She's a Golden-laced Wyandotte, and that one there is a Silver Dorking. Aren't they fabulous?"

"So, sister mine," Will said, putting an arm around me, "seems the chickens know how to handle the human. How long before you're scratching around in the dirt for your supper and they're inside with their feet up watching *New Zealand's Got Talent*?"

"Not long I expect. Lola insists on laying in the wardrobe. I keep finding eggs inside my shoes and I have to check them carefully before I put them on. She'll be moving in next week at this rate."

Needless to say, the kids loved the bus. Ben spent a lot of time behind the steering wheel "driving" us to various exotic places, like Legoland, Magasta (Madagascar), and Hayden's house.

Maia's favourite spot was the raised sleeping platform. She spent a long time up there playing out different scenarios and would eventually come down covered in sweat, the bedroom having only one window. However, neither child was particularly taken with the toileting facilities.

"Will, this is what happens when you spoil your children by providing them with decent sanitation, like a loo that takes all the mess away with the push of a button. They're completely ruined."

Yet, using the toilet was unavoidable and it only took one turn for Maia to be sold on the set-up. It was such a hit that she took to eking out her daily movement to at least three.

On the second morning the family was there, she announced. "Goodbye everyone, I'm off to The Office."

"Okay, see you after work," replied my brother. When she hadn't emerged after fifteen minutes I told Will we'd better check to see she hadn't fallen in.

"How's business?" asked Will when we entered the shed.

"Good thanks."

"Make any deposits in the National bank of Plopland?"

She looked between her legs. "Three little ones and one big one."

"Nice work, Maia," I said. "That's a sound investment strategy. You'll be able to reap your interest when you come to stay in two years' time and claim your fruit profit. Peaches or nectarines?"

Maia weighed up the options. "I think I'm a nectarine girl, Aunty Nan."

"Excellent choice, my love. I'll throw in some apples for good measure, in case you want to diversify your market share."

MARGOT JOINED us as often as she could, and when the temperature got too hot, we'd take a picnic to Saffron's Pool, or the adults would take their books and camping chairs down into the patch of bush while the kids played in the tree hut we had built together.

I had plenty of wood left over from my various projects, and I'd made a structure on one of the trees that the children could then add floorboards to. While I cut the wood to size up at the shed and carted it down to the bush, Will took on the tricky task of managing small children wielding hammers and nails. After Ben had fallen out of the – thankfully not too high – hut two times, I took a trip to the dump and acquired more wood to add handrails and balustrades. The hut became a pirate ship, a shop, a school, a hideout from the baddies, and Aunty Nan's magical touring bus.

"Aunty Nan, can you live here forever?" asked Ben after a long, involved game in the hut of chicken mothers and babies.

"That's the plan, little man," I replied. "Will you keep visiting me, even when you're too big for the tree hut?"

"We'll always come here, Aunty Nan," Maia answered. "This place is sublime."

I gave Will a questioning look, but he just shrugged his shoulders. "Her verbosity definitely doesn't come from me." He looked at Sina. "See what your superior genetics have done? She'll be outsmarting us with advanced logic and esoteric terminology by the time she's eight."

"Ben," Maia said, "are you still playing? I'm going to have another baby." She had a towel wrapped around her midriff. "Come under here so I can poo you out."

Margot let out a throaty laugh. "I think you're quite safe, Will."

Will made a show of relaxing back into his chair. "Phew, thank goodness for that."

. . .

ON WILL and Sina's last night, we sat outside their tent watching the children play in the sheep shelters I'd built. They crawled in and out of them, baa-ing and giving chase to each other.

Behind them, the mountains were ablaze in the red of the setting sun. I closed my eyes and presented my face to them as if to the first of the rains after a long drought.

Will sighed. "It's a shame Skye's not with us. She'd be loving this."

"I know, love," Sina said, "but there'll be other opportunities."

"I wonder how she's getting on. She's working two jobs at the moment, did you know, Nan? Daycare for a wealthy couple during the week, and kitchen handing at night and on the weekends. She'll be exhausted by the time she's saved enough to go."

"Nah, she's young and strong and completely driven to make her trip happen," I replied. "She'll be fine. I have absolutely no doubt about that."

"Thank goodness that surgeon had her head screwed on and didn't see a need for surgery. She's out on her bike most mornings building the strength up around her knee. How she has the energy after getting to bed so late..."

I raised my wine glass in toast to Will. "To be eighteen again."

"Look at me everyone, I'm a sheep." Ben had scrabbled up the hill and stood in front of us with his legs apart. He had his hands behind his back and dropped a handful of sheep nuggets between his legs. "I can poo raisins."

Sina clapped her hands and laughed in delight. "What have you done to my children, Nan?"

"Yeah, thanks for feralising the kids," Will added. "I was worried I was raising city kids who were too precious to get their hands dirty, but you've staged a successful poo-fest."

"Hey, whenever you're concerned about their rate of urban sickliness, send them to me for an immunity boost. I'll throw in some optional tapeworm if you want. Good for controlling allergies, I hear."

Will momentarily wrinkled his nose before looking at Ben in alarm. "Come on little guy, let's go wash your hands."

"And after that, Ben, we can go to Saffron's Pool for a quick swim before bed. Is that a good idea?" I asked.

"Yeah! I love Saffron's Pool." He wrapped his arms around my neck. "And I love *you* Aunty Nan." I peeled his hands off and held them away from me as I leaned down to give him a kiss. "And I love you, my little lamb."

I RANG Margot and told her I had an idea for a business that had been marinating for a while and could I come over with a bottle of wine so we could discuss it.

She told me to take my bottle of wine over to the place of a couple named Martin and Anoushka. They were hosting a barbeque and had extended Margot's invitation to include me, though Margot could feel a migraine coming on and I would have to navigate there myself.

She encouraged me to use the opportunity to make connections that could provide help with the build or find me a job.

I wanted to prove to her that I was committed to making the money plan work, so I obliged, wondering if I might have another opportunity to view a particular set of knees.

Anoushka was very welcoming and was quick to express her concern when I offered Margot's apologies. She asked me how I was going on my land and listened with interest as I outlined what I had achieved so far and what my plans were for the house. "I've never seen a tiny home before. Will it be like the ones you see on that tv show, with George what's-his-name?"

Before I had time to explain my "No, not really" answer, Martin came over, grabbed my elbow and pushed me into the growing throng of guests.

"Have you met any of your neighbours yet?" he asked.

"Not really. A bit...maybe," I answered with the

confidence and articulation of a post-thirties woman who had forged her place in the world.

"Well, there's one of them. Nothing like the present." He steered me towards a solitary Farmer Hot Knees, who was dressed in a faded Sex Pistols t-shirt and jeans that accentuated the muscular thighs I'd glimpsed the other day.

Only mildly disappointed he'd chosen not to wear shorts, I concentrated on affecting a look of polite interest that was aimed at his face. Two beads of sweat rolled synchronously down the insides of my arms.

"Right. Do you two know each other?" Martin asked, planting me firmly in Farmer Hot Knees' eyeline.

"Not at all, though we're intimately acquainted," Farmer HK said, looking me directly in the eye.

Heat rose to my face and I desperately hoped it wasn't noticeable, thanks to the sinking sun behind me.

Martin looked puzzled, shook his head and said, "Angus, this is Nancy, Nancy this is Angus," and moved off, satisfied he'd met his duties as a host.

"Angus? Beef farmer, are you?" I quipped, expecting at least an eye roll in retort.

I was met by an impassive face. "Yes."

Pause.

"No. Really?" I laughed.

"Yes, really. Sorry, were you making a joke?

About four hundred people got there before you, Nancy. I can't be bothered even pretending to be amused anymore."

"Sorry, it is actually quite funny."

"Yes, when it's novel," Angus said softly and looked down at his shoes.

From across the deck, Derek shrugged his shoulders and offered me the smile of a parent comforting a losing child.

I decided to take a punt.

"Okay. In all seriousness it is a good profession. I s'pose it was a calling? Something you felt in your blood?"

Angus looked up at me without a hint of amusement around his mouth, but I could see a twinkle in his eye.

I stepped to the side so that Angus blocked Derek's raised eyebrow. "So," I said, inviting Angus into the joke, "what's your last name?"

He surveyed me over the top of his beer bottle and the twinkle turned playful.

"Stockman."

"Hah. I would have picked you for a 'Fields' or a 'Horn'."

"My middle name's Russell."

I snorted my mouthful of beer out my nostrils, narrowly missing his shoes.

"Oh God. Sorry. I *was* aiming for Sid Vicious."

He rubbed at the front of his t-shirt. "Nothing

wrong with your aim, I think you got the whole band."

Derek's head appeared from behind Angus'. He peered over the farmer's shoulder and down at his front with an expression of distaste. *Way to put your smooth on, Nancy. Gross.*

It really was. "I'm *so* sorry."

"Hey, they'd understand. Having beery snot sprayed over you is very rock'n'roll. I'm sure they've snorted much worse things." He wiped his hand across the back of his jeans. "My real name's Angus Ross."

"Well, that's a relief Mr Ross –"

"Nancy!" A penetrating voice that could only be Mona's carried across the hubbub of the other guests.

I flinched and ducked my head.

"It's too late, she's seen you," Angus said. "The fact she used your name was a bit of a giveaway."

On arrival, Mona stood as close as she could to both of us, presumably to create the illusion of group intimacy and exclusivity for the benefit of the other guests.

"Tell me all about your building plans, babe. I am *quite* intrigued. I hear you're thinking about building a tiny home," she said, wrinkling her nose as if the notion of a tiny house carried an unsavoury aromatic mix of patchouli oil and unwashed armpits.

I drew a deep breath to steady myself and answered, "Not technically a tiny home, no, Mona. It'll be permanent, but it will be small – just one bedroom."

She looked aghast. "One bedroom? That's very short-sighted of you. Don't you want to future proof?"

The muscles in my shoulders began to cinch together and I hoped the woman wouldn't provoke me into calling forth The Barbed Tongue Beast. I could feel it prowling just behind my teeth.

"Um...given that I have no idea what the future will look like, how can I 'proof' for it?"

"You should put at least one other bedroom on so that the resale value is decent. In fact, three bedrooms and two bathrooms would ensure a tidy profit down the track."

I glimpsed Angus rolling his eyes and giving me a small smile for moral support. It helped me to reign the beast in a little, even if the muzzle had fallen off.

"Okay, let me get this right. You think I should build *my* home for someone else I've never met, and that I should guess what that unknown person wants?"

"Oh, I wouldn't put it quite like that, but a house is an investment, babe, and every new build is an opportunity to make the most of the booming real estate market. It's just common sense."

"What if it's not an investment? What if it's my forever home?" I managed through gritted teeth.

"Oh. Well then," she faltered before regrouping. "Okay, what if you meet someone?"

"He'll have his own house."

"But," Mona said, momentarily brain-struck by this revolutionary notion. "Won't you want to live with your life partner?"

"Not necessarily. I'll see. I like the idea of living separately, actually. I'm not too fussed on mopping up his urine because he can't aim straight or picking his back hair out of the shower plug hole. I like to keep the romance alive, thanks. But you know, Mona, I might never meet anyone, and that is just fine. I'm certainly not going to plan my life around possibilities. I'm only interested in what *I* want and what *I* can control. And everybody else can..." I raised my beer and said quietly into its neck, "fuck off," and took a sip.

"Right." Mona did an excellent impression of fucking off. She raised her chin and spun quickly on her heels so that her hair whipped across my face, then she threw an ominous, "I'm watching you, Angus," over her shoulder.

He laughed good-naturedly. "I've no doubt, Mona." He turned to me. "You handled that well. That's the best bit of entertainment I've had since you leapt out of my stream like your arse was on fire."

I grimaced by way of apology, then abruptly stopped. "Angus, why would she be watching you? Has this anything to do with an easement she mentioned to me the other day?"

"Yep, I reckon so. But surely you know about the

easement. It would have been disclosed at the point of sale."

"Um," I tried to look as if I were a responsible land buyer and had done my due diligence before signing the papers, but Derek's salutation to the heavens prevented me from pulling it off effectively.

"How much did you pay your lawyer?"

"The GDP of a small African nation."

"Okay. Look, Nancy, it's not a big deal, don't worry. The easement is for access to lots we're subdividing off the farm. It's at the eastern end of your property – nowhere near where you'll build so it won't have much impact. Originally, we'd approached Mona and Stu to have the easement through their land, but Mona wasn't keen on having her 360-degree view of seamless green ruined by being reminded other people exist. I'm guessing she's not aware we signed with the previous owner."

I took a large sip of my beer. "How big will the subdivision be?"

"Four lots, about an acre each."

"And they'll border my property?"

Angus hesitated. "Ah, yeah, they run right down the boundary between your property and mine. Shit, Nancy, I'm sorry you weren't aware of it. It must be a hell of a surprise."

Derek, cheeks sucked in, glided past, stirring his drink with a straw.

I drained my beer. "I need another drink. Preferably one in each hand."

I TRIED to use the party as an opportunity to network, I really did, but the two drinks I downed in quick succession after the subdivision revelation went straight to my head, and Martin kept handing me more. I didn't want to get off on the wrong foot with him by seeming like an ungrateful guest, so what could I do but indulge him by over-indulging?

The problem was that several glasses of alcohol doesn't do much for enhancing your judgement, and I discovered that my philosophical approach to most things in life was a little on the left of some of the guests. It's possible that I might have been a bit too forward with expressing my opinions.

One man, Jim somebody, bravely introduced that notorious party killer – politics. "I don't know why the government keeps harping on about child poverty. There's no true poverty in this country. Put some of those so-called 'desperately poor' in an African country and they'll know the meaning of the words. It seems 'poverty' is defined in New Zealand by one's lack of unlimited Wi-Fi."

"But, Jim," Angus countered, "poverty is relative, mate. By third-world standards the poor in this country appear moderately well-off, yes, but by first-world standards there are thousands of people below the poverty line. If you can't afford to feed your children every day, or keep them warm and healthy, I'd say that's pretty desperate."

"Nicely put, Angus," I added, "couldn't have put it better myself. I'll tell you one thing, Jim, you could certainly do with sharing your plenty with some of the less fortunate. Looks like you're running out of holes on your belt buckle to keep your paunch in."

Silence.

Angus grabbed my arm and steered me away from the group as Derek gave me two thumbs up from behind Jim's head. "I think I'd better take you home, Captain Tactful. We can pick your car up in the morning."

"Yes, good idea. I think there's three people left that I haven't offended. Best save them for the next occasion."

He took my still half-full drink out of my hand, placed it on a table and steered me towards his ute, shouting farewells en route.

"You could of let me finish that one," I complained.

"Could *have*. And you don't need to finish that one. You've had enough to knock out a bull."

Martin and Anoushka came to wave us off and I gave each a hug that was slightly longer than anyone was comfortable with and declared their party the best I'd ever been to. Ever!

Fortunately, they were both three sheets to the

wind themselves, so they accepted my praise with the good grace of drunks, generously inviting me back anytime I wanted.

I climbed into the ute, banging my forehead on the closed passenger window as I turned to give one last farewell.

"Ow!" I whined.

"Smooth." Angus looked at me pityingly and explained with as much sarcasm as he could muster, "I know windows can be hard to see, but that's the magic of glass. It's see-through, so you can see through it."

He started the ute and the stereo came on automatically, playing a banjo instrumental.

"Who's this? Kermit unplugged?" I laughed uproariously at the genius of my witticism, snorting attractively.

"No, Miss Piggy." He carefully navigated between the cars parked on either side of the long driveway. "This is Béla Fleck, a banjo maestro. This music is from a documentary he made when he travelled to Africa to discover the musical roots of the instrument. Watch it, you might learn the banjo has many more musical facets to it than moonshine and rocking chairs."

"*You've* obviously got plenty of facets – a bowls enthusiast, a lover of obscure music, ninja warrior. What else are you that distinguishes you from the stereotypical farmer?" I looked him right in the eye and said with mock sincerity, "What defines you, Angus Russell Stockman?"

"Well – and you'll have to promise to remember this in the morning, because it's the main thing that gets me up every day to happily chase tiny profit margins – I'm working on getting the farm certified carbon neutral."

"That, Angus, sounds highly ambitious and extraordinarily difficult, but is extremely admirable and I wish you complete success," I said in a rare moment of verbal fluency. Then I ruined it by inhaling sharply and saying reverently, "You're a carbon zero hero."

Angus looked at me with the corners of his mouth upturned and a bubble of laughter burst from his chest. "That's quite catchy. Thanks, Nancy."

"You're welcome," I said thickly as I swallowed back down what tasted like a minted lamb sausage. "Can you drive straighter? Why does there have to be so many curvy bits in the road?"

"Corners?"

"Yep." I waved my hand about. "Just drive through the paddocks." I slapped the dash. "I bet this beast can drive over anything."

"I could do that, or I could just drop you off at your bus. Which is right there." He pointed up the hill we were climbing.

"Okey doke. See if you can get there without turning the wheel."

"Ah, no. I'm not going to do that."

When we pulled up to the bus a few wheel turns later, I turned to Angus, my hand resting on the door release. I surveyed him through heavy eyelids and offered a slow smile.

Derek slid into view from between the back seats. *Are you going to pull a move, Nancy? You look like you're about to pull a move.*

"Oh, fuck off, Derek," I said into the car door as I turned to open it. I climbed out, gave a salute from the bus steps, and after I closed the door, tripped on the top one. It took me a long time to decide that my bed was a better stopping place than the floor.

LATE THE FOLLOWING DAY, when I'd got back from picking up my car and slept off the remainder of my hangover, I rang Hanita.

"His name's Angus."

"Angus? Does he farm cattle?"

"That's what I asked him, but he didn't find it very amusing to begin with. Turns out he does actually farm cattle."

"That's hilarious!"

"I know. He mostly farms sheep, though, apparently. The farm's been handed over to him from his parents and he has to split the profit with his two siblings – minus his salary – to pay them out."

"Did you do some knee perving?"

"He was wearing jeans, alas, but his t-shirt was quite tight, so I perved at other things." I paused. "He's also really eloquent for a farmer."

Hanita waited a beat before saying, "Ah, Nance, that sounds just a teeny bit prejudiced."

"I didn't mean it like that, just that he sounds like he's highly educated, you know, gone to uni or something."

"Plenty of farmers have degrees in Agricultural Studies. And even those that don't can be well-spoken. You, Nance, are not sounding particularly educated right now. You're coming across as a small-minded, ignorant urbanite. Are you sure you're not still drunk?"

"Perfectly sober. Maybe the alcohol sucked all my common sense out along with my brain fluid."

"Don't go saying stupid things like that to anybody there, will you? You'll alienate yourself before you've even had a chance to make friends."

I groaned. "I think I've already made a bit of a start on that. Luckily Angus rescued me last night before I could do too much damage. God, I was awful. That poor man. I really let rip on him." I closed my eyes as the scene replayed itself. "What must Angus think of me?"

"Nance, do you realise a reasonable amount of your conversation revolves around Angus? I think you're more interested than window shopping."

"No I'm not, Hanita! Besides, he's only thirty-four. Even if I was nurturing the smallest flicker of curiosity about seeing him naked, and I'm not saying that I am, he won't be interested in me. I mean, I'm old enough to be his—"

"What? Older sister? Slightly more senior cousin? Get a grip. You're not even old enough to be considered a cougar. What's the biggest difference in age between you and a younger man you've shagged?"

"Um," I wracked my brains. "It would be...negative two months."

"Negative two months?"

"They've all been older, okay? Isn't that normal?"

"It might be more common, but it doesn't have to be a convention that dictates who we choose in a sexual partner. Loosen up. Shift your shagging frame of reference. You might be shocked to discover that a) you are attractive to a younger man, and b) you quite enjoy the sex."

FEBRUARY.

I found a job working the busy weekends at the town's café and adjoining co-op. It didn't pay particularly well, but it was a start and it made a good contribution to my weekly budget.

Not having barista training, I wasn't allowed to make coffee, but I waited on tables, served at both the café and co-op counters, and helped with stocking the co-op when new produce came in.

The profits from the co-op went directly back to the farmers, growers, bakers, cheese-makers and apiarists who provided the goods, while the café was run on a more conventional business model by the woman who established the co-op, Barbara.

Because staff were shared between the two, and some of the produce was used by the café, Barbara spent a lot of her time in the office managing the paperwork.

Barbara was beautiful. She was in her fifties and had large, deep-set eyes above a long, slightly hooked nose. The lines around her mouth were like concentric circles when she smiled and I found I wanted to make her smile as often as I could. Luckily, she liked my sense of humour, so it wasn't too difficult a task.

She always wore bright, bold colours and her hairstyle repertoire could rival that of Princess Leia. She was also organised, decisive, exceptionally good with people and completely comfortable in her own skin. I wanted to be her when I grew up.

Today, Barbara's hair had a purple hydrangea in it above a loose bun, the colour of the flower complimenting the dark grey of her hair. She wore a pale yellow puffed-sleeve blouse above a red polka-dotted skirt and knee-high green boots.

I had been called into her office to discuss the

prospect of me filling in for someone who was on leave the following week.

"It'll be no problem at all, Barbara. I've got no pressing plans and, to be honest, I'd be grateful for the money."

"Okay, great. Thanks Nancy." She shifted her focus back to her computer.

I stood still, watching her. "Barbara?"

"Hmm?" She looked back at me and smiled.

"How do you do it? Age so unbelievably gracefully? I'm trying not to be bitter about the fact that my cells are slowly breaking down and I'll end up a group of molecules dispersing through time and space, but I've recently discovered two black hairs on my chin and I now say 'oomph' every time I have to get up from a seated position. How do you go about life without being crushed by an impending sense of doom?"

Barbara laughed, framing her mouth in her concentric-circle wrinkles. "Well, it helps to have Ngāti Mamoe genetics, but look Nancy, there's nothing you can do about aging, so you might as well embrace it. Take heart in the fact that everyone goes through it – there's no way of avoiding it. Also take heart in the fact that you're aging rather better than a lot of people your age."

God I loved her. If I were not forty and in full view of the coffee-drinking public, I would have done a happy dance. Instead, I mustered my maturity and said, "Thanks, Barbara. That's a really nice thing to say."

She added, "You should celebrate your aging. That's what I do every day. No way in hell am I going to fade into some little grey woman."

"Yeah well, speaking of grey, judging from the amount I've been cultivating recently, that's another thing I'm going to have to embrace."

"Let me see." Barbara stood up, held my face in both hands and turned me so I stood in the light better. "You're not going grey, you're going silver. What a beautiful colour! You've got a shock of it in the front and it looks amazing against your fair hair." She let go of my head and looked into my face. "You're a silver fox."

I was puzzled. "Aren't men silver foxes? You know, DILFs, the George Clooneys of this world...?"

"Ever heard of a man being called 'foxy'? Jimi Hendrix certainly didn't write his song about a man. Claim it, Nancy. Make it yours."

"I am a silver fox" became my mantra. I said it when gorgeous twenty-something bronzed European men came in to order coffee and looked right through me. I said it when I looked in the mirror of the staff toilets and the harsh, fluorescent lighting threw all my fine lines into relief. I said it during a staff reminiscence about what we were doing to celebrate the new millennium and eighteen-year-old Gracie volunteered that she didn't remember the party very well because she was too busy being conceived. And I said it when Angus came into the café and sat down at a window seat.

I had just wrapped my new "hot older lady" confidence around me and was about to go over and take his order, when a young, attractive woman entered the café, gave him a kiss and sat down opposite him.

While I dallied watching the pair of them begin an involved conversation, Gracie clucked her tongue, glided past me and threw a "Too slow, old woman" over her shoulder.

I watched her take their orders with the easy grace of the young – one hip cocked, her ponytail bobbing as she nodded, listening to what they wanted.

However, I made sure I was the first to reach the barista when the coffees were up, and I made my way over to Angus and companion miraculously without tripping, walking into a table or slopping any of the coffee.

"Latte for the lady, flat white for the gentleman."

Angus looked up at me with a surprise that hinted at a level of discomfort. "Nancy! I didn't know you worked here."

"Yep, needs must," I said with a perky smile and stood there hoping he'd introduce me to his lovely younger sister.

He nodded and continued to look at me.

"Riiiiiight, well, enjoy your coffee." I retreated

behind the counter and found something to do that would allow me to surreptitiously watch their table.

The conversation seemed fairly intense. The woman was asking questions and taking notes and it looked like it could be a business meeting of some sort. Not his sister, then.

So, when they had finished an hour and two more coffees later, and she kissed him goodbye with tenderness and love, I was at a complete loss.

Face it, Nancy, said Derek from where he stirred his coffee at a nearby table, *there was never any way he was going to look at you and associate,* he raised his index fingers, *"silvering" hair with hot. But it shouldn't matter, because you're not interested anyway. Right?*

I turned my back on him and it was then, with sudden clarity and impeccable timing, that I remembered the subdivision conversation. I closed my eyes and groaned. How on earth did I miss an important detail like a small village about to be built next to my land?

Nancy, you're a mess. I looked around at Derek and he pointed to my feet.

In my distraction, I'd tipped the plate I had just cleared from a table and oily pesto juice pooled on my left sneaker.

"Fuuuuuck," I said under my breath and marched into the kitchen to clean myself up.

TO: alison.mckendry@mckendrylaw.co.nz
From: nancypants01@getwired.co.nz
Subject: Easement
Hi Alison, can you please look through the file on my property and see what information there is about easement rights to the property behind mine? Apparently, it was all signed off by the previous owner, but I don't recall taking note of it.
Thanks very much,
Nancy

THE PSYCHOLOGIST. *Session one:*

Dr Stevenson, or as she insisted I call her, Lou, sat calmly waiting for my answer, her alarmingly blue eyes fixed on mine, and her hands resting together, not quite steepled.

"I have some baggage from a recent relationship. It's big." I spread my arms wide to indicate its enormity. "Bigger than a Kardashian butt implant. You can see it from space."

Lou offered a small, obligatory smile.

I ran my fingers through my hair. "And no matter what I do, I can't get rid of it. I feel like I'm losing it, you know? Like, my grasp on reality is slowly slipping."

"Okay. And how does this baggage present itself?"

"My ex, Derek, talks to me sometimes, but not in my head. He's physically there with me. I can see him." I laughed. "Crazy, right?"

She shook her head and brushed her dark hair from her eyes. "Many people see loved ones that aren't actually present, particularly those that have passed on. It doesn't make them crazy." She offered a smile, then inhaled slowly through her nose. "What sorts of things does he say?"

"He tells me what a useless twit I am when things get...difficult, or out of my control."

"Hmm. If you were to describe the relationship you had with Derek in three words, what would they be?"

I was quiet for some time. "Inadequate, dominated, old," I offered eventually.

"Interesting. All those words describe how *you* felt while in the relationship, not the relationship itself. None of those words are 'we' words, like, 'loving' or 'toxic' or 'cold'. Do you see the difference?"

I nodded.

"But that's okay, because it helps me see that the relationship was balanced in Derek's favour, and you felt some degree of powerlessness. Would that be accurate?"

I nodded again, slowly, thinking it over. "Yeah, I've never thought terribly hard about it before. I guess I loved him enough that I couldn't see things objectively, or I didn't want to. And since it all ended, I have to admit I've done a lot of brooding, but not a lot of reflection."

"It's very easy to allow anger to wall us in so we can't see over the other side. It prevents us from thinking clearly, from getting perspective. I think it's time you started pulling down those bricks, Nancy."

FIVE

A BLOODY GOOD SHINDIG

"I'M GOING to start a carpentry business." I stood in Margot's kitchen still wrapped in my towel after a shower, chopping beef for a red curry.

She didn't so much as raise an eyebrow. "Good."

"You're not surprised? You don't think it's a bloody stupid idea?"

"I think it's exactly what you need to do."

I had been expecting at least an *Are you sure?*, but more likely a *Have you weighed up the pros and cons, researched what's needed to set up a business, evaluated the likely costs?*

"You should always be happy in what you do. Working's a huge part of your life and what could be more miserable than grinding yourself down toiling away in a thankless job?" She put the curry paste into the frying pan and the oil hissed its welcome. "You

74

were never cut out for an office. You're a doer, a maker."

"No. There's only so much reviewing a policy planner can make of the district plan before it sucks your will to live." I scraped the meat off the board into the pan. "I'm being dramatic, it wasn't that bad. Working for council had its perks, like a secure, regular income." I sighed. "I kind of miss that."

"You'll have to get used to not having those comforts when you own a business, but your advantage is that you won't be starting out with many overheads. You already have most of your equipment, so you'll be able to turn a profit quite quickly."

"*If* I can get work. Do you reckon people would consider hiring a woman to do a job that guys usually do?"

"I think some of them will need to have their opinions shifted. You'd have to prove yourself first, I expect, but with the thousands of hours you've put into renovation over the years, I've no doubt you have enough experience."

I nodded and thought back to the half dozen houses I had tirelessly worked on whenever time allowed. It had never been about turning a profit (well, a bit, maybe), but mostly it had been about the job, about the gratification of transforming a tired, often badly designed space into a thing of beauty.

"There's nothing holding you back, Nancy. If you've got the confidence to present yourself to this community as a skilled workwoman in a male-dominated field and you get the clientele – and I know you can do both – then you are going to do just fine."

She retrieved a bottle of wine from the fridge. "Let's drink to your new venture." Pouring out two glasses, she clinked hers against mine.

I took a sip. "It's going to take a while to get off the ground, isn't it?"

"You are going to have to exercise the patience of a virgin on her wedding night."

THAT NIGHT I rang Hanita from the comfort of the bus' couch to bounce business names off her. "I'm thinking about having something with a pun, like 'Off the Shelf Joinery' or something with a 'x' in it, like 'Woodworx'."

"Ew, don't you dare! I will not associate with you if you debase your fledgling business in such a tacky way."

"Point taken. What if I called it 'Petrified Woodcraft' and have a logo of a really scared looking tree."

Silence. Then, "You're just playing with me."

Laughing, I said, "Sorry, you're just so easy to wind up. And I've got a bit of nervous energy at the moment. Turns me into Jokester Nancy."

"Why?"

"I don't know. Because it's better than being Bitchy Nancy?"

"No, why the nervous energy?"

"I'm worried that no one will want to hire a woman to do what they think should be a man's job."

I pushed myself further into the cushions. "Then you've got to build a really good reputation. Set up a website that showcases your skills. You can start by putting up photos of the interior of the bus. Have you got before shots?"

"Yes."

"Perfect. You can add to your gallery the more jobs you do. Plus, in a small town a lot of work will be got via word of mouth. Make sure you pull a stunner on your first job and encourage the client to tell everyone what excellent work you did."

"Okay."

"Oooh, I know what you should do to promote your business – start a Facebook page and post funny stuff so that people will be drawn into liking your page and share the content. I saw this meme once with a rugged-looking builder dude smiling into the camera. At the bottom it said, 'Sawdust is man-glitter'. You need to be posting stuff like that."

I had just taken the first sip of my evening chamomile tea and the urge to laugh was confused with my urge to swallow. "That is awesome!" I croaked when my coughing fit subsided.

"I'll help you do the website. It's pretty cheap and easy these days to build your own site and have it look sexy and professional."

I gasped with the suddenness of an idea. "What about 'Sawcraft'? It's short and simple and easy to remember. I could have 'carpenter and renovator' as a subtitle."

"Yeah, that could work."

"And I could change the 'c' in 'craft' to a 'k'."

"Nancy, don't make me come over there to knock some good taste into you."

"Snob."

"At least I'm a snob with a job. Maybe you shouldn't be too quick to dismiss my ideas."

"Sure. Is that ideas with a 'z'?"

———

LATER THAT MONTH was Margot's eightieth. She'd hired the municipal hall, citing her need as a grand old lady to celebrate such a significant milestone in a grand old hall.

I felt it only appropriate to rise to the occasion and wear my one and only dress-up dress. It was maroon red, mid-calf, figure hugging and off the shoulder.

I thought I looked quite nice, but with no decent mirror and minimal lighting in the bus it was hard to tell. It could have been inside out and back to front for all I knew.

When I arrived, Margot and her children were at the door greeting everyone. The grandchildren and great-grandchildren were in the hall, already making a concerted effort to get the party underway.

I'd met all of her kids before and greeted them warmly, but I only knew a handful of her grandchildren and none of the youngest generation.

Of the grandchildren, only a couple were near my age, and I had fond memories of two in particular. Wheturangi and his sister, Teremoana, had played with Will and me during the summers they also visited, and although I hadn't seen them in years, I recognised them instantly.

"Whetu, is that you?"

"Nancy? Wow, look at you. You're looking great. You've got to be what, fifty now? Not bad, girl, not bad."

I gave him a playful punch on the shoulder and patted his well-padded stomach. "What happened? You used to be stick thin. Remember, we used to call you invisi-boy because when you turned sideways we couldn't see you anymore."

"I know, too much of the good life. That and faulty contraception." He nodded to the throng of little people, running and squealing their way around the tables.

"Oh yeah? How many of those are you responsible for?"

"Just two. Could be worse. Tere's hapu with her fourth."

"Blimey. And I think having six chickens is a handful. I bet she's very good at it though."

"Getting pregnant?"

"No, being a mum. She was always such a considerate little girl and I bet those kids know exactly where they stand. Where is she anyway? I can't see anybody with an enormous stomach. Except you." I grinned and kissed his cheek.

"There she is. Tere!" Whetu shouted above the music and din of children. "It's Nancy-Pants Myers. She wants to know what your secret to eternal fertility is."

Tere waddled over to where we stood and leaned in awkwardly for a kiss. "So lovely to see you, Nancy. Nana said you would be here."

"It's been too long, aye?" I patted her stomach. "Bloody hell, you're enormous."

"I know. I'm worried that with the weight of it and after having three big babies it'll just fall out onto the floor."

I laughed and Whetu said, "How are your parents?"

"The question is, *where* are my parents. They've retired into backpacking the globe. I don't think they want to come back, to be honest. Currently, they're yoga-ing themselves into enlightenment at a retreat in Sri Lanka."

As I talked, my eyes, in disregard of the etiquette of polite conversation, felt compelled to keep checking the activity at the door. It may or may not have had anything to do with the expectation that Angus and companion would arrive at any moment.

"Who are you waiting for, Nancy?" asked Tere. "Must be someone pretty special. You got them nervous love eyes. Relax, girl. Whoever he is you're gonna scare him off with your jittery energy."

I absolutely *did not* have love eyes. I cleared up any confusion by shouting, "I do not have love eyes!" and adding, "I don't believe in love anymore, so how could I possibly project that particular emotion through my eyeballs?"

Tere and Whetu exchanged a look and Derek materialised between them, a hand on each of their shoulders. *Do you recognise that expression, Nancy? It's the one that communicates words like 'doth' and 'protest'.*

"It does not. Piss off."

"Okay, okay, you don't have love eyes! Here," Tere reached for a glass of sparkling wine, "maybe you should have a drink."

"Yeah, but just one, mind," Whetu added. "*Should* you want to impress him, best not to do it by showcasing your floor hugging skills."

WHEN ANGUS DID ARRIVE some time later, and stepped into the room alone, my stomach disassociated itself from my body and settled back into place with a snap. He was dressed in a fitting, dark shirt with the top two buttons undone to reveal the hollow between his clavicle, and smart black trousers.

He made his way over to an older couple, gave each of them a hug and exchanged a few words, then started circulating round the room, chatting with people.

Eventually, he spotted me and came over to where I was standing grazing on olive tapenade and honeyed feta.

"Nice dress."

"Thanks. This is my wedding dress."

Angus gave me a puzzled, slightly alarmed look.

"Wait, no. Let me rephrase. I don't want to sound like some sort of Miss Havisham, walking around in a decaying shrine to failed matrimony. It's the dress I wear to *other people's* weddings. The only occasion I have for dressing up is weddings, and I get invited so infrequently I might as well save money and wear the same outfit. It also provides continuity between the wedding photos. It looks like I've been to ten weddings in one day."

"Sooo, you don't have an actual wedding dress stashed somewhere?"

"Nope. I am definitely not a divorcee," I answered, energised by the conversational direction.

"And you haven't left a broken heart in the city, hoping the land thing is just a phase, that you'll eventually get it out of your system and go back to him?"

"That's an excellent question. The answer is definitively and unequivocally 'no'."

"Okay, good."

I smiled into my shoes and imagined I was standing on Derek's face, the 'o' of his mouth collapsing under my weight. "And you, Angus?"

He looked away over my right shoulder, inhaled deeply through his nose, looked back at me and exhaled.

"I have some complications, yes. But that is a conversation for another time. Let me introduce you to my parents," he said, quickly changing the subject *almost* before I had time to think of café woman. "Just to warn you. Dad has one major interest — farming. Talk about anything else and you'll likely lose him." Angus took my elbow and gently steered me towards the couple he had greeted when he came in.

I had no idea such a bony part of the body could be an erogenous zone, but my pleasure centre seemed to have relocated to the wrinkled skin around the joint.

When Angus said, "Mum, Dad, this is Nancy. Nancy, this is Rob and Liz," and dropped his hand, my elbow felt exposed, as if it were a more private, secret place.

"Nancy," Liz said. "I've heard a lot about you."

I glanced at Angus and glued my smile in place. "Have you?" I tallied the number of times I'd embarrassed myself in front of him and pictured the three of them, their heads thrown back in laughter.

"You know we have a lot in common?" She placed a hand on her husband's arm. "Rob and I downsized a couple of years ago. We swapped living in the main house for the two-bedroom farm cottage Angus was in and it's the best move we could have made. To be perfectly honest, I don't know why anybody would want a large house. Unless you had a lot of children."

I had to agree. "My ex-partner and I had a four bedroomer before and I ended up suffering from space guilt. Why on earth would two people need that many rooms? It belongs to a family now, as it should."

Rob said, "Angus tells me you've got some sheep. Do you know much about looking after them?"

Angus placed his hand on the small of my back. No doubt it was intended as a 'dig in – the onslaught of farming verbiage is about to rain down upon you' gesture, but with the heat that pooled under this touch and radiated across the rest of my flesh I needed the space of an "Um" to redirect my thoughts. "Above drenching them and hiring a shearer? No."

"Okay, well this time of year you've got to be aware of facial eczema. When fungal spore counts get high in the grass, it can affect their liver. Once you see the eczema it's too late."

The heat of Angus' hand receded under a violent surge of freak out.

That particular piece of information seemed the kind a responsible sheep mother would know and then done everything in her power to mitigate the risk of.

I didn't want to ask the question, because I wasn't sure I'd like the answer. "It's not...too late, is it?"

"No, I believe spore counts are climbing, but they're not at critical mass yet."

Thank Christ.

"However, you should get them protected now."

"How do I do that?"

"You insert a zinc tablet down their throat using a special gun to administer it. That will sit in their stomach and act as a prophylactic. It lasts about a month."

"When you said 'you', you meant someone else that wasn't me, right? It would be like wielding the needle when you immunise your children."

Rob gave me a sympathetic smile. "Tell you what, I'll come over and we'll do it together. You can hold the sheep and I'll do the nasty bit."

We were interrupted by another couple who had come to say hello to Liz and Rob, and I turned to Angus. "That was really generous of your dad."

"You'll find most people are around here. We're a small community – it pays to look out for each other."

"How do I repay something like that?"

"Any chocolate-based baking should do it. Of the 30 teeth he has left, 28 of them are sweet." Angus took a swig of his beer. "So, how're things at the co-op?"

"Fine. I think I'm in love with Barbara. She is one super funky lady and she doesn't seem to mind that I'm a bit rubbish with delivering un-spilt coffee and always being polite. And she called me a silver fox."

"A silver fox?"

"Yeah, on account of me going grey. And being foxy."

Angus threw his head back and laughed. Then he looked me right in the eye and said, "She's right. You are definitely a silver fox."

All the saliva in my mouth disappeared and I knew I was no longer a captain at the helm of SS *Just Looking*. I had to work my tongue furiously to unglue it from the roof of my mouth.

I dropped my eyes to the floor and said in a fast ramble, "But it's only two days a week. I could really do with a couple more, you know? The cost of the build is starting to get very real, and it's freaking me out a bit. I thought I had enough to get the project started, but I've got to live as well, and I'm already starting to eat into the build budget..."

"Nancy," Angus grabbed my upper arms and made me look at him. "It's okay. I think I have something for you. Some work on the farm. Can I come over to your place sometime to talk it through with you?"

I started to answer that, "Yes, that would be unbelievably incredible," hoping that as an officer of the grammar police he wouldn't pick up on my tautology, when I was interrupted by a microphoned announcement that entries for the caption competition would be closing in five minutes, then winners would be announced before a short speech from Margot.

We wandered over to a wall that had photos of Margot tacked to it with numerous captions already lined up underneath. I chose a photo showing Margot unwrapping a large, cylindrical object, clearly chosen for its phallic quality. I wrote:

Margot read the speed settings for her new vibrator with eager anticipation:

1. Thunder Downunder

2. Rumble in the Jungle

3. Chernobyl

Angus laughed so much he had to wipe his eyes. "You are one funny lady, Nancy. You know that, right?"

I grinned at him and squished Derek's face further under my heel.

A few minutes later the music faded and Margot took the stage.

Everyone turned towards the front of the hall, the chatter dying.

"Good evening everyone, I've had the happy job of judging the caption competition for photos I thought I'd burned two decades ago. Thank you to my delightful children for digging them up. I think they were filed under 'Stone Age'. Firstly, let me say how disappointed I am that none of the contestants attempted to bribe the judge with promises of back rubs and pedicures."

"Is it too late?" someone called out. "I've got a good hoof pick. I'll scrape your toenails for you."

"Yes, Mac, unfortunately it is too late, because the judging's been done. The winner of the competition is...Nancy Myers, with her caption for this photo." Margot held it up for everyone to see then read out my entry.

It received a gratifying amount of laughter from the floor as I was called up on stage and handed a bottle of Marlborough Sauvignon Blanc from Margot's daughter.

Emboldened by the Derek brain goo oozing across the floor, I said to Angus on my return, "This is too good to waste on just me. Come over tomorrow night and we can crack it during our business meeting."

"That could be dangerous," he replied suggestively.

My stomach fluttered wildly.

"You might take advantage of me and persuade me into agreeing to an exorbitant hourly rate."

"Angus, I'll have you know I am worth every penny of an exorbitant hourly rate."

Margot addressed the guests again and I had to wrench my attention away from his grin.

"Alright, and now for the speech. I am going to keep this short because I know how tedious speeches can be, especially when there's the important task of carousing to get on with. I've also had five too many aperitifs, so there's a high risk I'll end up drivelling on into the small hours. Whetu?"

A "Yup" boomed from the back of the hall.

"Set the timer on your phone to thirty seconds please. Right. I'd like to thank everyone who's come here tonight – my beautiful family and wonderful friends – to help an old lady celebrate a very impressive milestone. I know. Even I'm surprised that after all the drug taking and unprotected promiscuity of the late sixties I've made it this far."

"Mum, you were married with three children by the late sixties!" her eldest son called out.

"Yes, Michael. Your point being? Anyway, as I was saying before I was rudely interrupted by a child whose mother obviously neglected to teach him good manners, I'm eighty!"

Whoops and whistles rang out across the hall.

"And I reckon even an old duck like me can throw a bloody good shindig, so I challenge you to make merry to the last eighty-year-old standing!"

Whetu's alarm went off as the hall erupted with applause.

. . .

AS PEOPLE DRANK MORE and the volume in the hall increased, it became harder and harder to have a conversation. Angus had to stand very close and lean into my ear to make himself heard, his jawline nearly brushing mine. Concentration became rather difficult and my vagina, studiously ignoring my brain, started its own conversation with Angus.

"How about we dance?" I suggested in a bid to a) avoid the discomfort of a shouted conversation so close to our cochleae and b) give my knickers time to dry out.

Angus liked the idea.

As soon as we got on the dance floor, I realised I'd made a big mistake. Angus could dance. Angus could *really* dance. And a man who can dance is the mother lode of all aphrodisiacs. I felt like I was mainlining dopamine just watching him.

"Where did you learn to dance like that?" I shouted, rather breathily.

Angus shrugged. "I come from a musical family. I just can. Dance, I mean."

"Do you play an instrument?"

"Nah, not really. I'm okay with the guitar, but I'm a better singer than a player." He smiled and said, "I listen to music a lot. As Blur put it, 'Music is my Radar'. It makes me very happy. In fact, Margot entrusted me with the playlist. It's got a little something for everybody, but I think we're about to enter a musical genre that might bring a bit of nostalgia for you."

Gary Numan's 'Are Friends Electric?' pulsated across the dance floor.

"Eighties electro-pop? Aren't you too young to even know what that is?"

"Hey, I'm not that much younger than you, and this has a shitload more soul than mere electro-pop, even if Numan wasn't recognised for it at the time." He looked down at my feet. "You know, you're not so much of a bad dancer yourself, Nancy Myers. Though how you jungle boogie in those ridiculous, ankle-snapping shoes, I don't know."

"That, Angus, is why women are the superior sex – adopting a gravity-defying, ergonomically eye-watering shoe design, that was probably created by men for the benefit of men, and mastering its use with skill and poise. If it was the other way around, you'd be constantly flat on your arse."

Several musical genres later, we had just started dancing to Justin Bieber's 'What Do You Mean?' when Whetu sidled up.

"Nancy, I didn't know you were a Belieber."

"I try not to be too much of a musical snob, Whetu. This is actually quite a good song. Surprisingly."

"Yeah, it's got really great syncopation," Angus added. "Listen to the off-beats that are stressed with the synth."

"We haven't met," Whetu extended his hand. "I'm Margot's grandson, Wheturangi."

"Nice to meet you. Angus."

"So, Angus" – Whetu directed a very unsubtle wink at me – "you've been monopolising a lot of our Nancy's time this evening. What makes your company more valuable than anybody else's?"

Angus required all the loin girding of a single blink before replying, "The question is, Wheturangi, what makes Nancy worthy of such undivided attention? She's demonstrated tonight that she can dress up for an occasion and not break a tibia, that she has a full dance repertoire, including the hand jive *and* the funky chicken, and that she can be funny without offending anybody. Her behaviour's improved a lot since the last party we both attended, where she left several obnoxious people in no doubt of their place in the natural order of the universe and abused Kermit the Frog."

Impressed by the speed and verbosity of Angus' calm response under Whetu's scrutiny, I naturally said, "Yeah well, he deserved it, the whiny amphibian. Try being peri-menopausal. See how hard that is. I'd choose to be green any day."

BY ONE IN the morning I felt broken. My shoes had long been discarded, my throat was sore from yelling, my ears were ringing from the noise, and my body was acutely aware of every minute that had gone by since my usual bedtime. When I yawned for the seventh time Angus said, "Come on. I'll walk you to your car."

Stepping out into the still warm night, we walked the short distance to my car in silence. I stood against the door, looking at him, my brain empty and my heart racing.

Angus broke the silence. "Great dancing, partner."

"Yep. We did good."

He put his hands in his pockets.

I drew a breath. And exhaled.

And accepted that the appropriate thing to do was to get in my car and leave. I stood on my tiptoes and gave him a kiss goodnight on the cheek. "See you tomorrow night, Angus."

"See you tomorrow night." He held up a hand in farewell as I drove off.

THE NEXT DAY I rang Hanita from the cocoon of my bed to discuss the nerve-wracking prospect of entertaining Angus in the bus.

"I've decided it's safe to enter the shop and do some product sampling."

"Okay! That's good."

I agreed and rolled over to peer through the crack in the curtains at the rain.

"Are you sure it's not just a business meeting,

though? I don't want you to get your hopes up if all he actually wants to do is offer you a job."

"All the signs were there. He pretty much asked me directly if I was single and emotionally unattached, he danced with me all evening, and he walked me to my car in awkward but meaningful silence. I don't think it could be much clearer." I dropped my voice. "I'm gonna make my signature move."

Hanita laughed. "Your signature move? Which one is that again? Impressing him with the ability to pick your nose with your tongue? Making a bong out of a coconut and modified apple corer?"

"That's unfair!" I countered. "I haven't done the bong party trick since high school. And besides, it's not much of a trick when the coconut fibre catches fire and burns your eyebrows off."

"Look, Nance, just play it cool, okay? If you read into his behaviour too much, your imagination will fill in the gaps. Let him make the first move."

I sighed. "Okay. I guess."

"And call me straight away and tell me all about it."

I'D ARRANGED with Angus to have a post-dinner meeting early enough in the evening that the bus would still be well-lit by daylight. I was very keen for my mostly finished wee home to be looking its impressive best, given that he'd only seen it from the outside.

I spent half an hour pacing the bus, ensuring everything was perfect. Then I stood by the bus' rear wheels and watched the changing light in the alps. Slowly, like sand settling on the ocean floor, my mind calmed and I felt ready for whatever the evening would present.

Angus arrived at seven-thirty bearing crackers and cheese to go with the wine. When he stepped inside the bus, he took a few seconds to take it all in.

"Whoa."

"I know."

"This is an awesome set-up!"

"Thanks. I did it all myself."

"You did it yourself?"

"Yep. I've spent the last month or so refitting it from top to bottom."

He ran a hand over the macrocarpa kitchen joinery. "And you marvel at *my* facets. I'm totally blown away. The workmanship, sorry work*woman*ship, is bloody brilliant." He looked up from inspecting the cupboards and drawers and met my eyes. "You are an unusual and very surprising woman, Nancy Myers. I imagine Margot's very proud of you."

Heat flooded my chest and I busied myself with the wine. "Margot's very encouraging, which is great, because I need it." I handed him his glass and asked, "So, what's this job you've got for me?"

"Well, do you remember what I told you in the car on the way home from Martin and Anoushka's?"

"Yes, I remember saying something cheesy about you being a 'carbon zero hero', because I'm very good at embarrassing myself." I arranged the crackers and cheese on a wooden board. "You want to get the farm to a point where it has no carbon footprint?"

"It's a bit of a crazy goal and I'm not sure I can do it, but I'm working pretty hard at it. I'm lucky in that the farm has large tracts of untouched native bush in the least accessible gullies, so I've been able to have them covenanted. They'll provide a reasonable carbon offset, but nowhere near enough." He took a sip of wine. "So, what I'm doing to try to plug the massive gap is propagate more natives. That's where you come in."

I gestured for us to sit down at the foldaway table. "Okay. I've got no experience at all in that area, but I'm intrigued to hear what you're going to say next."

"Well, for years I've been collecting local seeds and sowing them with a lot of hit and miss, but I've got my growing conditions just right now and I've got approximately ten thousand plants at varying stages of development. And that's great – I'm really happy with the progress I've made, but the reality is I'm just too busy elsewhere on the farm to manage the project properly. I need someone who can continue to collect seeds and specimens, get them germinating and growing to a point where they're ready to plant. The seedlings need to be looked after so they're healthy and planted when they're ready." He exhaled sharply. "I know it sounds like a lot, but it's mostly straight forward stuff, and I'll be around to help. I reckon it will be two days total work a week, but I want it spread over four. Which days is totally negotiable. What do you think?"

I knew what I *shouldn't* think. Sitting opposite me was an attractive man with not only a full head of hair and a sense of rhythm, but such strong environmental principles that he was prepared to throw money into a project he might not see a return on. The word "perfect" flittered across my mind.

I dismissed it and pretended to think about his proposition over a sip of wine. When enough time had elapsed to give a convincing impression that I'd been engaged in careful deliberation, I said, "I'll do it. I admire what you want to achieve, Angus, and I believe in it. I can see how important success is to you, but I also see that regardless of whether you get to the point of certification or not, you'll be setting an important example *and* precedent for sustainable farming practices. I would absolutely love to support you."

Angus looked at me for a beat, then said quietly, "Thanks, Nance."

It was the first time he'd used the shortened, more

familiar version of my name, and a warmth germinated in my chest and spread through my limbs. I placed the cool backs of my hands on my warm cheeks before reaching for the stem of my wine glass. "Right, I think the sensible thing to do would be to finish this bottle of wine before we start discussing my hourly rate."

For the next half an hour we talked about his parents' positive attitude towards the farm's new direction, the range of reactions from other farmers, and the support he'd received from the regional council. Eventually, Angus produced a well-thumbed book on the propagation of native plants in New Zealand and said it had been his bible for the project.

"I'll leave it here with you so that you can have a look through and get a feel for what's required."

"Blimey, it's been about fifteen years since I've had to swot for anything. Please tell me it's picture rather than text-based. I'm a visual learner. I know that because in sex ed when we were shown those photos of nasty sexually transmitted diseases, the ones designed to put you off having sex until marriage, I scored one hundred percent on the Name That Disease test afterwards."

"Um."

"I know, right? Herpes and chancroids look remarkably similar."

"Okaaaaay. Is that a real story or was that supposed to make me laugh, because either way, it's pretty gross."

"I made it up. Sorry, I'm a little nervous right now and I tend to turn into somewhat of a clown when I'm out of my comfort zone. It can make hitting the entertaining mark a bit like aiming for a mosquito with a shotgun."

"You're not shy of the challenge, though. I guess that in itself is admirable."

"Thanks. I appreciate your hesitant appreciation."

Angus' chuckle rumbled around the bus. "No problem. Anyway, the book's not strictly picture-based, but the propagation methodology is clearly set out. Here, I'll show you."

He moved around to my side of the table, and because of the small size of the book, he had to sit very close so that we could both get a good view.

"See here, how it has a picture of the plant or seed followed by headed descriptions about how to treat the seeds and spores?" He had draped his arm along the back of my chair and in the tight confines of the small table his thigh was forced up against mine.

"Mmmhmm," I answered.

He said something else, but all I could hear was the delighted squeal of my inner fox.

"Nancy?"

"Yes?"

"I asked you a question."

"Did you? Sorry, I *am* trying to focus, but my brain has gone into pheromone overload courtesy of four out of my five senses. If you sat any closer we could add the fifth, but then I think my brain would melt."

Angus took a moment to process this. "You want to lick me?"

"I admit, I have thought about it." I said, staring at the hollow underneath his Adam's apple. "You probably taste of sunshine and grassy meadows."

"Nah, roast beef," Angus attempted to quip, but his smile disappeared as he looked at me and the space between us crackled with tension.

He held my gaze for several long seconds. Then he looked down at the book, closed it and shifted his feet under himself in readiness to stand up.

"Okay..." I exhaled through pursed lips. "That was..."

He slumped back in his seat. "Sorry."

We were quiet for a moment, then I ventured, "I take it your 'complication' complicated things just then?"

He laughed. A single humourless chuckle. Then he looked at me, one side of his mouth turned up in a smile. "Yeah."

"Do you think, perhaps, that 'other time' could be now?"

Angus drew in a deep breath and looked down at the book. "Alright." He started fidgeting with its corners. "I reckon I owe you that, but" – he looked back up at me – "this is something I am keeping very private, so I need to be able to trust you with it. This can't go any further."

"Of course."

"Well, I have, until recently, been in a very long-term relationship, about eleven years. Things got progressively sour towards the end, and it all unravelled quickly and bitterly. She lived with me on the farm for most of the time we were together, and that has allowed her to think," he paused, swallowing audibly, "that she can make a claim on my portion of the farm, which I only recently inherited. I have no idea why she's doing it – out of spite? I don't know, but apparently she can do this and there's a possibility that I will have to pay her out."

I was quiet for a couple of beats. Eleven years. The most I'd managed was a poxy two and a half, but even I'd unquestioningly accepted the requirements of de facto property law. "That sounds very...stressful."

He snorted. "Yeah, you've no idea. Luckily, I've got a very supportive family, including a cousin who practices family law. That was who I was meeting with at the café a couple of weeks back."

"Ah," I said with guilty relief. Then, "Angus, eleven years is a long time."

"I know. And that could weigh it in her favour. I know what you're thinking, but her contribution to the farm was minimal. She had her own career and didn't have much of a financial loss as far as I can see when the relationship broke up."

I shifted in my seat, edging ever so slightly away from his chair. "Why did things fall apart?"

"Lots of reasons. I guess the main sticking point was that she wanted marriage and kids, and I couldn't say with certainty that I wanted those things with her. You know, a lot of farmers put their farm into trust for their children to protect them from things like this happening, but my parents didn't think about it." He looked up at me from under his brows and said, "It's all pretty bloody awful, really."

And goddamn him, after he gave me a fleeting half-smile, his eyes began to well. The resulting rush of tenderness overrode any indignation I might have had on behalf of his ex and I reached out my hand and placed it on his cheek.

He looked at me for a good, long moment, shifted his eyes to my lips, then leaned forward and placed a soft kiss on them.

Everything narrowed to that single point of contact and any thought of disenfranchised exes evaporated. His breath, warming my skin, was at once intimate and erotic and my stomach and groin competed in theatrics.

Angus drew back a few inches and held my gaze. It was up to me to decide what happened next and I debated for all of three seconds before leaning towards him and finding his lips again.

He didn't taste of sunshine or grass, but of the sharpness of the wine and an earthy sweetness, like yams, that was all him.

His lips parted and his tongue tentatively touched mine.

An electric charge zip-lined between the tip of my tongue and my belly button and a sudden heaviness sat between my legs.

Angus' hand inched its way up the outside of my thigh and he pulled me to him, swinging my leg around so that I straddled his lap. His arousal pressed into me and when I shifted my hips to get better contact, he emitted an involuntary "huh".

The gentle exploration became a press of tongue and lips. The desire to get as close as possible now a need.

He pulled back. "Listen, Nance," he said breathily, his focus shifting between my eyes and my lips. "Before this goes any further, I want to be really clear on one thing. Obviously, I'm not in any space to think about a relationship. If we do this, it can only be casual. Are you okay with that?"

I nodded. "I'm not looking for anything serious either."

I closed the gap between us, nibbling on his bottom lip.

Angus' hands made their way under my top, his

fingertips travelling the length of my back and I shivered at the thrill of his touch. When his hands eventually started to make their slow way towards my breasts, another face pressed between ours and hummed hungrily. *This is nice*, it mumbled into the sides of our mouths.

I jerked backwards and sat upright, breathing heavily. Derek was gone.

Angus regarded me quizzically. "Everything okay?"

"Ah. Yeah." I gave him a smile. "Everything's fine."

He pulled me back into the kiss and started to work on the clasp of my bra.

I slid my hands under his shirt and felt the smooth, warm skin of his back.

To my left, someone started clapping.

Way to go, Nancy – straight into the arms of another man who doesn't appreciate the worth of his women.

I looked at Derek out of the corner of my eye.

He leant against the pantry doors, arms and ankles crossed, his mouth in a smirk.

I straightened up again. "You know, I do need to think about this. I'm sorry, Angus."

"Okay."

"Really sorry."

"It's okay, Nance. I understand. Logic and desire don't often work well together."

With slightly trembling legs, I climbed off him and he stood up. "I'd better go," he said softly.

I nodded.

"Look at the book, and I'll see you next Monday morning, at eight. Don't forget to set your alarm."

"I won't."

"And wear something loose and baggy. The uglier, the better."

"Roger, Captain."

SIX

LIVE LONG AND PROSPER

THE PSYCHOLOGIST. *Session two:*

"It's just so creepy. What's wrong with my brain?"

Lou cocked her head and fixed me with her pale eyes. "It sounds like you're allowing Derek to act out your conscience."

"I'm not allowing him anything. I mean, why would I willingly invite him into my head?" I shuddered. "You're saying I *let* him be part of that kiss?"

"Yes."

"Oh God. I *am* crazy."

"No, you're just insecure."

"No I'm not!"

Ignoring my outburst, Lou continued, "Derek is an...expression of that."

"I am *not* insecure. I know what I want and I'm driven to get it and...and I'm forging a new path with a shitload of confidence." I stabbed the air with my pointer finger.

"And therein lies the rub, Nancy. You have this wonderful inner conflict. Fiercely proud, independent Nancy and vulnerable, uncertain Nancy. Proud Nancy's in denial and won't acknowledge Insecure Nancy, and Insecure Nancy is desperate to be heard, so she's created Derek to get Proud Nancy's attention."

"Maybe Proud Nancy's too busy shifting bricks."

"Well, let's help her so she *can* pay attention. Why are you so angry?"

That was an easy one. "Betrayal." I took a deep breath and told Lou about the circumstances of my break up with Derek, about how I hadn't seen it coming, about how he had made me a fool. "I felt," I stopped and corrected myself, "I *feel* so incredibly humiliated."

Lou suggested we "unpack" that statement.

I shifted in my chair, pulling my sticky shirt away from my back, then pinning my hands under my thighs.

"You said you felt old, inadequate and dominated in your relationship with Derek. Yes?"

I nodded.

"Your anger, a consequence of feeling humiliated, is knitted to your insecurity, Nancy. Let's tease them apart. I'm going to start with 'old'. Did you feel old while in the relationship?"

"No."

"Right, so that's actually a consequence of feeling humiliated, being cuckolded if I can use a male term. Things have changed though. A younger man finds you attractive. This man, in fact, finds you attractive enough to want to sleep with you. How do you feel about your age now?"

"I feel like I'm trying really hard to be the fox, but it's just a stole draped around my neck. I'm an impostor."

Lou asked me to explain and I told her about Barbara's encouragement in assuming proprietary rights over "silver fox".

"I see."

I didn't. I looked down at the shirt button I was fiddling with and muttered, "Said the blind man while peeing into the wind."

Lou didn't laugh. "Your humiliation, your hurt, is preventing you from acknowledging the beauty of your Self. And I don't just mean your physical self."

The beauty of my Self? I wasn't interested in a pep-talk about self-love. "Look, at the end of the day, I might be able to get a younger man to sleep with me, but not *be* with me. There's no way he'd ever consider me girlfriend material."

"How do you know?"

"Because that's the way things work. Men only want younger women. Younger women like to have older men. It's biological, it's out of our control. Young equals fertile, more mature equals security – better provision for future children. Even men *my* age are no longer looking at me."

"I can guarantee they are. You're right, there's a biological pull to select partners who optimise our breeding potential, but we're no longer simple creatures driven to procreate. The modern human is far more discerning. Our way of life – our social pulls, our drivers, our material desires – is incredibly sophisticated and we have the privilege of being able to make decisions about how we lead our lives that our Homo sapiens ancestors could never dream of. Don't be in a hurry to minimise our motives. It won't always serve you well."

Feeling slightly chastened, I took a long drink of water from the glass Lou had provided. It bought me time to shuffle my thoughts around, if not exactly to the place Lou was pointing, at least to a loosening of the roots tying them to my emotions.

Lou waited until I'd finished drinking, as if she knew I needed the pause to recalibrate. "Now, I'm going to momentarily digress to your other words – dominated and inadequate. They're heavy words. I want you to take those words, put one into each of your palms and feel the weight of them."

I closed my eyes and thought about why I had given voice to each word, all the things that had made me feel those ways, and I *could* feel the weight of them. They sat on my outstretched hands, each a dense and dark mass undulating in a cloud of something even darker. Anger. Its energy rolled off them.

It might have been alarming, but I wasn't scared by the force of it. I was saddened. I opened my eyes and looked at Lou through a watery lens.

She smiled and said, "Good. Now that you can look at them, feel them outside yourself, do you think you were happy in your relationship?"

I slowly shook my head. "No. I guess I wasn't. I was so in love with him, I think I blamed any issues on me. I can't have been happy."

"And do you think he was happy in the relationship? Do you think an imbalanced one satisfied him?"

I snorted. "Well, obviously not."

"Exactly. Derek's philandering probably had less to do with wanting someone younger, and more to do with wanting someone *different*, someone who might provide the equal partnership we all want. Her age is irrelevant."

I said nothing, wanting what she said to be true, but not finding it within myself to believe her.

With gentleness, Lou said, "Start paying attention, Nancy. Don't allow yourself to dismiss admiration because of assumptions based on hurt and not likelihood. Then you'll find you can accept your self-truths, truths often revealed by how others treat you and react to you."

I HAD a week until I started work for Angus. I told myself I had to have the paperwork for my build into council before I propagated a single plant.

The plans came back from the draftsman on Tuesday. By Wednesday I had eleven quotes from potential contractors for various jobs and a logo designed for my new business. And on Thursday, Rob made good on his offer and the sheep were safe from fungal spores. In compensation, I made him Hazelnut Rocky Road.

He looked like Angus when he smiled.

Angus. I tried not to think about the awkward encounter with him, but with his book on propagation lying on the table as a reminder, it was difficult to stop replaying it.

I phoned Hanita, not sure if I needed sympathy, or distraction, or advice, or all of the above.

"He's a very good kisser. Shame he's just another one of those blokes."

"Another of what kind of bloke?"

"The type that undervalues their partner." I sighed. "But what do I know? I imagine it's pretty difficult splitting up farms that have been in one family for generations when a marriage or relationship fails."

"That's right. Maybe you should reserve your judgment."

"Well, anyway, I'll definitely be steering clear of him, even if he is lovely to the touch."

Hanita paused before saying, "It must be flattering having a young, attractive man keen to get their jiggy on with you."

I thought back to my session with Lou. Pay attention. Accept. "You have no idea. How on earth am I going to manage working four days a week with him? It's going to be an exercise in clitoral torture."

"It doesn't sound like you'll be working with him that much. He'll teach you what to do and then you'll be on your own for most of the week. And besides, he'll probably be sweaty and stinky and covered in cow shit most of the time. I know you most likely picture him as the gorgeous man that stepped into the hall at Margot's eightieth, but the reality of Angus' day-to-day life is not particularly glamorous."

"At the very least he's going to have to start wearing trousers. It's only fair if I have to wear old, shapeless castoffs from ex-Buffy the Vampire Slayer fans. You should see the church charity shop. It has a whole room dedicated to T-shirt merchandising. I could wear a shirt paying homage to the wrinkles in Dylan's brow from *Beverly Hills 90210* one day and the torso of Mr T the next."

"Did they have any Star Trek T-shirts?" asked Hanita provocatively.

"I would rather lance my own arse boils than advertise that science fiction travesty."

"Unless it has Benedict Cumberbatch on it."

"Absolutely. He can Vulcanise my final frontier with his photon torpedo anytime."

Hanita laughed throatily. "That has tickled me pink." She sniffed. "You just made me cry a little bit. I had no idea Trekkie words were so innuendo-y."

"They're probably not. It just takes a juvenile brain like mine to twist them into a cheap laugh."

"I don't know. The fans are pretty hardcore. I bet there's a whole sub-culture dedicated to dirty Trekkie talk. I wonder if Klingon gets a look in."

"I doubt it. 'Klingon' sounds like a stubborn case of crabs. 'Captain, I appear to be having trouble phasing the Klingons from my holodeck.'"

Hanita wheezed out another laugh, then fell quiet. "You know, Nancy, for someone with Treko-phobia, you have a suspiciously acute knowledge of Star Trek terms."

"Okay, you got me. I have a thing for Mr Spock. It's that kinky Vulcan Salute. He knew *exactly* how best to put that to use."

WORK ON SATURDAY morning started with a long tale of Gracie's exploits the previous night.

I paused from filling the sugar bowls. "So, you're telling me that you drank enough alcohol to anaes-thetise a sumo wrestler, you got home at four in the morning, and you're bright-eyed and bushy-tailed now, at eight?"

"Yup."

"Man, being eighteen is like being superhuman. Make the most of it, because it's only going to last another six years when you'll suddenly find you're a proper adult with chronic exhaustion and boring problems, like wondering if you'll get iodine deficiency from only using sea salt in your cooking."

My phone pinged with a WhatsApp notification and I took it out of my back pocket to check the screen. I gasped, "It's Skye!" and held the phone for Gracie to see the photo Skye had sent me.

Her eyebrows slowly rose. "She's...I know her!"

"You do?'

Gracie coloured. "No, I, um, served her once. She was with you. You probably don't remember."

"Right, yeah I do. That was when she drove my bus here."

"She's very beautiful," was said so quietly I almost didn't catch it.

"Yes."

Gracie refolded a napkin that was already a perfect triangle. I'd never seen her uncomfortable or uncertain before. She wore her smart-mouthed, tough-girl persona like a badge of honour.

Or so I had thought. Maybe Gracie had a need for armour. And that I understood very well.

Wanting to nurture this tiny glimmer of vulnerability, I offered another morsel. "She's cycle touring in France at the moment."

Gracie looked up from the napkin. "Oh, wow."

"Would you like to hear her message?"

She smiled and nodded.

I read:

I've had the most incredible first week!! I've done the Normandy coast from Cherbourg down to the Northern coast of Brittany and am now camped outside a town called Brest (hee hee). The weather has been very mild for early spring and I've been doing OK for warmth. The local cider helps. It's cheaper than buying water and has an interesting effect in that you get drunk from the waist down. True, I polished off half a bottle last night and was completely clear-headed, but my legs were numb. Thankfully there was no leg hangover today or I would have had a pretty challenging 80km to get through. OMG my saddle rash! I spent hours on the bike training for this trip, but nothing prepared me for the terrible tenderness of a chafed bum. I have to spend a reasonable amount of my day standing up while peddling, even on the flat bits. Can you develop buttock callouses? I'm hoping to wake up with some tomorrow. Love you. Skye xx

Gracie snorted at Skye's last comment and asked, "She's doing that on her own?"

"Yeah."

"Man, I wish I had the guts to do that."

"Me too, Gracie, me too."

I wrote a reply and as I was tapping the last 'x', Gracie groaned. "Urgh, it's that horrible Mona woman. She always makes you feel like you're a piece of dog turd she's just scraped off the bottom of her faux Gucci wedges. You wait on her, Nancy."

I had already ducked down behind the counter and was sitting on the floor, making myself as small as possible. "No," I whispered. "You do it. You saw her first."

"I'll paper, scissors, rock you for it."

"Okay, you're on. Best of three."

Gracie sat on the floor next to me and held out her fist in preparation. "Paper, scissors, rock!" Gracie's rock blunted my scissors. "Not a good start, old woman."

"It's not over until the goat yodels," I retorted cryptically, hoping to distract her.

"Paper, scissors, rock!" My scissors cut her paper. "Yes! Take that, baby-face."

We papered each other on the next round, chorusing our "oh" of disappointment.

"Okay, this time, grey dog, you're going down."

"It's silver fox. I'm a silver fox!"

"Whatever. Let's do this."

Gracie's paper wrapped my rock. "Yussssss! In your face, Nancy. Get out there and take the humiliation for the team."

Barbara put her head around the door and frowned. "Why are you both sitting on the floor?"

"Someone needs to serve Mona. That someone is

Nancy because she lost our hand duel fair and square," Gracie hissed, eye-balling me.

"Do I have to, Barbara? Can't we just keep hiding and pretend that we're all in Tijuana on conference and forgot to lock the door?"

Barbara clucked her tongue. "I'll do it. Remind me why I pay you two again." She plastered a smile on her face and walked over to where Mona and another woman were sitting.

"Ata mārie, Mona. And friend. What can we get you today?"

"Good morning, Barbara. I couldn't help noticing you're rather slow on service today. If you want to ensure that your customers return then it's critical you're prompt on attendance, babe. I want to offer constructive feedback, because I want you to succeed."

"Right. I appreciate your support, Mona. So, what'll it be? Just coffees or cake as well?"

"I'll have a double shot, soy flat white with the soy on the side. Bridget, you'll have a super trim latte, won't you?" Mona looked at Barbara. "And no cake for either of us. We don't want to negate the calories we've just power-walked off. Thanks, babe." I could see Bridget glance longingly at the cake cabinet.

"Okay, just the two coffees then." Barbara turned to give Gracie the order, then stopped and pivoted around. "By the way, Mona, please don't call me 'babe'. I find it over-familiar and patronising, as probably does everyone else."

I low-fived Barbara when she came behind the counter so Mona wouldn't see.

Gracie offered one word. "Respect."

TO: nancypants@getwired.co.nz
From: alison.mckendry@mckendrylaw.co.nz
Subject: RE Easement
Hi Nancy, sorry it's taken so long for me to get back to you. I can't find any documentation in your property file relating to easement rights. I will need to get in touch with the conveyancing lawyer who acted on behalf of the party you bought the property from.
Stand by,
Alison

SEVEN
THE DRIVING LESSON

MARCH.

On Monday morning I was up at six. I'd fed the chickens and myself, made a snack to take and had drunk a whole pot of tea in bed with my book by 7.40am. By 7.45am, I was dressed in my newly purchased XL *The Last Unicorn* T-shirt, and was ready to go.

Although I'd walked fairly extensively over the land that was closest to me, I'd never been to farm central where Angus' sheds were. I parked in front of a three-bay barn and walked around behind it to a large greenhouse where Angus' e-motorbike was parked outside.

I approached the door and two dogs ran out, barking, but tails wagging. They each gave me a good sniff, then ran back inside the greenhouse to Angus, who was bent over some plants several metres away.

I was early.

"Morning," I called.

Angus glanced at his watch. "Keen to make a good impression on your first day?" He turned, registered my outfit and let out a bark of laughter. "Excellent choice. That is definitely not going to work for me."

"Wait 'til tomorrow. I've got something that will make your eyes hurt."

"It'll certainly help things if I can't bear to look at you." He gestured towards his dogs.

"These are my right-hand ladies. This one with the grey muzzle and stiff back legs is my old girl, Rosie, and this is her granddaughter, Tess. Tess is my number one dog now that Rosie struggles to keep up."

They were good-looking dogs. The pair of them had the black and tan colouring of the Huntaway breed, but they also had the white stomachs and fine, white snouts of an eye dog – the type who round up stock by staring them down. They had both lain at Angus' feet with their paws crossed.

"Hey girls." I crouched to give each of them a rub behind the ears as Angus said, "This area is the nursery. You can see over there where the trays are seeded." He pointed to four long benches covered in plastic trays filled with what looked like potting mix.

"The younger plants live in here until they can tolerate being outside more easily."

He led me to the right of the structure where there was a large area surrounded by netting to provide wind protection for the older plants.

"These beauties over here are my sensitive large species. They'll grow really big, like this red beech here, but they need the protection of other plants while they get established. I've worked on a system for succession planting in open areas so they get that protection."

"This one's tītoki, isn't it?" I said, pointing to a plant with crinkly, dull leaves.

"Yes, it is." He looked at me suspiciously. "Have you been doing extra study?"

"Are you presuming that because I've spent ninety-nine percent of my life inside an urban boundary that I can't tell a tītoki from a rewarewa?"

"Yeah."

"Well, Angus, if I hadn't borrowed Margot's book on New Zealand native tree identification, I'd be really offended right now."

"I'm actually quite impressed."

"Are you? Good. I hoped you'd be."

The look on Angus' face spurred images from the other night to flit distractingly across my brain. The last clip in the make-out montage was one that had liked to present itself over the last week at any opportunity, preferably an inconvenient one – Angus' "huh" as I shifted my pelvis above his.

A heat rose from the pit of my stomach and the ridged veins of the tītoki's leaves suddenly demanded closer examination.

Angus shifted his feet, his boots scraping across the grit on the concrete. "Um, I thought for this week, I'd spend the first part of the morning showing you a process or two, then I'll set you up for the rest of the morning with tasks you can manage on your own. Does that sound okay?"

"Sure."

"There's going to be times when you'll need to get to places to either plant, source seed, or collect earth and you're going to have to use a four-wheel drive vehicle and a trailer. What's your experience like with either of those?"

"Well, at uni I mastered the art of trolley racing."

"Super market trolleys?"

"Yeah. They have four wheels wanting to go in different directions at the same time, which makes them bloody hard to steer. That's got to count for something."

"Ah, nope, it really doesn't. I guess we'd better pencil in some lessons for later this week." He clapped his hands and rubbed them together. "Right, let's start with seed sowing. I've got miro seed here that I've collected, which can take two years to germinate, so we'll label it, put it aside and see what happens. It'll be pretty hit and miss with these ones unfortunately, which is what happens with seeds that have a dormancy period."

He handed me a mask and a pair of gloves and took me through the procedure. Then we moved onto trays with seeds that had germinated, where he showed me how to prick out the seedlings and put them in individual containers with potting mix.

"I buy in my potting mix for this part of the process, but I use soil from bush areas on the farm for the older plants. It's localised soil for local seed, so it should suit the plants well. Collecting it will be something you'll do. All good so far?"

"Yeah, I think I've got it."

"Excellent. I'm going to leave you for an hour to carry on with what I've shown you. If you finish before I get back, give everything a water. The nozzle on the hose has been modified so it sprays finely. Keep it at that setting and make sure all the plants are well soaked. I don't want the plants to root shallowly."

"Of course. No one likes a shallow rooter."

I WAS SLOW. I was very careful to do everything right so that Angus felt justified in employing me based on the selection criteria of pity.

When he came back, I was potting up the last of the seedlings.

"Good job. Not the fastest work, but that'll improve once you get used to what you're doing. You ready for some planting?"

"You betcha."

"There's a small gully nearby that I've started planting out, but it needs thickening up." He gestured for me to come outside where there was a 4WD buggy with a trailer full of plants attached.

"I see you've pre-loaded it."

"No, Nancy, I've just plain old *loaded* the trailer. The prefix 'pre' is totally unnecessary. It seems to be some kind of lingual fad at the moment to add it to words to create emphasis. I mean, take 'pre-book' as an example. To 'book' already means to organise ahead of time, but everybody adds the 'pre' to it anyway."

"I know," I teased, "such a waste of precious verbal energy."

"It just sounds unintelligent." He turned to look at me. "You know the other thing that really ties my undies in a knot?"

"Not being able to tell the difference between chancroids and herpes?"

Angus looked distinctly un-amused. "The abuse of the apostrophe. No one seems to know where to put one these days."

"Which one's the apostrophe? Is it the little line with a full stop under it or the flying comma?"

"And don't get me started on the word 'learnings'."

"I can safely promise you I have no intention. Wow, Angus. The desecration of the English language is clearly an issue dear to your heart."

"Felt acutely in my spleen, more like. Come on, let's go. You can amaze me with your tree identification proficiency on the way."

THE NEXT MORNING, I sent Angus a text: I'm just pre-warning you that I'm very tired this morning from all your slave driving yesterday. I suggest putting the jug on and having two coffee's ready to put in each hand when I get there.

I got a reply back immediately: You mean one coffee ready to put in each hand. Unless you plan on drinking four.

TO: nancypants@getwired.co.nz
From: alison.mckendry@mckendrylaw.co.nz
Subject: Re. Easement
Hi Nancy, I've just heard back from the vendor's lawyer. I can confirm that there is no agreement to an easement through your property. I hope this is the news you were after.
Regards,

Alison

ANGUS HAD SET ASIDE the whole of day four for teaching me how to drive the 4WD buggy and manoeuvre a trailer. He decided the first thing to do was to get me comfortable driving the buggy on its own before I tackled mastering the art of towing a trailer.

"Okay, the first lesson is remembering which side to get in. For some reason these things are all left-hand drive, so it's a little counterintuitive first off, but you'll get the hang of it with practise." We climbed in and he got me to start it.

"The good thing is that you won't have to negotiate changing gears with your right hand, as it's automatic, but this next bit is very important. When it's in Drive it'll only go forward when the accelerator's compressed – I guess for safety's sake when you're parked on slopes. But, and I really want you to pay attention to the 'but', it does mean it's easy to accidentally leave it in gear. Never do that when you stop, which you will have to do often because of all the farm gates you'll need to get through. It's easy enough to absent-mindedly put your foot on the accelerator and shoot forward, which hopefully will only give you a fright, but it could move the buggy into a difficult or dangerous place to manoeuvre out of. Okay? And always use the handbrake."

"When I'm stopped or when I'm cornering?"

Angus gave me The Frown.

"Sorry, I *am* taking this seriously. Take it out of gear when I'm stopped, and put the handbrake on. Got it."

"Right, put it in Drive and have a go at accelerating and decelerating so you can get a feel for how it responds."

I had just started to creep forward when Rosie and Tess got up and made themselves ready to leap into the vehicle.

"Sorry, not today, ladies. Stay here." At Angus' command, they obediently retreated and lay down in the shade of the shed. "Good girls."

I drove around the barn a couple of times, speeding up and slowing down to stop, then doing it all in reverse.

"Great, I think you've pretty much got it. Let's do some practise driving through paddocks and having to deal with gates."

Angus directed me down a farm track, then indicated an empty paddock where he wanted me to stop.

"I will never get you to go through paddocks with cattle in them. Most of them are young bulls and they can be pretty amped with testosterone. If, for any reason, a bull has got into a paddock you need to go through, you'll be safe in the buggy. These boys are intimidated by it. Just keep it running when you open the gate and make sure it's between you and the bull, though you shouldn't have any trouble with a stray bull unless there's one in the next-door paddock. But look, if you don't want to run the risk, just give me a call."

I came to a stop in front of the gate, put the hand-brake on and climbed out.

"Ah, are you forgetting something?"

"Oh, right. Take it out of gear. Sorry, Captain." I got back in, corrected my mistake, then opened the gate.

After I'd driven through and gone to close the gate, a gust of wind blew my hat off and sent it into the neighbouring paddock.

"Shit," I said and jogged over to the fence.

"Watch out for the electric wire," Angus called, "it's the third one down."

Acutely aware that Angus would be watching, I put my practise at fence-hopping to good use, using the bounce in the wires to neatly vault myself over.

"Nice technique!" Angus called. "Ten out of ten for the dismount."

I pivoted and bowed. When I turned back again, the wind had blown my hat another few metres and was starting to roll away from me down a slope.

"Stop, you little bugger," I called to it. "Come back here."

Ignoring me, it continued its lazy roll.

I finally caught up with it and stomped on it before it could go any further. When I bent down to pick it up, I made the mistake of looking up ahead of me.

Twenty cattle stood in a loose herd towards the bottom of the paddock. I hadn't spotted them earlier because of the lie of the slope, but they'd definitely spotted me.

They were stock-still, watching.

"Okaaaay, easy does it," I said, starting to retreat.

As soon as I moved, so did they.

Towards me.

I stopped.

The cattle stopped.

"Alright, boys. I'm going to walk slowly back to the fence. Keep your distance, that's it," I crooned, hoping to keep them pacified.

I took a few steps backwards and they took a few steps forwards. "That's it, nice and gentle, good boys."

Suddenly one leapt forward, its head high in the air, then he lowered it and looked up at me.

I didn't waste any time. I turned and ran as fast as I could for the fence.

Hoof beats thundered behind me.

"Shiiiiiiiiiiiiit. Anguuuuuuuuus!" I came over the rise to see him sitting in the buggy shaking with laughter. "Angus! ANGUS!"

He climbed out of the vehicle, still laughing and started walking towards me without any hurry.

"Stop, Nance. Stop running. Stop!"

I came to a halt and the hoof beats also stopped. I tentatively looked over my shoulder and could see all the cattle watching me warily, the ones at the back jostling to get to the front.

"Are you sure?" I yelled, not quite able to stifle the panic in my voice.

"Yes, they're just steer. They've had their balls removed – they won't hurt you. Walk calmly to the fence and climb over."

As I started to retreat, one came very close, sniffing at me, then it abruptly jumped backwards.

I shrieked, turning in panic to climb the fence. In my haste, I caught my foot in the top wire, the momentum flipping me over sideways.

I landed on my bum at Angus' feet.

He let out another bellow of laughter.

"You alright?" he managed when he could breathe.

"No, I am not bloody alright! That was really scary, thank you very much. I nearly peed my pants. But I'm comforted by the fact you were so well entertained. How are your poor abs, by the way? Not too fatigued from the workout?"

Angus reached down to help me up, then drew my head in to plant a kiss on my forehead. "You're alright. Just a bit of bruising to your ego. It'll recover quickly."

"You knew, didn't you?" I said into his shirt. "You knew they were there all along." I breathed in. Hanita was wrong. There was not a single whiff of dung, just pine laundry powder and a heady trace of fresh man-sweat. I inhaled deeply before stepping back.

"Yep. I wanted to see how you handled being in a challenging situation with the stock. Not very well, it would appear." He wiped a tear from his right eye and let out the contented sigh of the recently amused. "That was awesome."

I threw him my Death Ray Look, hoping to vaporise him on the spot, but, disappointingly, nothing happened.

He shrugged. "Look, you were perfectly safe. Steer are like over-curious, bumbling children. If there was any danger, I wouldn't have let you go into the paddock." He chuckled again. "I can't wait to see how disastrous you are with a trailer, city girl."

WE SPENT another hour practising with gates and driving on uneven, grassy terrain. Angus took the opportunity to show me a couple of areas that were next in line for planting, explaining which plants should go where, then we headed back to the shed for a cup of coffee and some cake I had brought with me.

Tess sat at our feet, watching us intently for stray crumbs.

"Tess, don't beg," Angus admonished. "Outside." She dutifully trotted out of the shed, then poked her head back through the doorway in the hope Angus had changed his mind.

"Out!" he commanded.

The head disappeared.

"They're such good dogs. I miss having a companion pet," I said, gazing at where Tess' head had been. "The chickens are friendly enough, but they're not very good for cuddling. They only like me because I feed them, and I tell you what, I've never seen a more food-motivated animal. They're like a pack of piranhas when it comes to dinnertime. I reckon if I tripped and fell, I'd be stripped clean in under a minute, starting with my eyeballs."

"Your eyeballs do look pretty delicious, to be fair," Angus responded with a sideways smile. He took a sip of his coffee. "You had a dog before?"

"No, a cat. She died not long before I moved here. Man, I loved her. She was like a dog in a cat's body – she came when you called, she even wagged her tail when she was happy. I want to get another one, but I think I should wait until the house is built so I can settle it more easily."

"Have you thought about changing species? You could get a dog."

"I'm firmly in the feline camp, thanks. I like an

animal I can curl up with and not come away smelling like I've romped in unlaundered jock straps."

Angus laughed.

I was quiet for a moment. "Angus?"

"Yeah?"

"Tell me more about this subdivision. What point are you at with it?"

"The subdivision's my parents' retirement plan. Because they handed the farm over to us kids, they don't have much capital to see them through their twilight years. It's really stretching them."

He swirled the coffee in the bottom of his cup, watching it with a frown before looking up at me. "You wouldn't believe how expensive the process is. We've already spent over forty thousand getting the resource consent together, and it's not finished yet. Plus, there'll be the outlay for the infrastructure, and that's assuming the council give it the green light. It's pretty stressful for them." He sighed. "I can't wait until it's all over, really."

"I bet." I swallowed the last of my coffee. "Can I have a look at the plans some time?"

Derek materialised in my peripheral vision. *Nancy, Nancy, Nancy,* he said into my right ear. He walked behind me. *Are you going to tell him there's still an "i" they've yet to dot?* was said into my left.

"Yeah, sure," Angus answered.

It's for his parents. And they're such nice people, Nancy.

"I know!"

Angus furrowed his brow. "You know what?"

"I know..." I paused, placing my empty cup on the bench. "That it's time to get the farce over and done with. I wouldn't want to delay you from the rest of your morning's entertainment any longer."

Angus took me outside and taught me how to hitch the trailer onto the back of the buggy. Then he got me to drive forwards and turn in both directions so that I got a feel for the weight of it on the back.

"Okay, now for the true test of right and left-brain function. Backing!" He rubbed his hands together in eager anticipation of my imminent failure.

I really wanted to prove him wrong, but his belief in my incompetence didn't do much for boosting my confidence.

"Now, the first thing to remember when backing a trailer is that the steering wheel moves in the opposite direction to what you think it should, but if you do it slowly, you can easily correct yourself if you get it wrong on the first go."

I tried directing the trailer to points that Angus made me aim for and he was right, I had to flip my brain over to think in the right direction, but I quickly got the feel for it.

"One of the trickiest manoeuvres is backing a

trailer into a driveway, because of the tight turning involved. You can easily jack-knife if you oversteer."

Angus got me to practise on one of the farm gates. I got it first time.

I gave him a look of defiant self-satisfaction and said, "Close your mouth, farm boy, you'll catch a nasty case of urban emancipation."

"Beginner's luck. Have another go from the other direction."

I managed that one first time, too. "Angus, did you see that? Are you sure? I'd be happy to show you again, just in case you missed it. See, what I did was drive a trailer-load of 'up yours' *backwards* through your rural prejudice."

"Alright, Miss Smug. Let's see how you go backing into a tight spot while avoiding obstacles like trees and large rocks."

He grabbed some of the larger plants from the nursery and placed them around the forecourt of the barn. "You're aiming to go between these two trees here, while coming from the left. You've got all these other trees to avoid when you swing into the gap. Are you ready?"

"Bring it on!"

I avoided the first two obstacles, but had to re-position the trailer a couple of times for the third and fourth ones.

Angus stood watching with his arms crossed,

nodding in encouragement. "Great Nance, you're doing really bloody well."

Obstacle five and six proved a little tricky, but I was able to move around them with fine tweaks of the steering wheel.

I was just lining up the final two trees, when Tess spotted a rabbit and took off, running behind the moving trailer. Deep in concentration, I was alarmed by the sudden movement and slammed my foot down to apply the brake. Only I misjudged and hit the accelerator, sending the buggy and trailer backwards towards the race where stock were loaded onto trucks.

I was brought to an abrupt halt with an ear-splitting crunch and a shower of wood.

I looked at Angus.

He stood with his hands over his eyes. He slowly moved his fingers to peer through the gap. "Nancy? What have you done to my race?"

The trailer sat snugly between two sets of fence posts, both sides of the race between the posts having been completely demolished.

"It'll be alright. I can reattach the" – I counted on my fingers – "twelve planks back onto the posts." I grimaced. "I might have to replace a couple, or six, but it'll be fine. You won't know the difference."

I shifted the buggy into Drive to ease the trailer out of the mess, put my foot gently on the accelerator and went nowhere. I checked the handbrake. It was off. I accelerated again. Still nothing. I put my foot flat and revved the engine until it was screaming, but all that resulted was a lot of wheel spinning and flying gravel.

One of the dogs yelped.

There was always reverse. I shifted gear and gingerly pressed the accelerator. The buggy didn't move a millimetre.

I turned the engine off and climbed out. "Ah well, I guess it'll have to stay there forever." I looked at Angus.

He'd removed his hands from his eyes, and now had them clamped over his mouth.

"Coffee?"

FRIDAY, my one day off, had a gritty-eyed start. I dreamt Derek had slept beside me with his arm resting heavily across my throat. When I finally pulled myself out of the murky depths of sleep and broke the surface with a gasp, his weight still sat on me.

I didn't need Lou to interpret the dream for me. Despite my sessions with her, I was still allowing Derek to control me. Insecure Nancy was shouting to be heard and I needed to learn how to listen to her.

I rose and went outside to look at the mountains. Their peaks were orange in the dawn light, and I watched the shadow of night roll down the slopes and into the foothills with the ascending sun.

Since I'd moved onto the land, I was constantly surprised at how powerful a tonic my view of the mountains was. I would never get tired of looking at them.

Invigorated, I decided today was the day I would launch Sawcraft to the Pukeroa community.

After breakfast, I shared my new business Facebook page on the Pukeroa Noticeboard page and waited.

Within two minutes I had a comment: Darryl Thompson – A chick? Is this free advertising for Tui beer? "Lady carpenters. Yeah right!"

20 seconds later: Marie Alsthrop – Get off the noticeboard. Advertising is not a notice. Non-profit only.

I sighed and closed my computer. I knew when I dreamt up the business there'd be some shit pushing. I just didn't realise how steep the hill would be.

LATER THAT MORNING I finally heard from the builder Stu had found for me – Andre Wharekawa.

I arranged with him to come out and have a look at the plans and the site and he arrived in a new-looking 4WD ute with "Pukeroa Building Company" decals on the side.

When Andre got out, boy, what an exit. One

highly polished work boot emerged, attached to a long, shapely calf, then the other. His crisp, plaid shirt was under serious strain from his muscular shoulders and his knee-length baggy jean shorts were spotless. Then his head appeared.

He had beautiful curvature to his lips, thickly lashed eyes below perfectly plucked eyebrows, and short, immaculately styled hair.

Andre was enormous, gorgeous, and one hundred percent metro.

He bent down a foot to give me a kiss on the cheek and I was hit by the scent of orange blossom and lemon grass.

I tended to prefer men au natural so that I could snort their pheromones more easily, but he was dangerously good-smelling. I had an image of him walking around with a gaggle of people hanging off, suctioned on by their nostrils. Unbidden, another image forced the first one out. Angus with his arms around me. A kiss on my forehead. Pine and fresh sweat.

I told Andre he smelled delicious and he smiled. "Thanks. Niamh, my partner, makes organic skin creams. This one's in her new range." He patted his pockets. "I've probably got a business card somewhere."

He eventually managed to locate a card tucked in his wallet and handed it to me. "Derm by Niamh" it said. Even the card smelled exotic and tasty. I refrained from licking it and put it in one of my cargo pants' pockets.

"I've just put the jug on." I said, craning my neck to look up at him. "Shall we go have a cuppa while we look at the plans, and visit the site after?"

Andre's bulk seem to fill the bus. I hadn't thought of it as small before, because it adequately provided for the vast majority of my needs, but he gave it the proportions of a hobbit hole. His knees barely fit under the table.

I handed him a cup of tea while he looked through the various A3 sheets of plans.

"These are good. Something like this should get through the consent process pretty quickly."

"Well, so far, the council haven't called anything into question, so if it's plain sailing, you should be able to start building in about three weeks."

He turned around and caught me sniffing the air around the back of his neck.

I jumped back. "Sorry. I imagine you have this problem all the time."

"Um, no? Most people don't take sniffing liberties."

"Well," I faltered, "they're missing out."

Andre rescued me with a smile. "I'll tell Niamh her new range is on the money."

I sat down opposite him, turning sideways due to the lack of space under the table.

He took a slurp of tea, then said, "Stu tells me you're keen to be a roustabout on-site."

I nodded.

"I have no problem with that in theory, but what can you do? For the sake of efficiency, I'm not keen on having to teach you new skills."

"I did all this." I gestured with a sweep of my hand around the interior of the bus.

Andre raised one shapely eyebrow. "No way! This is..." He looked over my shoulder, then craned his neck around to peer down the back of the bus. "Sheee-it, Nancy, you can obviously handle your tools." He swivelled back to face me. "You should be able to do a lot of the finishing work no prob and I'm sure I can talk you through the initial structural stuff. You've got to understand, though, you're just an extra pair of hands. No mavericking or initiative-taking without my say-so. You okay with that?"

"Absolutely. I want to be a help and not a hindrance, but I'm sure you understand I need to save money by doing as much as I can."

"Hey, I'm all for mana wāhine. If you got the skills, you are absolutely welcome on my build site."

"There's one other thing. I want to project manage the build – it's such a small one, I don't think it will be too complicated a task."

Andre took a moment to mull it over. "Alright, but there will be times when I might have to step in. With all respect, I know this business and you've never built a house before. I want you to talk to me every step of the way – no surprises. Is that a deal?"

"Deal," I said, holding out my hand to have it swallowed by his massive one.

LATER THAT NIGHT I checked my Facebook notifications. Thirty-three comments. Darryl Thompson's had eleven likes and six laugh emojis. But it also had seven angry emojis. Alice Thompson had written, **Darryl you chauvinist. Get a life.** I hoped she wasn't his mother.

I decided I wasn't brave enough to read the comments. I told myself there was no such thing as bad publicity and even if my post had started some digital chest shoving, my name was out there.

Instead, I texted Hanita and asked her to read them to see if anyone had inquired about my services.

She texted back: **No. Lots of debate on gender roles, tho. Not all of it intelligible. U made quite an entrance to the Puke business table. Nice going!**

Then: **Who is Jim Carter?**

An image of the round-bellied man at Martin and Anoushka's barbecue came into technicolour focus.

Oh God. I replied: **Could be some dude I owe a sorry to. What did he say?**

Hanita's message took longer than I would have liked to woosh its way onto my phone: **Most popular comment. You should read it.**

The milky tea I was drinking turned sour in my mouth and I had to pace the floor of the bus four times before I felt up to the task. I quickly scrolled through the comments until I found his name and read: To all you nay-sayers out there who sit comfortably behind the facelessness of your computers and phones, how about giving the lady a chance? She's new to our community. Let's welcome her in a way that shows we are deserving of her desire to be one of us. Come on Puke, show your best side because I for one like living in a town I'm proud of.

It had twenty-one likes.

From the tiny photo accompanying his name, I could tell it was him. He smiled widely out at me, the black head of a pig propped on his left shoulder, its body draped across his broad back.

Derek peered at me over the top of my computer screen. His eyebrows were raised in the centre of his forehead in smarmy dubiousness. *Well, well, well. You certainly don't deserve that. Why on earth would he champion your cause when you humiliated him in such a nasty way at Martin and Anoushka's? Surely, he dislikes you as much as I do.*

There was nothing I could say in return. No pithy comeback, no telling him where to go. Because I had to agree with him.

EIGHT
METALLICA LIVES ON

ANGUS and I had gone to collect seedlings from a forested gully a few hectares from the sheds. It had been a cool morning and I'd dressed warmly in a thick jersey, but now that the sun was high, the temperature had risen and I pulled the jersey off, discarding it in the buggy.

Angus peered at the band picture on my over-sized "Metallica Lives On" T-shirt. "Is that the Jonas Brothers?" He began to laugh. "That is awesome!"

"Someone either had a great sense of irony, or this is one epic T-shirt fail."

"I know you like to complain about having to wear a 'uniform' to work, but I think you secretly love finding these rejected gems. The church shop must be doing a roaring trade."

"I believe they now have an official quirky T-shirt scout to keep up with demand."

We stopped to crack the thermos of coffee Angus had brought and the oat slice I'd made the day before.

Through a mouthful Angus said, "Oh, I brought the plans for you to look at." He collected them from the buggy, laid them out on the trailer next to where we were sitting and ran a finger over the paper. "This is your land here, and this is Stu and Mona's farm. You can see our farm has no road boundary in this area, but the land is some of our most gentle hill country and it makes for good build sites. That's why we asked for the easement." He moved his finger towards my east boundary. "You can see it marked on your property here."

I could, and he had been right – it was in an area that didn't look like it would impact on my use of the property much at all. As far as I could tell, Lots 1 and 2 wouldn't be visible from my build site. Lot 3 would, but it was far enough away that I would retain a decent level of privacy, and lot 4...

I held out the front of my T-shirt to vent my sudden flush. "Do you have a contour map?"

"Yeah, but I didn't bring it with me."

I nodded. "It looks, um... They'll be nice pieces of land."

"I know, right? I don't think we'll have any problem selling them."

I moved away from the subject, rapidly launching

into a series of Maia and Ben stories from when they came to stay.

Angus was particularly tickled by The Tale of the Sheep Raisins.

"I can't wait to have nieces and nephews. I'm not too fussed on the idea of having my own children, but I reckon I'd be a shit-hot uncle."

"You can't really fail with being an uncle or an aunt. You don't have to do any disciplining, you hand them back when you've had enough, and it gives you the perfect excuse to tap into your inner child. My level of maturity drops thirty-seven years when I'm around them."

"And alcohol, and when you name your animals, or demolish my property." He took another bite and said through a mouthful, "Mona also does a pretty good job of helping you lose sight of what it means to be a responsible adult. In fact, I'd say you don't need much of an excuse to behave like a three-year-old, Nancy Myers. Maybe you're in denial about turning forty and have just inverted the numbers."

"My behaviour's not that bad...is it?" I asked, not liking how small my voice sounded.

Angus put his arm around me and pulled me close so he could kiss my brow. "No. I love your childish energy. And apart from anything else it keeps me entertained." He looked me in the eye. "Don't change."

I swallowed and tried to look away, but there

were beautiful flecks of gold and hazel in his irises that I hadn't noticed before.

Angus' eyes dropped to my lips. "Have you thought any more about...us? You know..." he trailed off.

"Yes."

He leaned closer. "And?" The word was barely a whisper.

"And, I..." My brain stopped. At least, the part that connects thought with speaking had ceased to function. The primal part of my brain was working fine. It had the pom-poms out and was cheering for me to reach the scoreline.

He closed the small gap between us and kissed me softly.

I closed my eyes and the image of a faceless woman drifted across the underside of my eyelids. Angus' ex-girlfriend. "Angus..."

"Sorry. It was just very difficult not to kiss you right now."

"Well, don't!" I snapped. "I haven't made a deci-sion yet and you are a very good kisser. I don't think my resolve would last very long if you took advantage of any of the *many* moments I have secretly wanted you to kiss me. I have made a real effort to repel you, on your request, and you can't even go to the trouble of wearing trousers."

"Trousers?"

"Yeah!" I looked away and said into my shoulder, "You have really hot knees."

Angus barked out a laugh that startled a couple of kererū in a nearby tree, their wings swishing loudly above our heads as they took flight. "Hot knees? Right, well, trousers it is from now on. Are you sure about this? You're giving away your chance to view my finely-sculptured patella on an almost daily basis."

"Yes. Fair's fair. The uglier the better. I can source you some MC Hammer poo-pants if you want. I think there's a whole room dedicated to them at the church charity shop."

AS SOON AS I got home, I Dropboxed the photo Angus had allowed me to take of the plans, opened it up on my computer and studied Lot 4 again.

It didn't look any better the second time around.

I pocketed my phone, stepped into my gumboots and headed in the direction of the lot. After I'd climbed the boundary fence and walked down into a dip, I had to navigate by my phone to make sure I got it exactly right.

I walked up a gentle rise to my destination at the top of the hill. I stood on the build site marked on the plan, looked at the mountains, then turned back to locate the position of my build site.

Oh dear, oh dear. That does make things tricky,

doesn't it, Nancy? Derek stood beside me, arms crossed. He tutted. *What a waste. I told you this was a useless venture. Sell up before you make more of an investment.*

He started walking down the hill. When he got to the bottom he shouted over his shoulder, *Unless you refuse to renegotiate the easement...*

I CALLED Hanita that evening to relay kissing event number two and assure her that I had put my foot down about respecting boundaries.

"I know I said I was ready for merchandise sampling, but I'm not. I'm terrified of letting my guard down and getting hurt again." I exhaled with a sharp *huff.* "The problem is I don't actually want him to respect any boundaries at all. I'd much prefer he tore my T-shirt off with his teeth and ran his tongue the length of my body with a prolonged stopover at my tropical hot spot."

Hanita "Hmm"ed. "We need to remove some of the complications in this situation. Can you kill off his ex-girlfriend?"

"Probably. I'm pretty good with plyers and a nail gun."

"I'm not sure torture is necessary before you ice her."

"Angus may beg to differ. And anyway, killing her changes nothing about him."

"Well, then, just stay away from him. Can't you do stuff with the plants that doesn't involve him?"

"Yeah, maybe I'll have to do that. I'm probably capable enough with the plants now. You know, I think I'm starting to get quite good at this farming stuff."

Hanita's laugh sounded like it was aimed at me, but her, "That's good," was said kindly. "What can you do?"

"Well, I can drive a 4WD and trailer forwards *and* backwards."

"*And* into a fence."

"It was a race."

"So really, you backed into two fences."

I clucked my tongue. "That's just semantics."

"Man, I wish I'd seen it. I don't s'pose Angus managed to get his phone out?"

"No, he was too busy covering his eyes."

Hanita wheezed out an "Oh jeez" through a laugh. "The poor guy. Have you fixed it yet?"

"No. It's on my 'to do' list, but it's about number eighteen of thirty."

"So...what else can you do?"

"I can whistle Angus' dogs with my fingers."

"You could already do that."

"But I never used it for anything."

"Yes, you were very good at using it to deafen old Bumface Lovelace. Remember, the class would gradually talk quieter and quieter throughout the lesson until we were just mouthing stuff to make him turn his hearing-aids up. Then you would pounce with your whistle of fury."

"Oh yeah. That was a good trick, wasn't it? He was a right old bastard. Remember how he used to bring his cane out of the cupboard and lovingly oil it, watching us the whole time over the top of his glasses? Then he'd stand over you to check your work, bouncing it on one hand. He used to offer a daily lamentation on the cessation of corporal punishment."

"I think he started petitioning for reinstating *capital* punishment after you got him the second time with the whistle trick."

I chuckled, then sighed. "Maybe I need to find another week-day job until my business kicks off. I really like the work, though. I've spent my whole career at a desk. I'm feeling so much happier being outdoors, and I'm learning so much. I really don't want to have to give it up."

"How about you start looking around for something else that would allow you to work outside? It won't hurt. If you come across something, then I'm sure Angus will understand. And if you don't, well, there's nothing for it. You'll have to go on Tinder."

I snorted. "Go on Tinder? Everyone here knows everybody else. And their business. In a community this small I might as well wear a large sign around my neck that says 'Single and desperate'."

"My love, you don't need a sign."

"Look, I'll be fine. I just need to replace the batteries on my vibrator."

"Nance?"

"Yes?"

"I love you. I want you to look out for yourself, okay? If that's as simple as making sure you choose the rechargeable batteries so you're never again left feeling lonely *and* horny, then so be it. But, somehow, I don't think it's that simple. Promise you'll come and see me soon."

"Okay. Love you, Nita. Oh, wait, Hanita?"

"Yeah?"

"Something else has, ah, come up."

"You've heard about Derek?"

"No, I haven't heard about Derek."

"Oh. Shit, Nance, God I'm an idiot – this is no way to break it to you."

"Break what?"

"Are you sitting down?""

"Just tell me. Rip it off quickly like a plaster."

Hanita said hurriedly, "He's married. He and his twelve-year-old lover took a holiday to Fiji and came back husband and wife."

Silence.

"Bit of a bombshell, huh?"

More like a full-frontal assault.

"You okay?"

"Um," I managed, "I...don't know." I completed the lie with, "I have to process it."

"I'm so sorry, my lovely. I'll call you tomorrow and see how you are."

"Okay."

"What did you want to tell me?"

"Nah, nothing. Don't worry about it."

When I hung up, I allowed myself the indulgence of a good, old-fashioned ugly cry – the type where the tears, snot and saliva mingle into one viscous mess.

Derek hadn't been my first love, but he'd been the one I fell most for. When I first saw him, everything around us blurred into insignificance and I knew I would love him. He was the only man I'd invited to live with me, to share my every intimacy with. Now, he'd made the ultimate commitment to share his every intimacy with someone else.

And in that moment, the death of my beloved cat seemed incredibly unjust. Of anyone to give me comfort, it was her I wanted. She'd offer no judgment, no awkward condolences, no unwanted advice, just unconditional love. I cried for her, too.

NINE
A BIG LOAD OF BULL

THE PSYCHOLOGIST. *Session three:*

"Fuck him. I want him gone from my head. I'm ready to start listening."

"I take it you mean addressing your insecurities?"

"Yeah. I've accepted I have...some."

"Good. That's great, Nancy." Lou repositioned herself in her chair, as if settling in for a demanding session. "I'd like to go back to your previous visit. I want you to describe to me how you felt when you had those two words sitting in the palms of your hands."

"Sad," I said without hesitation. "I mean, I could see the words were weighed down by my anger, and I felt sad when I saw that."

"And what was your reaction to that emotion?"

"Surprise. I feel like there's a whole part of me

I've been neglecting that needs nurturing. I feel like I'm completely out of touch with what's going on in here." I pointed to my chest.

"I don't think you are out of touch. Not unconsciously. If you're feeling sad about being angry, then you're ready to move on from that anger. You need to forgive him."

"Forgive him for cheating on me?"

"Yes. And for having some responsibility for you feeling inadequate and dominated."

"For having *some*? *I* didn't make me feel that way. That was all Derek. He still makes me feel inadequate and dominated."

Lou smiled as if I'd made the same textbook mistake as her last ten clients. "Nancy, nobody can *make* you feel anything. You feel that way because of how you have chosen to respond to them. *You* control how you feel. Nobody else. Don't let him have that power over you."

We sat in silence for a minute while Lou allowed her words to sink in.

It made sense. It made complete sense, but it also sounded like something that was easy to say and hard to do.

"When Derek talks to you, telling you what a failure you are, don't ignore him or get angry at his words. Being passive or aggressive is not constructive. Instead, I want you to acknowledge his words. Like this: 'Derek, I hear you. You're telling me I'm a self-interested loser.'"

I winced.

"Then, calmly inform him how you are not like that. Use a positive statement, an 'I am' statement instead of an 'I'm not' statement: 'However, I am actually a considerate person who often thinks of what is best for others.' The aim is to be as strongly self-affirming as you can."

I tried it out. "Hey Derek, I am a skill saw wielding goddess, you arsewipe. That feels good. Can I use abuse when I'm being self-affirming?"

"Absolutely not. You're not abusing Derek, Nancy. Derek is *you*. His voice is your voice. Your job is to convince *yourself*, not him, of your worth. So, use those affirmation opportunities to remind yourself just how wonderful you are."

My nod was given more out of obligation than any agreement to what she'd said. Was there a wonderfulness lurking somewhere inside me? Right now, under the fierce gaze of Lou's microscope, it was proving tricky to locate.

"And be prepared for it to take time for Derek to leave. You're going to have to keep working at it."

I clucked my tongue. "I'll add it to the list."

ON SATURDAY, Gracie asked me if I had heard from Skye again and, happy to have someone to share her with, I got out my phone. Gracie spent a long time looking at the pictures Skye had sent and chuckled into the cutlery tray as I read out the message:

Here are some observations of the French:

1. They are all under 5 feet 8 inches and have 1.4 children. They have to be to fit in the ridiculously small cars they all drive.

2. They all smoke. It's a rite of passage and they start at the tender age of ten. I kid you not – I've seen numerous pre-pubescents puffing.

3. All the young men are gorgeous. All the old men aren't.

4. All the women wear copious amounts of perfume so that when they pass you with their window wound down you suffocate in their backdraft.

5. They are all excessively friendly, but only after I've told them I'm a New Zealander (might have something to do with the English).

6. The number one accessory is a baguette, preferably two, either hand-held, bagged, or stowed in a bicycle pannier. The most sought after look is to clothe your baguette with a specialised, tubular jute bag with "pain" neatly embroidered on the side.

Skye xx

P.S. Oh, and my knee is perfectly mended

(shame my bum is not). The heavy amount of cycling has worked wonders. Hoorah!

"How long is she gone for?" Gracie asked when I'd finished.

"Her intention's to be back in time to start uni next year, but I don't know. She's the kind of kid – young woman," I corrected myself, "who could get carried away on the adventure. It wouldn't surprise me if she didn't come back. Not for a while, anyway."

"Oh." She shone a fork with renewed vigour and, with a shrug of her shoulders, hard Gracie re-emerged. "Whatevs."

LATER THAT MORNING, Barbara introduced me to a customer who was planning a small renovation.

"How good are you?" were the first words out of her mouth. Standing a few steps behind Barbara, she fixed me with a frown.

"Ah," I faltered, taken aback by her directness, "I'm as good as any other experienced carpenter."

She continued to look at me dubiously.

"Here," I brought up the Sawcraft website on my phone, "this is some of my work."

She flicked through the photos, peering at them closely. "It looks alright, but I don't know," she said slowly. "I'll need to talk to my husband."

"Okay, no problem. Take my card." I pulled one out from a pocket on my phone case.

She nodded and walked towards the door.

"And I'll never hear from her again. Thanks anyway, Barbara."

"Hey, these things take time to get going, but you'll get momentum soon enough." She laid a hand on my forearm. "I'll keep plugging you as much as I can. Once you get one job, the rest will roll in. Have faith."

And an inordinate amount of patience. It wasn't just the time it was taking that was testing mine, it was the attitude towards tradeswomen that was preventing people from giving me a go. I needed to do something that would prove without any question that I had the right skill set.

"Gracie?" I shouted over the grinding of the coffee machine.

She deftly created a fern in the surface of a latte. "Yuh?" she said eventually, without looking up.

"What do you know about YouTube channels?"

ON A VERY MILD AUTUMN DAY, I arrived at the farm to find Angus loading up the trailer with plants.

He was dressed in gumboots, a singlet, and skin-tight pants with an American flag print on them.

"Good God, what on earth are you wearing?" I

asked, fighting the laughter bubbling up from my chest and losing.

"These are my meggings."

"Your what?"

"Man leggings."

I laughed harder. "You look like a bizarre parody of Axl Rose."

Angus put his hands on his hips. "I wanted to prove to you that I'm taking your trouser request seriously."

"You're not doing a very good job. Looks like what you're taking is the piss."

"I'm not. This was the most startling pair of pants they had at the church charity shop. I have to meet the high level of ridiculousness you've set."

"But you've kind of missed the point, Angus. Those pants leave *very* little to the imagination." I peered more closely at him. "Did you stuff a zucchini down the front of them?"

"No."

"Oh." I tore my eyes away, only to find them drifting back whenever he moved.

He pushed a couple of pots towards the back of the trailer and the back of his singlet rode up, revealing his buttocks. Their rounds flexed, accentuating the hollows at the sides and I had a strong urge to sink my teeth into them. I gasped with the thought and covered my mouth with my hand to ensure my jaw remained firmly closed.

"I want you to plant these up in Hector's Gully."

"Mmmhmm."

"Don't forget the optimum spacing between them. I've put a box of fertiliser tablets in for you already, so you're good to go."

"Great. Really nice," I mumbled through my hand.

"Ah, Nancy, it's customary to look a person in the eyes when you're talking to them."

"I don't want to look at your eyes today. I've seen them before."

"Fuck's sake. I'll put my toolbelt on."

"No!" I answered hurriedly. "Please don't add a toolbelt to your already fine display of masculinity. I'll end up a little puddle of goo in the gravel, which won't make for very productive planting."

Angus clucked his tongue, grabbed his jersey from where it was draped over the trailer, and tied it around his waist.

My "oh" of disappointment was louder than intended.

He pointed to the buggy. "Get! Take Rosie with you. I'm going to get changed."

I climbed in the buggy and whistled for Rosie to come.

She jumped in beside me and we headed off towards Hector's Gully, which was a good ten-minute drive, mostly along farm tracks.

I had to pass through two paddocks to get to the

gully, and when I got to the first gate, Rosie got out to relieve herself in the paddock. I didn't wait for her, knowing she would catch up at the next gate.

When I got to it, I could see that it opened away from me, so I parked close. I jumped out of the buggy and had just climbed onto the gate to reach the latch on the other side, when I heard Rosie leap into the vehicle.

The engine roared and I turned to see the buggy hurtling towards me, Rosie's tail poking out of the side of the footwell.

I had no time to do anything but momentarily appreciate the inevitability of my folly. The buggy hit the gate and sent it violently swinging and me flying.

In most situations there's an opportunity to weigh up the positives with the negatives. On the downside, I managed to break the fall with my face. On the upside, I had a soft landing.

I sat up, spitting dung out of my mouth. I couldn't breathe through my nose and checked to make sure nothing was broken. It felt fine, if a little swollen and tight. I gingerly pinched my nostrils and a plug of shit fell out of the left one. "Oh God," I groaned and snorted the remaining faecal matter out of my other nostril.

In the meantime, Rosie had jumped down from the buggy, which had come to a halt, and now trotted over to me. "What the fuck, Rosie? I bet bloody

Angus planted you to test how well I paid attention in buggy driving bloody lessons."

I got up and wiped my face on my shirt, then went to close the gate. The force of the collision had swung it so wide that it was hard up against the fence line. I grabbed the gate and realised, too late, that because it was against the fence, it was now live.

Cattle-strength voltage surged through me, the pain searing into my hand. I jerked backwards.

"Fuuuuuuuuuuuuuck! Rosie, you little fucking, good for nothing fuck-face. Fuck off!" I screamed at the dog.

Rosie wasted no time in putting her tail between her legs and heading back the way we came.

I edged the gate away from the fence with my gumbooted foot, then marched it back to position, slamming home the latch.

"Stupid, *fucking* buggy," I railed as I climbed in, putting my foot hard on the accelerator and shooting off across the paddock at buggy break-neck speed.

Derek, sporting a shiny band of gold on his ring finger, sat beside me, watching as I started to shiver. *That was quite some show, Nancy. Hardly fair to take it out on Rosie, though, when you were the one who was carefully given the instruction. I can't imagine my wife ignoring my advice so readily. She's so...*

"Impressionable?" I offered through chattering teeth. "Servile?"

Sensible.

I was in no humour to practise Lou's "self-affirming" technique. I shoved him out the side of the buggy and turned around to drive back to the shed.

Angus was working on the tractor when I returned, having changed back into the usual shorts.

"That was quick. Everything okay?"

"Yep, fine," I mumbled. "Just need a coffee."

He raised a suspecting eyebrow, then walked over to me. "What have you been eating?" He peered closely at my face. "Is that shit? Jeez, Nance, you're covered in it. It's in your hair! What happened?"

"I don't want to talk about it."

"Okay," Angus said hesitantly. "Would it have anything to do with Rosie slinking back here ten minutes ago?"

"Yeah," I answered, unable to meet his gaze. "Where is she? I have to give her my profuse apologies. I was...pretty horrible."

He paused before asking in a tone that suggested he knew I had created a shit storm (almost, but not quite, literally), "Why were you horrible to my dog?"

"Can I sit? I need to sit down. I'm feeling a bit funny," I deflected, truthfully.

Angus gestured towards the buggy I had vacated and said, "By all means, sit. Then tell me what happened. And don't skip anything important."

Once I had positioned myself, I took a deep breath in, then said in a rush, "I might have left the buggy in gear with the handbrake off at one of the gates, and Rosie might have jumped in and landed on the accelerator, and the buggy might have hit the gate I was opening and sent me headlong into a pile of poo."

"Jesus bloody Christ, Nancy," Angus erupted. "I told you. I made a careful point of telling you not to leave that thing in gear. You weren't due back for a couple of hours at least. You could have been seriously hurt and I wouldn't have known. What the bloody hell were you thinking?"

"I know! I know, alright? I did a stupid, unthinking, dangerous thing, and I feel humiliated and very, very sorry for myself, for Rosie, and for disappointing you. I don't need your anger as well." The hot burn of tears prickled behind my eyes and I desperately fought them off.

Angus looked broodily at me for a few moments. "Alright. Just don't bloody well do it again." He took a deep breath. "Are you sure you're okay? Why are you feeling funny?"

"Just shock, I think."

He put his torque wrench back into its casing. "Come on, I'll take you back to the house and make you a cuppa. You can have a shower."

THE FARM HOUSE WAS A LARGE, white villa with curved-roofed verandahs running around all four sides. The inside had been modernised and polished matai floors ran along the hallway and into every room.

Angus showed me where the bathroom was, handed me a towel and said, "I'll put the jug on. Take your time."

I stood under the hot water, reliving the episode and cringing at every "fuck" I'd directed at Rosie.

After rehashing the event for the eighth time, a ball of laughter rose from the pit of my stomach and burst its way out. It reverberated loudly around the shower cubicle.

Once the animal abuse and narrowly-avoided tragedy was put aside, it was just so funny.

I imagined Angus' stern face telling me I was lucky to be in a position to laugh about it, and another ball erupted guiltily into the jet of water.

When I got out and dried myself, I saw that my clothes were thoroughly grass-stained and flecks of manure decorated their front.

I walked out of the bathroom with just the towel wrapped around me and went into the kitchen.

"Um, Angus, do you have something I can wear? My clothes have crap all over them."

He looked up from what he was doing and ran his eyes up and down my body. They darkened. "Sure. I'll get you a shirt. I don't think any of my pants will fit you, though."

He left the kitchen and came back a couple of minutes later with a dark blue T-shirt.

I went back to the bathroom to put it on and was relieved to find it was sufficiently long enough to protect my decency. But only just. I gave way to a suspicion that Angus had deliberately chosen his smallest T-shirt.

When I re-entered the kitchen, he was leaning against the far bench with his arms crossed, waiting for me. He took a good long moment to grab my cup of tea and hand it to me.

Normally, I would have addressed the questionable selection of my attire with a facetious quip, but my tongue suctioned itself to the roof of my mouth under the intensity of his gaze.

"I put some sugar and lots of milk in it," he said. "I figure you need it."

I released my tongue with a pop. "Thanks," I whispered and took a sip. It tasted wonderful. I gulped the tea greedily, let out a sigh and looked up at Angus. "This is just what the doctor ordered."

"So, can I trust you to be left on your own from now on? No more stupid mistakes or ignoring my sage advice?"

"Yes. I think I well and truly learned my lesson."

"Good. I'm going to set one more rule. You must have your phone on you at all times and have it turned on at all times. Sound sensible?"

"Perfectly reasonable."

He went and got a cold sausage out of the fridge and cut it in half. "Here," he said, handing one half to me. "You need to make good with my dog. This'll be the quickest way to win her trust back."

"Okay, thanks." I put my cup on the kitchen island. "Angus?"

"Yeah?" He looked at me with a face that betrayed some kind of hope or expectation.

"You doing anything with the other half of that sausage?"

OF COURSE, the first thing I did when I got home was tell Hanita. She laughed so hard she lost all vocal cord capacity.

It took her a full twenty seconds to make a sound. I thought I'd killed her, but then Death by Slapstick wouldn't be a bad way to go.

"This move was the best thing you've ever done, if only to keep me entertained. Please, please keep doing stupid shit. When I said before you left that I wanted to live vicariously through you, I had no idea how heady the result would be. You are quality sport, Nance."

"But I don't want to go through life making a name for myself as the biggest muppet out."

"Look, being a total tool means you're safe now with Angus. He probably thinks you're a raging incompetent who's a complete liability."

"No. My idiocy did nothing to put him off. He

couldn't have made his desire clearer when he saw me half-naked. Twice."

"Oh, geez, you're not doing much to help yourself."

"On the plus side, I think my heart's been shocked back into rhythm."

Hanita set off on another paroxysm of laughter. "Look, I shouldn't laugh so much. You could have been really hurt. I mean, are you okay? You don't sound okay. You sound all blocked up, like you've got a cold or something."

"Yeah, I think my sinuses are full of bull shit."

I BLEW green mucus out of my nose for two days until I'd cleared it all out. I was in pain, and miserable and dreading a trip to the doctor to get a course of antibiotics.

I called in sick with Angus and spent two days in bed watching movies and seeking pain relief through sleep.

Margot called in on me to make sure I was looking after myself. She brought homemade vegetable soup with her and watched while I ate a bowl of it.

"The best thing you can do when you're sick is eat and sleep, but the last thing you'll want to do is cook, so this should last you a few days."

"Thanks, Margot. You're really very nice, do you know?"

I didn't tell her the reason for my sinus infection. I was not in any mood for another lecture. I just hoped there wasn't some poo-borne amoeba slowly eating its way through the bone and into my brain. There could be dozens chowing down on my grey matter from the way I felt.

"When you're better, I'm going to invite some couples around to dinner so you can all get to know each other more. I think you'll have a really good dynamic. It's past time you developed your social life in this town, my girl."

"Oh yeah? Who are you going to invite?"

"Anoushka and Martin, Andre and his partner, Niamh, and you and Angus."

"Angus and I are not a couple."

"Not yet."

"Margot, I am in no mood to humour your romantic fancies. Nor, I imagine, is Angus. Don't make life difficult for me. I have to work with him."

"That boy needs a good blow out, and after the dry spell you've had, you're just the person to do it."

"Do what? Oh God, don't say it."

"The blowing, Nancy."

"All I'm going to be blowing in the near future is my nose. Can we please stop talking about you pimping me out to needy farmers? I'm trying to be sick and you're distracting me from my need to wallow."

"Right. Don't let me get in your way." She got up to leave. "Make sure you keep eating and call me if you need anything."

"Alright. Thanks Margot."

I climbed back up to my bed and put my head under the pillow, groaning. I was not looking forward to the awkwardness of a "couples" dinner party. Angus would probably wear a shirt. And the top two buttons would be undone.

I groaned again. If I could only stay sick forever. Then I could keep concentrating on how well Angus, through the treatment of his ex, was single-handedly dragging gender equality back towards the twentieth century.

TEN

THE DINNER PARTY

APRIL.

I arrived at Margot's early to help with preparations.

Apparently, Angus had the same idea. He was in the kitchen in Margot's frill-trimmed apron, standing over her chopping board.

"Whoa, looking good," I said as I closed the front door behind me.

He grinned in greeting. "There's no place for gender roles in a kitchen. That goes for the protective wear, too." He deftly cut up some coriander with the manic chopping action of a professional chef.

"Impressive. You still got all your fingers?"

He held up a hand with a 'missing' finger, then made a show of looking for it. He gave up, shrugged, and said, "Who needs four on each hand, anyway?"

"That's right, a thumb and picking finger is all you need."

Angus looked at me, his mouth turned down in distaste. "What do you pick, Nance? Should I ask?"

"Well, I've recently discovered I'm a dab-hand at picking dung out of my nostrils."

"It went up your nose?"

"Yep. All the way."

"Is that how you got the sinus infection?" He guffawed. "Classic! That's going straight in my *Curious Tales from the Farm* book."

"You're writing a book?"

"Not yet, but with the amount of material you're giving me I reckon I could have a manuscript ready in a couple of months."

"Maybe I'll write my own book. It'll be called *The Smallholder's Guide to Sticking it to Your Neighbours*. It'll be about a beautiful, silvering woman who single-handedly creates a self-sufficient homestead despite the snide misgivings of her farming neighbours."

"It'll be a work of fiction, then?"

I placed my bottle of wine on the bench. "I was going to offer you a glass of wine, but my generosity seems to have vanished."

"I'd love one, thanks."

I retrieved glasses from a cupboard and poured us one each.

"Where's Margot?" I asked, handing him his wine.

"Getting changed."

"Good." I took a sip out of my glass. "You do know this whole thing has been staged for our benefit." Angus raised his eyebrows. "Margot's calling this 'couples' bonding'. At some point in the evening you and I are meant to realise that the most desirous thing is to join the couples party, with 'coupling' being the operative word."

"Really?" He chuckled into the capsicum he was julienning. "Well, we'll just have to have fun playing along, whether it's to Margot's script or one of our own making. She's canny, our Margot. Her finger's never too far from the pulse." He gave me a pointed look.

I returned it levelly, suppressing the heat rising from my stomach. "Alright. I'll happily follow your lead. Just try not to embarrass me. I do a good enough job of that on my own."

He grinned. "That you do. Or" – he paused his chopping – "we just go with the flow as it's already an option under consideration."

I didn't answer straight away, helping myself to a piece of chopped capsicum instead. Finally, I asked through my mouthful, "Do you need a hand with anything?"

"Yeah, can you set out the antipasto platter? It's all here, it just needs artful arranging."

"Sure."

"Nance, *is* it still on the cards?"

"I..." I squinted my eyes, trying to force an answer. "Yeeees?" I managed, the faceless ex hovering on the periphery of my mind's eye.

Angus laughed and shook his head. "I hope you're more decisive with your house. The thing'll never get built."

Ignoring him, I started removing cheeses from their packages and in the conversational lull, my brain focused on the woman, dragging her into full view. She'd changed since I last saw her. Her hair had gained colour – a rich honey-blonde – and her features, though still a blur, were starting to form. "So." I unwrapped a gouda. "How's everything going, you know, with the legal challenge?"

Angus sighed. "Slowly. Thankfully her lawyer's not pursuing it with any urgency, which makes me hope she's half-hearted about the whole thing, but it would be good to have it done, one way or the other. Things are really ramping up with the resource consent for the subdivision and it's a bit beyond mum and dad to manage, so I've been brought in to help."

"Oh." Oh indeed. If I didn't come to the party things were about to get a lot more complicated for everyone.

"It's a big project. It takes a lot of focus."

"I bet." I applied slightly too much force to the

packet of crackers I was opening and the contents scattered across the countertop. "Shit."

"Have you ever listened to an audio book?""

I looked up from my cracker retrieval, confused by the change in topic.

Angus continued without waiting for my answer. "There's a whole world of them out there I'm having fun discovering. I've been listening to them while I'm working to avoid wasting mental energy mulling over everything. It bloody well works. I've been to other galaxies, other centuries, alternative universes, Australia–"

"That's good," I interrupted, my discomfort far from being quieted. "I'm glad you've found a way to help deal with...stuff."

Angus caught my eye. "I'm thinking *Curious Tales from the Farm* would make a pretty entertaining audio book."

Happy at the chance for light relief, I affected a sigh. "Can you at least change my name to something more modern, more edgy?" I spotted a cracker under a plate and stretched to reach it. "Like Latiqua."

Angus laughed and Margot walked into the kitchen adjusting an earring. "Nancy, hello darling. You're looking very nice in your blue skirt. Isn't she looking nice, Angus?"

"Can't say I noticed, Margot," he answered, smiling at me over the back of Margot's head.

"Somehow, I doubt that, my boy. Now, where did I put my drink?"

NIAMH WAS JUST as striking as her partner. She had red hair cut into a French bob and finely freckled skin. Her dress was a fifties cupcake frock in pastel purples and greens and she wore red ballet flats to compliment her hair.

I couldn't take my eyes off her. She was tiny, made even smaller by Andre's large physique.

She and Andre had the night to themselves, having handed over responsibility of their two-year-old, Terence, to Andre's parents.

Martin, who'd greeted me by declaring he hadn't seen me since I quashed Jim Carter's conservatism with savage drunkenness, told them to make the most of the cute years when you're still the centre of your child's world. Putting up with the derision of his two teenage sons was, however, not without its disadvantages. "I can now interpret six dialects of grunt thanks to our boys and their friends. Who needs to waste energy on words when an expulsion of air from the diaphragm works just as well?"

I contributed to the child-rearing conversation by admitting I'd found Old Trousers standing on top of the coop crowing like a rooster that morning. "She has some identity issues. I keep finding random eggs in the middle of the garden or in the grass, like they just fell out where she happened to be standing. She hasn't worked out that laying eggs is part of her job. I think they're an inconvenience to her transgender lifestyle."

Talk of children and animals continued until dinner was ready, at which point Margot positioned herself at the head of the table with Angus and myself to her left, ostensibly to help with clearing and serving courses. "You two sit next to each other here," she said, "and I only want to see one hand on the table at all times."

"I quite like using both a knife and fork when I eat, Margot," I replied. "A bit radical, I know, but I'm not too fond of violating my nostrils with wayward asparagus spears."

"You save that for wayward manure missiles," Angus whispered out of the side of his mouth.

I gave him a horse bite above his left knee. He jumped in his seat and the whole table shook, the cutlery rattling.

"Not quite what I had in mind, Nancy, but at least you're warming up," said Margot.

Anoushka, watching the exchange, asked uncertainly, "Are you two...?"

"No," I interrupted.

"Definitely not," said Angus at the same time.

"They will be," said Margot, over the top of both of us.

"Right, that's all clarified nicely," Martin remarked, exchanging raised eyebrows with his wife.

Over the entrée, Margot, fascinated by Andre's appearance, asked him about his grooming regime.

"Do you do your eyebrows yourself or get them done by a professional?"

"Ah, Niamh does them for me."

"And do you remove other body hair?"

"Yes."

"All of it?"

"Most of it."

"That must be a job to maintain. Do you get that combination done, what do they call it, 'Back, sack, and crack'? Is the sack awfully painful?"

"Margot," I chided. "You're making Andre feel uncomfortable, let alone the rest of us, and it's hardly dinner conversation."

Andre just laughed. "Give me another couple of wines, Margot, and I'll happily tell you all the gory details."

"Excellent," she said, sliding the nearest wine bottle closer to him.

BY THE END of four courses, we had collectively consumed eight bottles of wine and were onto bottles nine and ten. Needless to say, the mood had become rather merry and the noise level, on the rowdy side of boisterous.

A conversation about best stress-relief methods was being held to my left.

"Have you tried 'dancing like nobody's watching'?" asked Andre. "Clear the furniture in the lounge, put your earphones on so as not to disturb anybody else, turn the music up and the lights off and go hell for leather."

"Have you tried secretly watching someone who's 'dancing like nobody's watching' when they're wearing earphones?" Niamh added. "It's pretty funny."

Andre looked at her aghast. "Niamh, you can't diss my unwinding time."

"It helps me relieve my stress watching you relieve yours."

Anoushka joined in. "We tend to book a childless island holiday once a year. Last year we went to Aitutaki. Martin slipped a disc hula-ing on Island Night, and I fell asleep by the pool and blistered my eyelids. We both had to go on a strict mai tai diet to help numb the pain. It ended up being quite a good holiday, from the bits I can remember."

On my right, Angus asked, "If you had intro music whenever you walked into a room, what would yours be?"

"Yours would be Weird Al's version of 'Blurred Lines' – 'Word Crimes'," I said before anyone else could answer.

"Yours would be *The Muppets* theme tune," Angus retorted.

Margot thought about it and said, "Mine would be 'Machine Gun' by the Commodores. That has a very funky opening."

"Huh, that's a perfect choice, Margot," said Martin, laughing. "You do have the ability to walk into a room and pepper it with your cutting wit. We all have to duck for cover."

When we retired to the lounge with post-dessert liqueurs, Margot suggested we play a game.

"How about Sardines?" Martin suggested. "One of us goes and hides, then the rest of us have to separately try and find them. When you do find them, you have to hide with them in the same place until the last person discovers everybody."

"Let's hope Andre's really bad at finding stuff," I stage-whispered to the group.

"I can tell you on good authority," Niamh said, slurring slightly, "that Andre is exceptional at locating small, elusive, secret places." She giggled and leaned into him, putting her arms around his waist.

"Right. Margot?" Martin directed. "You go and hide. We'll wait on the porch and give you one minute."

We filed outside with our drinks and waited for the clock to tick down. When it got to zero, Martin opened the door and said, "Fan out. There's no collaboration at all in this game."

I started in the kitchen, opening cupboards, the pantry – I even threw in the fridge for good measure.

"Good one," Angus said from where he was searching under the dining table.

"At least I can see from the outside that it's empty. Are you just checking in case Margot's wearing her Cloak of Invisibility?"

I went into the laundry and when I came back out, the kitchen and dining room were empty. I left Andre and Anoushka searching the lounge and headed for the bedrooms. Margot's room was clear, the only places to hide being under the bed and in the wardrobe.

I opened the door to the wardrobe in one of the spare rooms and saw that Niamh, Martin and Angus had found the hiding place before me, their grins wide and their eyes narrowed against the light. Angus grabbed me and squeezed me in next to him so we were facing each other. There was so little room all I could do was put my arms around him and rest my head on his chest. "This is nice," I said softly.

"Shhhh, someone's coming," Martin hissed.

Andre opened the door. There was a collective moan and we all shuffled a couple of inches to the left. Somehow, he managed to fold himself into the space that remained.

"Alright, nobody breathe," Martin whispered.

"Or fart," I added.

"You okay, Margot?" Andre murmured.

"Top notch. I haven't had this much fun since I discovered hotboxing in 1972."

A pair of hands slid over my buttocks and remained cupped around each cheek.

I looked up at Angus and whispered. "Are those *your* hands?"

He shrugged. "There's no room to put them anywhere else."

At that moment, Anoushka opened the door and we tumbled out, collapsing in a giggling heap.

"Again!" Margot commanded, clapping her hands in delight like a child. "I believe, according to the rules of the game, it's your turn to go and hide, Anoushka."

I WOKE up in Margot's spare bed with Angus, fully clothed, beside me, an arm draped over my ribs. I sat up and he opened one eye and looked at me.

"Water," I rasped.

He turned over with a grunt, grabbed a large glass from the bedside table and handed it to me.

I drained it and handed it back.

After refilling it from a pitcher, he drank a glass down himself. "I came to bed prepared," he offered in explanation.

"You are just referring to the water, right? Nothing, you know, happened...?"

"Nothing happened. The other spare bed has Niamh and Andre in it, and Martin and Anoushka are curled up on the couch. I thought about spending the night freezing in my ute, but this option was much better."

"Huh. We're not doing much for maintaining a front of disinterest."

"Nobody knows. I closed the door."

"It's just a case of counting people and beds. Plus, Margot's probably outside right now with a glass up against the door."

A shuffling sound came from the hallway and daylight appeared under the door.

"The cheek of that woman," I said loudly in feigned outrage. I looked at Angus and we both snickered.

With a long sigh, Angus reclined back on the bed, pulled me down next to him and wrapped his arms around me.

I put my head on his chest and listened to the slowing rhythm of his heart until I was lulled into a doze. Fragmented images of the previous night played out lazily in my sleep-and-hangover-addled brain. "You fondled my bottom," I slurred.

It took Angus a few seconds to respond and when he did, it was unapologetic. "You have a nice bum."

In my mind's eye a pair of American-flagged buttocks presented themselves to me for the second time, the muscles shifting under the tight fabric. "So do you."

I received a squeeze and an "I'm glad you think so", and I realised that if Angus were less of a gentleman and more the type to take advantage of my admission and close proximity, I wouldn't have resisted. Given my post-carousing state, I knew my resolve would crumble in a nanosecond.

And besides, it felt very nice lying in Angus' arms. They were just the right length to wrap around me. I drifted off to sleep trying not to think about the neat fit our bodies made.

ELEVEN
BURNING RUBBER

NOW THAT PUKEROA was attuning to the off-season lull, Barbara decided she didn't have need to employ me. I was given my weekends back until the busy ski season started in a couple of months.

While a three-day weekend was a luxurious thought, Angus' twenty hours wouldn't help me save money for the build.

I gritted my teeth and forked out for a renewed Sawcraft marketing campaign, paying for a regular advertising slot in a district newspaper and a promo to appear in Google searches. I assured myself it would pay off further down the line.

And then there was Angus. Angus was a growing concern for the following reasons:

1. I needed to make a call on us becoming bed fellows

2. That call was possibly complicated by the fact that I might, just a little bit, think he's a really nice guy

3. The shitty one – I needed to let him know he didn't have an easement through my land.

The outcome of what I wanted to do with each of those things scared me so much, I hoped to keep my head in the sand for as long as I could hold my breath. My lungs, however, were starting to feel the strain.

It was time for that visit I'd promised Hanita.

THE FOLLOWING FRIDAY AFTERNOON, I left enough food and water for the chickens to last them the weekend and, having organised to stay with my brother and his family, hit the road for the big smoke.

I arrived to a chorus of, "Aunty Nan! Aunty Nan!", the children having not long arrived home from kindergarten and school.

"Hello mein lieblings," I called from where I was getting my bag out of the car. "I didn't know you still lived here. I thought you'd grown up and moved away to make it big in New York."

I put my bag down and picked both children up with only minor "oomph"ing for a shared cuddle.

"No, we won't grow up for ages and ages," said Maia.

"I don't ever want to move away," added Ben. "But

maybe I can live in your tree house. Will you live there too, Aunty Nan?"

"Yep, I'll live in my new house. It'll be pretty close to the tree house. We can wave at each other every morning. And every evening you can make me gin and tonics."

"Okay. I don't like gin and tonics. Can I have lemonade?"

"Sure," I answered, putting the children down and picking up my bag to walk to the house. "How do you know you don't like gin and tonic?"

Maia said, "We tried some of Dad's when he wasn't looking. It tasted like earwax."

"Right." I nodded in mock solemnity. "Maybe stay off the earwax. It's probably safer to stick to bogeys if you don't like your taste buds being turned inside out."

Further sage aunty advice was offered over a fish and chips dinner, when I challenged the kids to find the longest chip. "Choose your weapon carefully, because in the ultimate chip duel, there can be only one."

The sword fights were short-lived, each chip lasting at most a two-thrust bout. The winner was allowed to refresh their weapon to face the next challenger.

After three rounds we paused to eat some dinner.

"Na-an," Sina said in the sing-song voice of half-hearted chastisement.

"Wha'?" Two chips stuck down from under my top lip and tomato sauce decorated my chin. "I only want to suck the sweet, innocent blood of your children," I said in a terrible attempt at a vampiric accent. I leaned over towards Ben's neck and he pushed me away, giggling.

"That's no way to teach children to play with food," said Will. He turned to Maia with a chip stuck up each nostril. "Is there something on my face?"

Maia shook her head, a small grin threatening to break through. "No, you look fine."

He pulled one out and handed it to her. "Here, I'm full. You eat it."

"Ewwwww," Maia squealed in delighted disgust.

Sina chuckled at the end of the table. "It's like having four children whenever you visit, Nan."

I wasn't embarrassed to admit I was proud of having that power. But I turned my adult back on after putting the kids to bed.

"So, Nan, what's going on?" Will asked, breaking off a piece of the chocolate I'd found hidden high in the pantry out of child eyesight.

"What do you mean? I've already told you all my news."

"No, you haven't. You've got a weight on you somewhere. I can see it hovering over you."

"Yeah, money's a going concern, especially now I'm not getting any work at the café."

"No, something else. If I was a betting man, I'd

put my money on this Angus fellow you work for."

"Really?"

"You've got a soft-eyed look whenever you mention him," Sina said.

"I absolutely do not. He's not the kind of man I want to be with. And besides, even if I was interested, he's off limits. A closed door. A one-way ticket to Shit-Out-of-Lucksville. So..." I shrugged my shoulders, leaned back in my chair and put my hands behind my head.

Will leaned forward to close the distance I had created. "I think your list of metaphors smacks slightly of denial."

"Fuck off, Will."

He smiled knowingly and I offered Sina an apology for my language.

"Why is he a closed door?" asked Sina.

I sighed. "He's got some pretty stressful complications with his ex-partner that he's working through and he hasn't got any emotional space left for anybody else, which" – I looked pointedly at Will – "*actually* suits me just fine. He is, however, keen for some Posh 'n' Becks."

"Some what?"

"It's cockney rhyming slang. You know, sex."

"Ah," Sina and Will said in unison. Will added, "So?"

"So," I started slowly, "I have other things on my mind, like," I paused to swallow, blinking rapidly,

"Derek marrying his child sweetheart and the fact there's going to be a great big, bloody subdivision next to my land and I will no longer have a view of the mountains."

"What?" said Will. "I mean, we heard about Derek – I'm so sorry about that, Nan. It must be a bitter pill to swallow..."

"But," Sina finished, "this subdivision – that's..."

"I'm so disappointed, you know." My voice wobbled. "Those mountains were why I moved there. I'm so in love with that piece of land and that view. It makes me extraordinarily happy, like, I can see me finally getting my life together there, you know? They keep me grounded." I sniffed wetly and Will got up to get me a tissue.

"Can't you petition the council? Don't neighbours have to be consulted on developments?"

I shook my head. "I don't think so. I figure that was why the land was up for sale. The last owners cut and run."

"And is it a certainty?"

"It's got to get through council, but they wouldn't be investing in such an expensive process if they weren't confident it would be approved. They'll have consultants making sure everything's square."

"I don't know what to say," Will said softly. "Maybe it won't be as bad as you think."

"The build site for one of the lots is directly between my build site and the mountains. Unlike me, people don't tend to build small houses on enormous pieces of land."

"You've got to talk to the council, Nan," Sina advised. "I'm sure there'll be some avenue you can raise an objection through."

"It's their retirement scheme!"

"Who?"

"Rob and Liz's. The people doing the subdivision. They're really nice," I added in a small voice.

"If you have the right to object, they'll have to accept that."

"That's right," Will added.

Across the coffee table Derek popped a piece of chocolate in his mouth. *But there's another way, isn't there, Nancy? You going to tell them about that?*

I dabbed at my nose with the tissue and surveyed Derek through slitted lids. It was time to pull out the therapy guns. I took a deep, shuddering breath and, taking aim, said loudly and firmly in my inner voice, *Derek, I understand you're implying I'm underhanded, selfish and cowardly. I am, in fact, trying to find a solution that is clear-cut, above-board and conflict-free.*

Then, still looking him in the eye, I reached out and broke off a piece of chocolate. "Good idea," I sniffed, not breaking eye contact with Derek. I slid the square between my lips. "I'll ring the council."

THE FOLLOWING EVENING, I went to Hanita's for dinner. "We'll have a late one," she had said, "so we can eat without having to manage children. Come at eight."

When I arrived, she met me at the door, chastised me in a low hiss for not dressing more smartly, then brought me into the lounge where she introduced me to her partner's handsome colleague, Bryce.

Hanita's partner, Jasper (the 'j' pronounced with a 'y'), hollered greetings from the kitchen, then asked if I wanted red or white.

"Ah," I answered decisively, shooting Hanita a look that I hoped effectively conveyed "What the fuck?" with as much pith as it was possible to produce with a single flare of the nostrils.

"White it is, then. Good choice," Jasper said, then went about pouring me a generous glass.

Bryce said how good it was to meet me and how much he had heard about me.

"Well, I've heard absolutely nothing about *you*, I'm sorry." I said, giving Hanita another glare.

"It was a bit last minute, wasn't it, Jasper?" Hanita looked to her partner for support and ushered me to sit next to Bryce on the couch.

"Mmmhmm," replied Jasper, handing me my wine. "We didn't know you were coming over until a few days ago."

"Right. It's not as if I speak to Hanita on the phone every other night or anything."

Bryce shifted in his seat. "Ah, should I go?"

"No," we replied in unison. Each of us talking over the top of one another to offer an explanation for our collective bad behaviour.

"I'm just not good with surprises," I said. "But what the heck. You look like a nice guy."

"Sorry, I should have warned her. I thought it would be better if she walked in to be surprised by a good-looking man," Hanita said.

Jasper said, "You've got nothing to lose, Bryce. Take a punt. You could do worse."

Hanita and I turned to frown at him.

He cleared his throat. "What I actually meant to say was, you can't do much better than our Nance. She's a good 'un." He reached over to pat my knee.

"Hanita, do you need a hand with anything in the kitchen?" I asked, giving her the big-eyed 'say yes, for fuck's sake or I will flay you alive later' look.

"Ah, yes, I need help with...turning the potatoes. It really is a two-person job."

"Great! Let's go turn the potatoes," I responded through a plastered smile.

Once in the kitchen we commenced a furiously whispered conversation:

Me: *Was that really the best you could come up with? Couldn't you have thought of something that made it look like you were at least making an effort to lie?*

Hanita: *I can't think quickly under pressure.*

Me: *You put yourself under this pressure, Hanita, by setting me up and not telling me.*

Hanita: *I knew you'd say "no". And I knew that by you saying "no" you'd miss a great opportunity to meet a really nice man. One who is interested in a woman his age.*

Me: *Oh yeah, how well do you know him?*

Hanita: *Not at all. He comes on Jasper's recommendation.*

Me: *I'm not sure I'd trust his recommendation after what he said about me just then. Does he actually like me?*

Hanita: *He loves you as much as I do.*

Me: *Hmph. I don't want to be set up with anyone Hanita. Okay? No. One. Not a single person.*

Hanita: *You need to get your mojo back, Nance. He's just the man to do it.*

Me: *Tongue cluck. Did you at least give Jasper some prerequisites?*

Hanita: *Of course – handsome, sane and no major baggage.*

Me: *I s'pose he's got kids.*

Hanita: *Of course he has kids, Nancy. You're old now. Most men your age have lived half their lives already. Wake up. The reality of being a forty-year-old single woman is there's going to be some complications with any eligible man. But you're a grown up. You can deal with it.*

Me: *I don't want to deal with it when it's been*

forced on me. Why couldn't you have bloody well given me some warning?

Hanita: *I told you. Because you wouldn't have been up for it. This way was much better.*

Me: *Yeah, it's got off to a great start.*

Hanita: *Look. Can you at least give it a go? I'm trying to help you move on from Derek's betrayal and Angus' knees, and right there in the lounge is a gorgeous man who was, until you opened your mouth, really interested in meeting you. Can't you make even a small effort, for fuck's sake?*

Me: *Alright. All fucking right!*

We made our way back out to the lounge, where Jasper was engaging Bryce in a louder than necessary conversation about a recent rugby match, presumably to cover up the whispering coming from the kitchen.

Hanita elbowed me. "Smile!" she hissed.

I offered Bryce my best I-do-want-to-get-to-know-you-despite-all-appearances smile.

"Potatoes alright?" he asked.

"Yep, all turned," I answered and sat back down next to him.

He really was a very good-looking man. He had a strong jawline and green eyes under wavy auburn hair. Maybe the evening wouldn't be a waste of time after all.

I surreptitiously sucked my teeth, wishing I'd brushed them before I came.

I could see he had made an effort. His smart-casual attire was good quality high street and he was wearing aftershave. It wasn't really my style, but I was willing to make concessions for someone who'd clearly set out to impress me.

"So, you're an architect, too?" I asked with a smile. Hanita and Jasper relaxed into their chairs.

"No, I do a lot of IT contract work for the company."

"Oh. Do you really ask people who have computer problems if they've tried turning it off and on again?"

"Yeah, we do. It's the number one fix. So many glitches are just minor system malfunctions that are sorted by rebooting the hard drive. The problem is that programs can become inefficient with memory and data usage and some of that can be misplaced from the hard drive the longer the computer is running for. Operating systems don't always do an effective job of tidying up the misdemeanours of wayward or tired programs, so you get those common issues like runtime errors and slow processing times. The best way to sort it is by restarting the computer and getting everything to reset."

"Fascinating." I didn't mean it to sound as sarcastic as it came out, and I quickly asked, "So, it's best to turn your computer off when you're not using it?"

"Yes. Absolutely. You use a laptop?"

"I do."

"Okay. In order to ensure its longevity, you need

to be defragging regularly, cleaning out redundant files and uninstall programs you're not using, keep your anti-virus software up to date, clean out the air vents so it doesn't overheat from dust build-up, and don't leave your battery charging all the time. You know, one of the biggest mistakes people make is continually using their laptop on a soft surface like a bed? The laptop can overheat because the air can't get into the vents to keep it cool."

I thought of all my indulgent evenings in the sleeping loft with a pot of tea, a block of chocolate and a couple of movies. Surely it was worth risking a technological meltdown for two hours with Michael Fassbender.

I decided to pretend I'd never heard his advice and changed the subject before he could kill more of my joy. In desperation, I chose my favourite of all topics – other people's children.

"Hanita tells me you have kids."

"Yes, I have..."

And that is as much as I heard, because I have to admit, I wasn't listening. I nodded and "uh huh"-ed to give the impression of being engaged by the same degree of minutiae he gave me about his children as he did with his passion for computer malpractice, but the truth was, my mind was two hours away in a certain small town.

I wondered what Angus was up to. I tried not to think of his knees, but that train of thought only made me think of all the other parts of his body I had since noticed were just as appealing.

I wondered if my ads had worked yet and whether I'd get a dozen calls on Monday asking for quotes.

I thought about my build site and how the simplest but most expensive solution would be to change its position. When my mind started wandering dangerously close to the "mortgage" word, I thought about Angus again. Two top shirt buttons popped open and, reluctantly, I forced myself to refocus before I opened the rest.

The evening ground on.

Bryce was courteous and asked me over dinner about my move and what I was trying to achieve. He seemed interested, if a little bemused by the desire to go country and radically downsize.

"So, when you've built your house without creating any debt, what then? How are you going to generate an income?"

"Well, I'll have the bus to rent out and hopefully a carpentry business that is in hot demand."

"A carpentry business? But..."

"I'm a woman?"

"Sorry, I meant no offence, I'm just surprised. It's a very unusual vocation for a woman."

"Yes," Hanita leaned forward. "Isn't it fabulous?"

"Um," answered Bryce, still getting his head around the notion of lady tradies.

Choosing to take offence, I moved the subject back to his original question before I said something that would make him feel more uncomfortable. "My land is well away from any flight paths. If my business fails, I can always run retreats for chemtrail conspiracists."

Hanita and Jasper offered an obligatory chuckle, but Bryce looked at me blank-faced.

"You know," I said, "the idea that vapour trails are in fact mysterious chemical agents sprayed by the government for nefarious purposes."

"Right. Why would you run a retreat for people who believe in that? You shouldn't be indulging them in their delusions."

"No, I don't..." I faltered, rendered inarticulate by the fact he thought I was being earnest. "I was actually..." I gave up. "You're right, Bryce. That would be irresponsible of me. It's a terrible idea."

WHEN BRYCE LEFT for the evening and said what a nice time he had, I hoped he was just being polite and could see as clearly as I did that we were a bad match.

Hanita turned to me with a hesitant smile. "Well?"

"He was lovely, Hanita, and nice to look at. Shame he was so boring."

"He wasn't *that* boring."

"I saw you shooting daggers at me when I asked him another question about his neighbour's rampant bindweed problem."

"And you just had to say that if you had a neglectful neighbour like that it would really wind you up."

"Oh come on, it was funny. *You* laughed. He just carried on talking, though."

"You're right. He was a dud. Jasper, what do you have to say for yourself?"

"Nothing. I was asked to find someone who met three selection criteria. I fulfilled my obligations."

Hanita turned back to me and shrugged. "Right, there's only one option left. We're going to have to pull out the big guns. You'll have to get a rabbit."

Jasper looked puzzled. "I'm not sure a pet is going to satisfactorily fill the hole Nance has in her life for the love of a good man."

"Oh, this is a very special pet, my love. I have no doubt that Nance's love hole will be filled to the satisfaction level of stratospheric. What are you doing tomorrow morning?" she asked me. "I'm taking you shopping."

ON MONDAY, I stared at the rabbit packaging, afraid to open it. It looked big and slightly akin to a medieval torture device with its rings of ball bearings at the base. I wasn't sure I was set up right for some-thing of its menacing bulk.

On Tuesday, I was feeling very relaxed, having worked my way through all the settings on the rabbit. Twice.

On Wednesday, I slept through my alarm after having the best sleep I'd had in months. I'd discovered that a single session with the rabbit was a more effective soporific than a John le Carré novel.

By Thursday, I was in a reasonable amount of discomfort. Angus wanted to plant a waterway that was on the far side of the farm. He decided to help as I'd never been in that area before and I had no confidence that I would find exactly where he wanted me to work.

When I emerged from behind a bush doing up the buttons of my fly (it had been the eighth toilet stop that morning), Angus asked, "Why do you need to pee all the time? What's wrong with you?"

"Nothing, it's fine," I said, unable to meet his eye. "It's just the sound of running water. Gets me every time."

"What, ten times in an hour? How do you explain the three stops we had to make on the way here when we were nowhere near running water?"

"I had a lot of tea this morning."

"Yeah, okay," he said dubiously. "If you're *fine*, we'd better get started. Come help me unload the plants."

I lasted ten minutes before I had to make another dash.

Angus' voice filtered through the leaves of the bush I was toileting behind.

"Nance?"

"Yeah?"

"Do you think, perhaps, you should go to the doctor?"

"It's fine. Nothing a bit of cranberry juice can't fix."

Angus was quiet. Then he asked slowly, "What on earth have you been up to?"

I stood up, unable to squeeze anything out despite the desperate pressure on my bladder. "You can't ask personal questions like that, Angus."

"Alright. I'll just have to draw my own conclusions."

I hoped that his conclusion was that I had been having an extraordinary amount of highly vigorous sex, and that he would be very jealous. That would be much preferable to him guessing the truth or assuming that my personal hygiene left a lot to be desired.

"You know, you can always have a shower at mine whenever you want," Angus said, dashing my hopes.

"I do not have a bladder infection because I don't know which direction to wipe in, thank you," I retorted as I emerged from behind the bush. "And I shower at Margot's. Most days."

"Okay, if you're sure."

Then it hit me. "You really want to know, don't you? You want to know if I've embarked in a sordid and steamy soirée with someone else and you're trying to manipulate me into telling you. Well, I'm not going to, so stop guessing."

Angus shrugged his shoulders. "Okay." He put his weight onto his spade and levered out a plug of dirt.

I stood still, watching him and he looked up at me. "Come on, you're on the clock, sister. Get that spade firing."

"You're giving up, just like that?"

"Yep. If you're determined not to tell me, why pursue it?"

I grabbed my spade. "How do you do that? Just turn it off and move on?" I didn't wait for him to answer. "Sometimes I wish I was a man so I could care less."

Angus smiled into the hole he was digging, unwilling to rise to my petulance. "I care," he said evenly. "I probably care a bit too much at times. I just don't waste time on trivialities."

"The state of my bladder isn't a triviality. It's rather painful, actually!"

He dropped a couple of fertiliser tablets into the hole. "Then see a doctor. I don't understand why you're being so stubb —"

I held up my index finger, stopping him mid-sentence. Then I turned and fled.

When I re-emerged, Angus was leaning against the side of the buggy with his arms crossed and his eyebrows raised. "Does it...have to do with a man?"

"No," I answered superciliously, before reconsidering. "It kind of does."

He raised his eyebrows even further.

I sighed and did my best to meet his eye. "My friend, Hanita, bought me a vibrator." I added quietly, "It's really good."

Angus smirked. "A vibrator?" After a pause he said, "You know I'd be more than happy to assist you in relieving your sexual frustration."

"Yeah, I know. But I bet you can't make me come seven times in a row."

Angus gaped. "Seven! Bloody hell." He laughed and shook his head. "You're right, I can't compete with that. I'm willing to give it a go, though. Nancy," he said formally, "I accept your wager."

Oh God. What had I just done?

"Whenever you're ready. Of course," Angus added.

I'd unknowingly invited him to a lengthy, multiple-orgasm-filled sex-fest. I needed to let him know I didn't say "bet" in the literal sense, but my mind was somewhat distracted, wondering at all the ways he might employ to win.

TWELVE
FOR THE LOVE OF A GOOD GIN

THE FOLLOWING WEEK, the pain in my urinary tract was replaced by the burning disappointment in my relationship with the local council. Not only did the subdivision developers not have to consult neighbours if they followed the rules of the district plan, apparently I'd neglected to provide something called a "Flooding Report" in my building consent. It had been a stipulation when my piece of land was carved off the original title, but that little piece of fine print was lost in the passing of ownership. Presumably, it was in the same mysterious hole as the easement agreement.

I got on the phone immediately and contacted several different companies who specialised in that type of thing. The soonest any of them could get out to the land to do their preliminary review was three weeks from now. I booked them anyhow and rang Andre to tell him there would be a delay.

Andre informed me he'd have to bring his other jobs forward to plug the gap – other jobs that required much longer than a mere three weeks. So, now my delay was looking like a couple of months.

While it was disappointing, it gave me breathing space to focus on the business and time to save more money.

It also gave me more time to dwell on the subdivision. I didn't know what options I had left and the more I thought about it, the heavier the block of concrete in my stomach sat.

These were the facts:

1. My consent was already with council. Changing it would cost more money. Not that I would, because:

2. Changing my build site would be something I couldn't afford. The only other areas of my property that would give me my view of the mountains were on slopes. I'd need to fork out tens of thousands in earthworks before I even got the piles in.

3. The build site on Lot 4 was bang in the middle of my view. Again, because of the hilly terrain, the lot had limited site alternatives, so a change in site would make it undesirable to prospective buyers.

4. The subdivision couldn't go ahead without my agreement to the easement.

5. Liz and Rob weren't aware they no longer had one.

6. They needed the money from the subdivision to live the rest of their lives in financial security.

7. I really didn't want to ruin my relationship with them by being difficult and negotiating an easement on the condition that Lot 4 was removed from the subdivision.

8. I couldn't think of an alternative.

I needed time. I needed time to come up with a plan that would leave everyone happy. And until I had that plan, I didn't want to make my working life with Angus difficult by informing his parents that the agreement had done a vanishing act and that I wanted Lot 4 to do the same.

MAY.

Barbara called me on Friday to see if I could work that weekend to cover staff illness. I arrived on Saturday morning and was immediately greeted by Gracie. "You're still alive. I thought you'd have passed away from old age by now."

"Gracie, lovely to see you out and about from the birth canal. I see you've mastered gross motor-mouth skills."

She flashed a grin at me. "You still rocking the fox?"

"Yep. I've gained the attention of *two* men recently."

"Two! That's not bad going for someone pushing retirement. You might want to be careful not to put a hip out with all the geriatric sex you must be having now."

"No, I'm not getting any, geriatric or otherwise." I sighed. "How do you get on, you know, meeting people in a town this size?"

"Okay. The local gene pool might be more on the grey-scale than rainbow spectrum, but there's plenty of tourists passing through, and if I'm lucky, some of them are hot *and* gay. I go up to the mountains as often as I can. Not to be some kind of vag vulture, necessarily." She shrugged. "I'm into rock climbing. It just happens to be a good way to meet people."

I'd been living in Pukeroa for nearly six months and never gone up to the mountains in all that time. It was a bit embarrassing. I admitted as much to Gracie.

"Yeah, that's pretty lame." She sighed dramatically. "I *guess* you could come up with me sometime. There will be three rules, though – no paying me out in front of other people, no shaming me with your agedness, and absolutely no box blocking."

I'd never gone rock climbing before. I imagined a silvering woman, effortlessly coordinating limbs up a rockface, like a spider. Or maybe something just as lithe, but less hairy. "I'd love that, Gracie. I'm pretty sure I could stick to at least two of those rules, though I mightn't have too much control over embarrassing you with forty-year-old-isms. They tend to present themselves somewhat organically. But I'm keen. I have absolutely no experience, mind, so you would have to put up with a reasonable amount of in-eptitude."

"All good. I want to instruct someday, so you can be my guinea pig. Though there's no guarantees that I won't be bossy, abusive and judgemental."

"No different to normal, then."

She grinned. "That's right."

"Look, just imagine you're taking one of the re-tirees from the rest home for a quiet day out. I'll even take the indignity of being severely patronised."

"You're on, granny." Gracie started filling a salt shaker. "So, ah, how's Skye's trip going?"

"Good. She'll be heading to Ireland soon."

"Oh yeah?" She stuck her tongue out of the side of her mouth as she eyed the salt level in the shaker.

"You...want to hear her last message?"

Gracie shrugged. "If you want to read it to me. I s'pose there's no photos though, aye?"

I smiled and showed her the two photos. One of a huge and very ornate castle-like building captioned "Chambord" and one of Skye in her swimwear pointing to her bike shorts' tan line captioned "cap-puccino legs". I read:

This may sound silly, but I heard my first sheep

today in France after how many weeks? Ten? Eleven? I couldn't see it as it was on the other side of a hedge from me, but I instantly felt really homesick and it brought a lump to my throat!! And I live in a city!! Makes you realise how entrenched sheep are in our national psyche. I have had an indulgent couple of weeks chateau hopping in the Loire Valley and have trained my way up to the Normandy coast and am now in a place called Grandcamp Maisie (great name!). I'm doing lots of monument hopping and have another observation to add to my list: French men are wonderful public pissers. It's a forced confidence due to all urinals being open for public viewing, but I'm beginning to suspect they actually prefer something of interest to tourists. The truth is I'm rather jealous and wish it was acceptable for women to pee where they stood. I'm so skinny now, despite my daily pastry overdose, that the bones in my chest are more prominent than my boobs. In fact, all I really have left is nipples. My thighs are positively thunderous now, though. I have man-quads, so I'm completely bottom heavy PLUS my tan line from riding in shorts every day is totally comical. When I went for a swim today at least three people stopped and pointed at me. Xx

Gracie's good mood held until she pulled rank over putting the rubbish out the back at the end of the day. Apparently, trash duties were a rite of passage for the newest cab off the rank. I called bullshit and promptly lost another game of Paper, Scissors, Rock.

Having dragged the rubbish sacks out the back door, I was struck by what a great space the neglected yard was. It was a mass of tall grass and weeds, but it was a reasonable size and got plenty of sun. With a good tidy-up it could be a superb extension of the café.

I went back inside and grabbed Barbara by the elbow, steering her towards the back door.

"Look at the potential of this space, Barbara. Have you ever thought of turning it into an eating area? People love to sit outside and eat and it'd be safe for kids because it's fully fenced." I waved my arm the length of the fence line. "You'd have to do some landscaping, maybe have planter boxes with kitchen herbs in them." I took three steps forward, flattening the grass. "You know, you probably won't even need to pave it, just keep the lawn mown, which will save you a lot of money." Pivoting, I added, "You could put in French doors here for access, maybe put a pergola over the top and grow a grape vine over it. It'd be perfect in the warmer months and it would take the pressure off your indoor seating, which gets pretty packed in the high season."

Barbara nodded her way through my feverish monologue. "It's definitely been on my radar over the last couple of years. It's just getting around to it. I'm working long hours as it is to manage what I've got."

"I'll do it. I'd love to do it. Anything structural you'll have to get a registered builder for, but I can do everything else. I could even make the outdoor furniture."

"Alright. Let me think about it. Things will get busy again once the ski season starts, so I don't know what window there'll be, but I promise you I'll look into it, okay?"

I beamed back at her, "Thanks, Barbara." Walking back into the café, I threw over my shoulder, "You won't regret a thing."

"I haven't agreed to anything yet," she called after me.

I put a little skip in my step as I approached Gracie who was cleaning the coffee machine. "Come on, let's make that video."

ON MONDAY after my usual four hours of planting work, I finally got around to fixing the race. I'd brought my tools with me and, after a hasty lunch in the back of my station wagon, I set to work.

I salvaged what I could, but much of the timber was too damaged to reuse and I was forced to replace it.

Rosie had forgiven me for my terrible behaviour and she kept me company while I cut each piece of wood to length and attached it.

When I was done, I noticed that a section of the loading ramp looked compromised, so I strengthened it with what I had to hand.

As I was finishing, Tess appeared and investigated my handiwork, and I knew Angus couldn't be far away.

Eventually, I heard his feet crunching on the gravel as he approached.

"Wow, Nance, it's looking better than it did before you waged war on it with the trailer."

"Thank you very much."

"What are you doing now?"

I stood on my tip toes trying to insert one of the bolts. "There's a section near the top of the loading ramp that looks weak. I've nearly finished, but I can't quite reach to get this blasted bolt back in."

"Can I help?"

"Sure. I've had a lot of help from Rosie today. She's been my shadow the whole aft– bugger!" As I'd moved out of the way and handed him the wrench and the bolt, I'd promptly dropped the nut.

I crouched down to search for it, and when I made the mistake of looking back up at Angus, he stretched up to place the bolt and his shirt rode up, revealing a line of hair that stretched from his belly button and disappeared into the top of his low-slung shorts.

My nether regions went on high alert.

"You alright down there? You've gone very quiet."

"Yep, it's just taking me a while to find your nut."

Angus cleared his throat. "Is it now?"

"The nut. *The* nut." I located it and straightened up, finding myself in the tight space between the loading ramp and Angus' body. "Here it is!" I said brightly and offered it to him in the palm of my hand. I swallowed hard, the small distance between us alive with a frenzied energy.

He reached for it without taking his eyes away from mine. When he did eventually look up to complete the job, I closed my eyes and inhaled deeply, sucking in the sharp scent of his sweat.

"Nancy," Angus said softly, "I'm finished. You can open your eyes and breathe normally now."

I opened them slowly and found his face very close to mine. "I'm going to step away now, okay? You're not going to collapse into the vacuum I create?"

"Quite possibly."

"Here." He placed my hands on the upright behind me, leaning in even closer to do so, his eyes still locked on mine and his mouth millimetres away from my lips. "You ready?"

Transfixed by the warmth of his breath on my face, I managed a small nod.

He slowly straightened up, then took a step backwards.

The cold air rushed in where his body had been.

He remained where he was, looking at me. "Right, I'm gonna go. Do some stuff."

"Yep. Good idea."

He didn't move and we continued to watch each other.

Tess came over to nuzzle his hand and Angus broke the spell, looking down at her and giving her a smile. "Alright, girl, let's go move some sheep."

He shot me a final look before he moved out, a soft smile on his lips.

I packed up my gear and went straight to Margot's for a stiff gin.

MARGOT ANSWERED the door and I pushed past her, heading for the kitchen and the calm of the blue bottle.

"I need gin. The neater, the better."

Margot raised an eyebrow, then went to the drinks cabinet in the lounge and returned with the gin and a crystal tumbler. I grabbed the bottle out of her hand and said, "Let's dispense with pleasantries. I'm in crisis."

She pulled the bottle from my fingers before I could upend the contents into my mouth. "A crisis is no excuse for a decay in decorum, Nancy," she said curtly, "and I will certainly not serve you neat gin. You can have your mother's ruin the proper, dignified way."

I paced the kitchen impatiently while she added ice, lemon, gin and tonic to the glass. When she handed it to me, her eyebrow still cocked, she did little to hide the smile tugging at the corners of her mouth.

"Am I to take it that the reason for your current state of agitation has to do with Angus?"

I held up one finger to let her know I would address her query in due course, but I was too busy slugging back the contents of the glass at that moment. I smacked my lips with an, "Aaaaah," and held out the now empty tumbler for her to refill.

"I will take that as a 'yes', I think."

By the time I'd reached the bottom of the second glass, I was feeling more relaxed. I sat down at the table opposite Margot and looked at my hands.

"I'm in a bit of a predicament and I don't know what to do."

"Do you want advice, or do you just want an ear?"

"I don't know," I said, my voice rising to a wail. "Bloody hell, I can't even make a decision on that. I'm hopeless."

"You're not hopeless, Nancy, you're just confused. Or perhaps you do know the answer and you don't want to face it. Tell me what's going on."

"Angus and I have a strong attraction for each other. He's expressed that he's keen to, you know..."

"Crash the custard cart?"

"Oh God. That's just a bit too visceral, even for

my sense of humour." I reconsidered her phrase. "Nice alliteration, though. Anyway, as I was saying, he's indicated that he'd like to," I fiddled with my glass, "do the horizontal tango."

"Not a very accurate analogy, that one, unless you're exclusively into missionary. I prefer a slow tango up against a wall, myself."

"Margot, I'm trying to explain the situation. Could you just let me do it without interrupting?"

"Well, if you keep talking in innuendo to skirt round the point..."

"You started it with your talk of explosive ejaculate!"

Margot eyed me before continuing. "We've at least established he wants to have sex with you. What's the issue?"

"The issue is, I want it too, but...I don't trust myself to keep it at just sex. I've got a bit of a record for falling for" – I carefully searched for diplomacy – "men that aren't best suited for me."

I shifted uncomfortably in my seat, moving my phone from my front pocket to the back pocket of my trousers.

"He left it up to me some time ago to make the next move, or not, and the problem is I've never given him a definitive answer on where I stand. All I've said is I need to think about it, and he's been very good at capitalising on the moments where my thinking is pro bonk-fest. I can't expect him to respect my position when *I* don't even know what it is. In the meantime, things are getting very heated. Like, nuclear fusion hot, and I'm starting to burn up."

"Nancy, I can't tell you what to do. If you think you can divorce sex from emotion, then by all means, give that boy the time of his life. If not, maybe you need to stay away from him if the tension is as heightened as you say."

"Get another job," I answered flatly.

"If necessary."

I was quiet for a moment. "I know. I know I need to." There was more than one reason to extract myself from the complications working for Angus created. But if I was honest with myself, I didn't want to. I liked the fun of trying to provoke The Frown. I liked the thrill I got each day when I'd see him for the first time. I liked making him laugh. A lot.

In fact, I liked it all a bit too much and they weren't things I could easily give up. "I'll start looking tomorrow," I promised, knowing very well that I wouldn't.

"That's the spirit, my girl." Margot slapped her hands on the table and pushed herself up. "Now, let's get some food into you before you fall over."

THANKFULLY, I didn't see Angus the following day while I potted up seedlings, his work taking him elsewhere on the farm. However, when it was time to go home, I climbed into my car, leaned forward to turn the ignition and heard a rap on the roof.

Angus walked around the back of the car towards the driver's door.

I wound the window down and he leaned over to talk to me, his arm resting on top of the car.

"Hey Nance. I, ah, received a call from you yesterday."

"What? No, you didn't. I definitely didn't call you yesterday."

"Your bum did."

"I pocket called you?" Please no. I didn't have to wrack my brain very long to remember a particular conversation that might lead to a reasonable amount of awkwardness now. My sphincter clenched.

"You were chatting to Margot."

"Ah." A hot flush crept from the pit of my stomach up towards my hairline. "What did you hear?" I asked tentatively.

"Not a lot, but enough." He crouched down. "Look. I don't want to put you under any pressure to sleep with me, and I'm sorry if you feel that I have. But I'm going to put you under pressure to make a decision, so that we're clear and there's no confusing behaviour that muddies our working relationship. So, the question is, what do you want? If it's nothing, then I will absolutely back right off. If it's a yes, I'm ready when you are. But you've got to decide. We can't keep going on the way we are."

"I know," I answered quietly. "I will. I'll let you know tomorrow. Probably."

Angus gave me a wry grin. "How about tomorrow, definitely?" He stood up, walked over to his e-motor bike, and with a wave, took off towards his house for lunch.

I sat in my car for ten minutes thinking things through.

My well-considered and carefully weighed-up conclusion was, "Fuck it."

I drove over to Angus' house and knocked on the door before I had time to change my mind. Angus opened it and said, "Hey, everything okay?"

I stared at him, my breathing rapid and shallow, not sure what to do or say next.

Angus held my gaze for several seconds, then took me by the hand and silently led me to his bedroom. When he closed the door, I knew there was no going back. I was choosing to court a whole lot of pleasure and, very possibly, a reasonable amount of disaster.

Angus turned to look at me, his eyes shining, his soft mouth slightly parted and I jumped feetfirst down the rabbit hole.

I stepped towards him, allowing him to pull me to him, letting his hands frame my face, and giving his mouth permission to press against mine with a firmness and urgency that left me breathless.

He pushed me up against the wall and moved his hips against mine. There was no finesse, no delicacy in his action, but in that moment, it was so erotic that a wave of heat washed from my stomach down through my feet and I lost the strength in my legs.

Before they could give out, Angus slid his hands up the outside of my thighs, hoisting me up the wall so my legs straddled his waist.

"Are you sure you want to do this?" Angus whispered against my lips.

"Yes," I whispered back, "I want to do it very badly."

I peeled his T-shirt off and slid my hands over his warm skin, feeling the muscles flex under my fingers as he worked to pull my shirt off. They were hard and ridged and perfect, their contours shifting in a series of small shivers beneath the feverish heat of my hands. I wanted to map the topography of his body, trace every dip, every curve.

Before I could venture too far into unchartered territory, Angus kissed my neck and all thought stopped. His breath was exquisitely hot against my skin.

A tingle, like the heat of a thousand tiny suns, emanated from where he placed his mouth and shot down to my groin. I groaned. While his lips softly explored the skin under my ear, his fingers traced my clavicle then brushed over my breasts to make their way around to my back, where they fumbled with the fastener of my bra.

"Just rip it," I panted.

Angus' lips curved into a smile against my neck as the clasp popped open.

When he removed my bra and leaned back to look at me, he breathed, "God, you're beautiful," and hoisted me up higher, dipping his head to lick and suck my left nipple. A small growl escaped from deep in his throat and he hungrily nuzzled my other breast.

Behind his back, my toes curled with each soft nip, each strike of his tongue.

Balancing me carefully, Angus moved to the bed and lowered me onto it. Seeking my mouth, he gently bit my lip and with a soft grunt shifted his pelvis against me.

My hands traced his spine, then found his hair and I tilted my hips to feel his arousal pressing against my own.

I tugged downward, encouraging him to collapse his weight so that I could feel the full, lovely heaviness of him. "God, yes," I wheezed, struggling to draw breath.

The contact of our bare skin, pressed together for the first time, generated a charged heat and I longed for the rest of him, for all of me to hold all of him. My gasps became progressively shallow and ragged the more I wanted and the more my lungs laboured.

Before I could suffocate, Angus lifted himself back up and looked down at me, his gaze shifting from my face to sweep along my body. He sighed and the corners of his mouth turned up in a slow smile as his eyes met mine again. His want was heady.

A frantic fluttering in my stomach rolled up into my chest and I raised my head to lick his lips, inviting him into a kiss that left me dizzy with the force of it.

Running my hands across his chest, I tracked the line of hair down his stomach to where it disappeared into his shorts. Desperate to know the secret place where the trail ended, I curled my fingers over his waistband and pulled his shorts over the swollen front of his underpants.

While Angus worked at my fly, I slid both hands inside his trunks and stroked his erection, circling the tip with my thumb. I was rewarded with a sharp intake of breath, and he quivered as if I'd delivered a shock.

With a small hiss he pulled himself out of my reach and started exploring the rounds and hollows of my exposed flesh with his mouth. He inched down my body, his deliberation a tease. When he reached my stomach, his stubble tickled the soft skin under my belly button and I gasped, biting my lip to stop from giggling.

Then I froze. Thoughts of the sweat-inducing

planting I'd done that morning flashed across my brain in brilliant neon. With growing horror, I couldn't remember if I'd had a shower in the last couple of days. And I had no idea when I'd last lady-scaped.

"You don't have to," I said hurriedly, my body rigid.

In reply, he lifted my hips and slid my shorts off.

I tried again. "You know, I'm more of a mains girl. Let's skip the entrée."

Defiantly, he began to nuzzle my clit through my underpants, sucking and lapping as if savouring an hors d'oeuvre.

My voice rose half an octave. "Angus, it's a nasty old swamp down there. Please stop."

Only Angus didn't stop. Instead, he looked up at me mid-lick and winked. Then, in one fluid movement, he removed my underpants and slid a tongue up the inside of my right thigh.

My eyes rolled back into my head and I collapsed onto the bed in defeat. My left thigh received a soft bite and I involuntarily clamped my legs, pinning Angus between them.

Gently, he eased my legs apart, kissing my stomach just above the line of my hair and continuing his caresses down over my mound towards the throbbing flesh at its base.

I arched my back as the heat from his breath unfurled over my wet flesh. He spread my lips and tasted me, his tongue dipping into my depths, then flicking lightly over my clitoris.

"Ungh," I offered in encouragement, my fingers digging into the bedclothes.

His mouth closed over me and he mapped my swollen nub with his tongue, sliding around its perimeter before slipping over its tender apex in one slow stroke.

Another flick.

Another teasing kiss.

The more his tongue quickened and slowed, the more I writhed, my moans coming louder.

With a strangled groan he stopped.

"Why did you do that?" I panted.

Angus' eyes were wide and black. "Condom," he croaked. He reached into the drawer of his bedside table, deftly removed the packaging and rolled the condom over his erection.

When he looked up at me, he drew a deep breath and pursed his lips as he exhaled, as if trying to establish calm.

I sat up and pulled him towards me, delivering a series of light kisses as he lowered me once again onto the bed.

As our tongues met, I guided him in, smiling as he gasped and groaning when he had completely filled me.

Angus let out another calming breath, then started to move his hips in a slow rhythm.

I clenched, holding him in place and he gritted his teeth and looked up at the ceiling.

Reaching up, I licked the hollow between his clavicle.

"Fuck," Angus muttered, his eyes shifting back to mine. After a moment, he resumed his slow slide and flex. A pause, another deep breath.

Impatient, I thrust my hips upwards, inviting him back into a shared rhythm.

His eyebrows met upwards in the middle and he looked at me as if I'd caused him pain. "Jesus, Nance," he murmured, a plea in his voice.

Ignoring it, I thrust again and with a moan Angus gave up, his pace rapidly increasing and his breathing becoming short and uneven.

As our bodies connected in a growing urgency, a dull energy built between my legs, growing in strength and clarity until I was overcome by that excruciatingly exquisite sensation.

Watching me as I came, Angus smiled, whether in enjoyment of my pleasure or relief or both, and he kissed me tenderly, his mouth at odds to the frantic movement of his body.

He didn't pull away to concentrate on his own climax, like many of the men I had slept with might, but remained where he was, his mouth against mine as his cries increased, and I was struck by the intimacy of it.

From somewhere deep in my belly a warmth

crept up into my chest and I pushed it away, choosing to laugh as Angus, with a hard thrust and wide eyes, silently shuddered with release.

WE LAY LOOKING at the ceiling getting our breath back. I turned my head to look at Angus and he swivelled his head towards me, a grin creasing his face.

"Angus," I said softly, "I have to go now."

His grin disappeared. "What? No, you don't. There's nothing I have to do that I can't put off. I'm already beginning to think about round two."

I reluctantly got up and started to put my clothes back on. "I do have to. If we're to keep things at a shagging-only level I'm definitely not hanging around for pillow talk. Helps, you know, keep the boundaries solid."

He paused before saying, "Okay, I respect that. Though I'm kinda feeling like a service bull right now."

I smiled at him and walked towards the door.

"Nance?" I turned to look at him lying naked and delicious on the bed. He had propped himself up on one elbow, his head resting on his hand, one leg cocked. "I want to be clear about another thing. I find you extraordinarily sexy, and I really want to do this again. Soon."

THIRTEEN

KICKING OVER THE PISS POT

NATURALLY, I immediately rang Hanita to confess to *Naked Encounters with my Neighbour Mark III.*

As soon as she answered, I blurted, "We did it."

"Who did what?"

"Weeee" – I stretched out the syllable to emphasise that the "who" should be obvious – "did IT."

"IT?"

"IT," I confirmed.

"Well, shit."

"Yep."

"You know, I'm not at all surprised that you gave in to the keening of your libido. I'm just amazed it took you so long. You must have lady-bits of titanium."

"Not any longer. He's penetrated my steely resolve."

Hanita laughed. "I take it IT was good?"

"Hanita, if he continues the way he started I'll have to put the rabbit into early retirement."

"Whoa."

"I know."

"Well, I'm glad the torturous wait was worth it. So, how are you going to manage the fact you don't like him very much?" She gasped. "You just had hate sex!"

I clucked my tongue. "I do like him. He's a really nice guy and we have a lot of fun together. I just don't like the way he's treating his ex-partner, as if living eleven years together on the farm amounts to nothing."

"So, you're only interested in the sex, then?"

"Yes."

"Good, then you're even. It would be rubbish if one of you actually did like the other one. Romantically."

"That's right." After a pause I added, "Though, I'm beginning to wonder if he is actually a bit interested. There's been a few instances where he's behaved like he might."

"Like how?"

"I don't know. Just like he might. Like he wants to start something but his other emotional complications are in the way."

Hanita sighed. "That is dangerous and wasted

thinking, Nance. Please don't be one of those women. Scourge it from your mind, right now."

I was quiet.

"Nance! Forget it, okay? If you can't, then you need to stop it now before you realise you're in love with him and he just rolls over and starts snoring. I am very fucking serious, Nancy Robyn Myers."

BEFORE I HAD the chance to forget it, my week threw me a series of challenges designed to test my shaky fortitude:

1. My finances were ambushed in a swift and vicious offensive by the United Front of Building Subbies. Deposits were demanded for the roofer, the waste water system, and the company fabricating the steel frame for the massive window that would effectively turn the end wall of the house into one of glass. The final bill came in for the water tank and the excavation work needed to bury it. And costs had increased for the manufacture of the windows. The company I'd contracted sent me a new several-thousand-dollars-heavier quote.

2. I spotted a pair of surveyors marking out the boundary lines of the lots. They had their lunch on top of Lot 4's perfectly positioned building site and sat facing the mountains to enjoy the breath-taking view.

3. One night, after I'd woken up needing the toilet for the second time, I skidded on the floor of the bus and kicked over the chamber pot much to Derek's delight. His laughter rumbled around the bus silencing my string of expletives. I'd managed to soak my socks, the bottom of my pyjamas and a good proportion of the floor in cold urine. Needless to say, sleep wasn't particularly forthcoming after I'd cleaned it up and I spent a good chunk of the next day exceedingly grumpy, unleashing The Barbed Tongue Beast on anyone or any animal who tested my patience.

4. Angus seduced me again before I could give any serious consideration to whether I was "one of those women" or not.

I stood at the potting bench easing a seedling out of its tray to place in a pot, when I sensed Angus watching me. I turned.

He stood at the door to the greenhouse, one shoulder leaning against the doorframe, his arms crossed.

"Hi," I said.

"Hi," he replied in such a suggestive way that my nipples contracted.

I turned back to the bench and took my gloves off.

His boots crunched on the concrete floor behind me and before I could turn around, he'd put his hands on my hips and pushed his pelvis against my buttocks. He was already hard.

Leaning forward, he kissed my neck with slow deliberation. When he started nibbling my ear and my knees went weak, I tried to turn around so I could kiss him, but his hands on my hips held me in place. Then he slipped them under my top, sliding my bra upwards and gently pinching each nipple.

"You have no idea how much I've been thinking about the other day and how much I want to do it again," he said unevenly.

I wanted to respond, but all I could manage was a squeak as one of his hands started to work its teasing way down my stomach. He softly bit my shoulder and slipped the hand under my waistband, pushing one of my legs aside with his knee so he could have better access.

I gripped the edges of the bench and threw my head back against his shoulder when, using the slickness between my legs, he started to gently massage my clit.

He pushed himself up against me again as the hand on my breast started kneading and the other slowly increased its rhythm.

Eventually, I couldn't take it any longer and forced myself around to find his mouth, my hands working furiously at the front of his trousers. He gasped as I took him in both hands and slid one down to caress his testicles.

"Condom," I panted.

"Shit, I didn't set out with the intention of ravishing you today." He gave me a mischievous grin. "I guess we'll just have to find other ways of entertaining ourselves." He hoisted me up onto the bench, removed my shorts and knickers and spread my legs. Then he lowered himself to his knees, keeping eye contact with me while he inserted a long finger and started to work his magic with his tongue.

Well, what was I to do? I was hardly going to protest at being treated in such a considerate *and* masterful way. Hanita would call Angus' approach, "the cunning of the cunnilingus seduction".

However, I for one was more than happy to be made the fool.

BY THE END of the week I felt like the steering shaft had snapped, the wheels were starting to fall off and I was wobbling helplessly on a direct route towards the cliff's edge.

I was tired and stressed and confused and feeling like a punching bag for Derek's continual jabs about my ineptitude.

As I had for much of my life, I sought direction from Margot.

I lay on her couch and unloaded while she sat in an armchair and practised sympathetic listening. I imagined we looked like a tableau from a Woody Allen film.

Awkwardly sipping my tea from to my position of

repose, I said, "I feel like the accident with the chamber pot is a metaphorical directive for life. 'Don't kick over the piss pot, you'll make an awful mess'."

"'Don't kick over the piss pot' has a good ring to it. You might have just coined a new idiom."

I harrumphed. "An idiom for an idiot."

"Don't you dare talk that way, Nancy. I will not tolerate self-abasement and you know very well that you are far from being an idiot."

"I just feel impotent. I feel like I'm not able to manage anything that's happening in my life right now, like I'm continually courting disaster." I sighed. "I wish I had the intelligence and mettle that Skye has. That girl has no fear. She'd walk up to a roaring lion's maw, berate it for not preventing tartar build-up and offer to floss its teeth."

"Nancy," Margot said gently, "you know Skye reminds me a lot of you?"

"Does she?" I asked, genuinely perplexed. "You're just saying that to make me feel better. How on earth are we similar?" I thought a moment and talked over the top of her. "I guess we both have an interest in riding things at the moment..."

"Yes, Skye's strong, yes, Skye's determined, but you have those traits too. You had the passion and energy and drive to move here without any security or knowing anyone but me. You single-handedly converted that eye-sore of a bus into a rustic dream home. That is a huge feat and one that takes rare and exceptional skill. You're brave enough to start a business despite the challenges that your chosen field will throw at you. But most of all, you're forging a firm and unique path in life when odds are, with the loose parenting you had, you'd either have all the direction of a blowfly spinning out its death throes on a window sill, or be living the pale existence of a woman who married the first man to offer some stability. I'd say those are excellent examples of someone who has inner strength."

Margot put her mug of tea down and swivelled in her chair to face me more squarely. "Look at me."

I shifted my gaze and found Margot eyeing me with a fierceness that I had to fight the urge to flinch from.

"You admire Skye greatly and are immensely proud of her, but she looks up to *you*. And there's very good reason for that. Don't be too hard on yourself because you've driven off-road and are having to negotiate some rough terrain. Remind yourself that you've got a four-wheel drive and you are in control. Wrestle that steering wheel until you're back on track."

THE PSYCHOLOGIST. *Session four:*
    "Tell me about your parents."
    "Ah," I said. "Yes." I had wondered when my

childhood would come under scrutiny. I took a deep breath, offering it up for easy dissection. "My parents provided a lot of love, but not a lot of direction."

Lou raised an eyebrow, inviting me to continue.

This I had thought a lot about and my description rolled off my tongue as if I had practised the answer. I kept it simple. "My parents were hippies. The freedom they enjoyed in the sixties and seventies became a core value of their parenting. My brother and I were encouraged to experience the world as much as we could with our imaginations and use our curiosity to answer our questions – growth through self-led learning, I guess."

"So, you had no boundaries?"

"They didn't believe in discipline or didacticism. I can't remember ever being told 'no', or 'yes' for that matter. It was always 'what do you think?', or 'why do you want to do that?'."

"Were you a happy child?"

"For the most part, yes. I think I was anxious at times. I relied a lot on my older brother. I followed him around constantly until I was old enough to be self-reliant."

"Right." Lou smiled at me. "I think you know what I'm going to say."

"My insecurity stems from the parenting I had."

She nodded. "You didn't get the security a child needs, Nancy. Unconditional love is wonderful and nurturing, but it's not enough. Children need boundaries. The world is a big and perplexing place and children need guidance to make sense of it. You were lucky that you had an older brother to look to for direction, but I imagine you felt quite lost at times."

"Probably."

"But you're not a child anymore."

"No."

"And you can be mistress of your own stability."

I didn't answer.

"When things get difficult and you have those feelings of impotence and helplessness, ask yourself what is within your power to control. Let go of the rest. Focusing on taking charge of just one detail will ease the sense that the ground is sliding out from under you."

"Like?"

"Like, I don't know, telling yourself you can't control what others say about you and your new business on social media, but you can control how you portray yourself to them. Remaining professional and positive in the face of conflicted public opinion and not being drawn into the debate will serve your business well. Or telling yourself that while you can't control the increasing cost of building materials, you can control the speed of the build. Slowing it down will allow you to save more money."

I tested the phrase, feeling it roll around in my mouth. "What can I control?"

"See how empowering asking that question is?"

I nodded.

"And Nancy, there is one thing you have absolute power over. You can control your negative thoughts about yourself. You can control Derek."

THAT EVENING, while I sat drinking in the mountains out the back window of the bus, the refrain "What can I control?" kept repeating itself and my gaze drifted towards Lot 4. If I made things difficult for Rob and Liz, I risked my friendship with Angus. And the thought of that...well, I didn't want to think about that. I couldn't. Instead, I focused my thinking and a plan that would keep everyone happy unfolded itself and started to flesh out.

I rang Jasper. "I need a massive favour," I told him when we'd dispensed with pleasantries.

WHEN I HUNG UP, I decided that tomorrow I'd put up the profiles for the house and I'd borrow Stu's post hole borer so I could make a start on the piles. I was so sure my plan would work, I figured there was no point in delaying the build, even if I didn't have consent yet. What the council didn't know, wouldn't hurt them.

I headed towards the kitchen to pour myself a celebratory glass of wine.

FOURTEEN
HITTING THE WALL

GRACIE WASN'T ROSTERED to work that weekend, so we arranged to go rock climbing on the Sunday. She had warned me that temperatures could be quite cold where we were going, so I was to bring warm clothes, including a woolly hat.

"If your feet get cold on the wall," she'd told me, "there's nothing you can do about it, but you can keep your head warm, which is the next best thing." I felt that her messaging was clear, professional and perfectly in line with her instructor aspirations, until she added, "Plus, I don't want to be shamed by your greyness."

I packed a thermos of hot chocolate with my lunch and picked Gracie up from her family home early in the morning.

She gave my car the once over and nodded her

approval, declaring it to have plenty of room for a kayak or a couple of bikes. "This is the perfect size for an outdoorsy vehicle. You don't want any gear on the outside, unless you're happy to risk never seeing it again. It's kind of wasted on you, though. You wanna swap? I have a 1994 two-tone Toyota Starlet."

"They made two-tone Starlets?"

"No. I've been cultivating mine through UV exposure and general neglect. It used to be red. Now it's what I like to call sun-streaked."

"Pink?"

"Yeah, with peeling scarlet highlights. It gives it something of a classic character. The fan might be broken and the bumper duct taped on, but she's honest and reliable and can reach a top speed of 115 kilometres per hour in twenty seconds."

"Gracie, as generous an offer as that is, I think I'll stick to driving my station wagon. And besides, I've named her, so it would be like abandoning one of my children. Once you name them, they're yours for life."

"Oh yeah, what's its name?"

"Her full name or what her friends call her?"

Gracie threw me a withering look.

I took a deep breath to buy some time while I thought one up. "Her full name is Captain Kazam Glitter Train of the Wayfaring Moonbeams, but I just call her Sparkles for short."

"Ew, that is seriously uncool, Nancy. You can keep your twinkle mobile."

"Thank you, Gracie, that is very magnanimous of you."

"Oh, hey, I checked YouTube this morning. Your channel has just over sixty subscribers now and the video on how to make floating shelves is doing best. It has nearly a thousand views."

"Really?"

"We need to make another one. You gotta keep the momentum going – keep the punters coming back. Any ideas?"

I did. "Those plastic trays we use at the café are horrible. They're ugly and they don't fit in with the style of the place. I was thinking I could make a set of wooden ones. Tongue and groove surface, maybe. What do you think? We could record me making one."

"K. Barbara'll be stoked."

"How long, do you reckon, before I'm spotted by someone in Puke and my video turns into a job?"

"Dunno. YouTube's a bottomless pit. You gotta tell people about your channel. Only way it'll work. Post it on your Facebook page and your website." Gracie sniffed. "Man, I'm hungry." She riffled in her bag and asked into its depths, "You didn't bring your phone with you, I s'pose?" A muesli bar was extracted.

I smiled. "It's in the console. Read it out. I'd like to hear it again."

Gracie opened up the photos first and I snuck a look at her. The corners of her mouth were slightly curled and her finger hovered over Skye's selfie, the only photo she appeared in. Gracie read:

I'm here in Eire! I'm actually now well into my trip and so have had plenty of opportunities to reflect on the things I love about Ireland (so far):

1. The way the Irish inflect their sentences at the end, like us.

2. The Irish living up to their stereotype and being friendly and VERY talkative. They conduct monologues, really.

3. Buttermilk scones. They are SO good, I'm considering risking arrest by smuggling them into New Zealand.

4. The way the "Give way" signs say "Yield" instead.

I had my second pang of homesickness since leaving New Zealand. The Wicklow Mountains, south of Dublin, reminded me so much of parts of New Zealand that it brought a lump to my throat (not ideal as it makes breathing difficult on the uphill). In fact, Ireland reminds me of home on an almost daily basis. In just a few days I've seen dramatic changes in the scenery and in accent. Dublin tends to be rough and broad, rural Cork sounds almost Welsh, today I met a man from an inland county who sounded Geordie. The most common accent is the soft, rounded one we're most familiar with, and there's also a plummy one adopted by newsreaders and uptown Dublin girls. Tomorrow I should hear what a Kerry one sounds like.

Skye xx

P.S. am SO excited your build has finally started!! Can't wait to see it. Make sure you get it finished by the time I'm back. No pressure.

Gracie gently put the phone back in the console and turned to look out the window.

AS WE DROVE into the foothills of the mountains, the sun had risen enough to bathe the snow-capped peaks in a golden, almost orange light. The mountains were heavily forested and the light threw their many ridges and valleys into sharp relief against the shadowed areas the sun was yet to touch.

Gracie directed me to a valley sculptured in limestone outcrops and crags and we drove along a gravel road for several kilometres until the valley narrowed and the road ended in a carpark. It already had half a dozen cars stationed near the entrance to a trail that disappeared into a patch of bush.

"You climbers like to start early," I observed.

"You gotta get up at sparrow's fart to get the best routes around here. This place is well-known and can get a little overcrowded, but it's got some great ascents for beginners."

Divvying up Gracie's climbing gear between our backpacks, we headed up the trail and passed a climbing pair. The person on the rockface was already so high it was hard to tell if they were a man or a woman.

"Bloody hell, that's high. You're not going to make me do anything like that, are you? Is now a good time to tell you I'm not the best with heights?"

Gracie chuckled in a delighted, fiendish manner. "I am really going to enjoy watching you squirm. I'll try to be gentle on you, but to be frank, I think the gene for compassion skipped a generation, so you might have to take what you're given."

"You're not helping ease the nervousness I'm starting to feel. Remember" – I pointed to myself – "geriatric out for a nice, *calm* day in the mountains. Treat me with the love and care and respect you would your own grandmother."

"My grandmother rides as Sergeant at Arms for the Hogs of Hell."

"Excellent news."

We had stopped below a sheer limestone wall. I craned my neck to take in the full scale of the towering rockface.

My jaw dropped. I looked back at Gracie who made no attempt to hide her glee at my uneasiness. Her shark's grin was truly terrifying.

"Oh God, what have I got myself into?" I muttered under my breath, slinging the backpack down next to Gracie's.

"This route is called Blazing Saddles on account of the guy who did the first ascent not adjusting his leg hoops tight enough and climbing it with a ball-popping wedgie. The legend goes that he got second-degree harness burn through his clothes, but that could just be a bit of wild climbing mythology."

She shrugged, then turned from the rock to look at me. "Okay. I'm going to secure the top rope from the anchor at the top of the route. You sit tight and keep warm." She juggled some gear between the bags, then set off along the path ahead of us, her feet lightly tripping across the dirt.

I watched her until she skipped out of sight, then groaned in annoyance and sunk to the ground to riffle in my bag for the hot chocolate. At least I could take comfort in the reliability of cacao beans and sugar.

I'd nearly drained my cup when I heard a call of, "Rope," from above me, followed shortly by the end of a climbing rope descending the length of the wall.

I got up and stepped backwards so I could sight the top of the climb.

Gracie leant out over the edge of the rockface until she was perpendicular to it and with a wave to me, casually rappelled down in a series of graceful backward leaps.

When she got to the bottom, I didn't waste any

time expressing my admiration for her skill. "Show off. I bet you can't do it front ways."

"Yeah, man. Front ways is a real rush. You wanna give it a go today, Nancy? I'm sure you'll enjoy the thrill of seeing the ground rushing up to meet you."

"Ah...You know, I'm not sure I want to give anything a go today. I think I'll just watch you. You go on without me." I made a shooing gesture.

"No way, José," Gracie replied, pronouncing the "J". "I am going to get you up that wall if I have to light a fire under your bum and let the route live up to its name. Give me some of your hot chocolate, then I'll get you geared up and we can have some fun." She growled out "fun" with the gentle purr of a sadist.

Gracie had lent me a pair of her climbing shoes and I stood shifting from foot to foot trying to get used to the cramped discomfort, while she tied a stopper knot in the rope attached to my harness.

"How can you bear wearing these shoes? My toes are filling a gap a third of their actual length."

"They've gotta be tight, so you can feel the rock with your toes. My toenails tend to turn black by the end of the season. I've lost the odd one, but that's just the name of the game."

I gaped at her.

"Relax, Nancy. One climb won't hurt you. Toenails are overrated anyway. It's not like you need them for anything."

"No, but I do prefer to have them all attached."

"I guarantee that when you're thirty metres up and hanging on by your teeth and one index finger, you're not going to be thinking about how little room you have in your shoes for your toes. Right, I think you're ready. Let's get started. Key pointers are stick to the route. If you stray too far to the right or left you risk pulling out loose stone, which will not be very fun for me belaying you at the bottom. Use your thighs to push your weight up, otherwise your arms are going to get tired very quickly. Most beginners want to get their knees in there too. Knees are for helping with leverage, they're not a climbing appendage. Oh, and if you get really tired, you can just sit back in the harness and take a rest – I've got you. Okay, you ready?"

"No, but if I don't do this you'll make sure I never live it down, so I think I'll choose the lesser of the two evils."

"It's only a grade 14, so it's not too difficult. You should be fine as long as you listen to me."

I took my first tentative hold of the rock, found a toe hold and pushed myself up, immediately finding another ledge to grab hold of.

"Great start. Keep this up and you'll be at the top in no time."

Once I was a few metres up I started to feel vulnerable and my legs seized up, allowing me minimal leverage. My progress slowed to a painful inching.

"Nancy, stop making love to the wall. Get your

legs cooperating with your brain, because if you keep going the way you are, you're going to exhaust your quads *and* your arms."

"My brain is currently overloaded with the fact that if I fell from this height I'd be a quadriplegic. It doesn't know *what* signals to send to my limbs."

"Isolate them. Concentrate on working one at a time. You've got a good grip with both hands, so forget about them. Think about your right leg. If you push up on it and extend it, you can give it and your other leg a rest."

"But my hands will then be too low and I'll lose balance."

"Your left hand is on the edge of a crack, so you can counter-balance against it, but the trick is always to look for the next hold. See up to your right, there's a small ledge? When you straighten your leg, you'll be able to reach that no problem, then you'll be perfectly balanced."

I put all my willpower into following her instruction, because I didn't want to have to live down the failure, but also because I suspected she knew what she was talking about.

I concentrated so hard, I didn't realise how high I was getting and when I finally paused to rest, I made that eternal mistake of looking down. Gracie was a good twenty metres below me, and I had a sudden attack of vertigo. I suctioned myself onto the rock and took in big gulps of air.

"Gracie?" I called down shakily. "I think I just peed in my pants a little bit."

"Don't worry, Nancy, happens all the time. When you're midway up a big wall, it can be pretty difficult to find a toilet. Climbers just let it flow. That's why it pays to lead the route."

All of a sudden, my terror and muscle exhaustion took over my body, and my legs started to shake violently.

"Oh yeah, Elvis has entered the building," Gracie called through a laugh. "You got some good sewing machine legs going, girl. But hey, not long to the top now, Nancy. Suck it up. You'll get there."

"Gracie, I can't do it. My muscles are in their death throes and I'm really bloody scared right now."

"Have a rest. Sit back and enjoy your air-cushion arm chair." I looked uncertainly down at her. "Nancy, the rope is taut. You're not going anywhere. Take a seat."

I tentatively put my weight on the harness and when I felt no give, I slumped with relief into it.

"The fear is mind over matter, okay?" Gracie called up to me. "You are one hundred percent safe up there. You cannot fall. Tell yourself that, then the height becomes irrelevant. You might as well be one metre up, let alone fifty."

I nodded mutely and took several deep breaths to get oxygen into my muscles and psych myself up for the last pitch. When I grabbed onto the wall, I felt weak, the fear over the height having drained my energy. I told myself I was bloody well going to do this or Gracie would forever hold one over me, and I slowly and carefully made my way up the last few metres until I could see the anchor at the very top.

"Woo hoo, Granny!" Gracie hollered. "Touch the anchor and you've done it!"

I reached up, gave it a slap and collapsed back into the harness. "Now what?"

"I've got to lower you."

"Wait, does that mean you're in control of the speed?"

"Sure does. Buckle up, Grandma."

"Um, can't I just do a Mission Impossible, like you?"

"No can do. It's controlled from the bottom of the rope."

"Oh, shit," I whispered into the rockface. I might have proven to Gracie that I wasn't a total piker, but she'd really been in control of the situation the whole time and now she would claim her puppet master victory.

"Nancy, you need to keep your feet on the rockface with your legs straight, so that you don't scrape up against it. Lean out like I did when I was rappelling."

I put my feet against the wall as high as I could.

"Your legs need to be ninety degrees to the wall. Walk them higher."

I managed a ginger shuffle and swore I could hear Gracie sigh thirty-five metres below me.

"For goodness sake. Keep your feet where they are, I'm going to lower you a bit. When I've got you in position, you're going to walk down the wall keeping your feet at the same level as your bum. Ready?"

"No."

"I'm lowering you now." The rope jerked downwards and I let out an involuntary shriek.

"God, Nancy, you're an embarrassment to our sex. Woman up!"

I didn't think I could. I'd used up all my womanliness on the ascent. "Just get me down so I can say I've done this and then I never ever have to do it again."

The rope jerked again and I shuffled downwards, getting a feel for it after a couple of metres and gaining in confidence.

"C'mon, Gracie," I called out, feeling unjustifiably cocky. "We'll be here all day at this rate."

"Challenge accepted," came the shouted reply.

The rope suddenly moved more quickly and I had to scrabble to catch up, fighting the feeling that I would tip over backwards.

"Keep up, Grandma. Put your money where your mouth is."

I managed to match her pace metre after exhilarating metre until I was about five from the ground. I went to put my foot under a ledge and missed my footing, my body swinging upright and my momentum pulling me into the wall. I collected my shins on the ledge and didn't quite get my hands off the rope in time to brace myself effectively.

My helmet took the brunt of the impact, but the bottom of my right eye socket connected solidly with a small protrusion of rock.

I heard an "Ooh, that's gotta hurt" from below me as I clamped my hands to my face and tried to recapture the air that had been sucked out of me.

"I think you've broken my face," I wheezed.

"No, Nancy. That was entirely of your making." Then she added more gently, "Let's get you down so I can take a look. Can you keep yourself away from the wall?"

I nodded and assumed my original position, noticing patches of blood seeping into the front of my trousers.

Once I was down and Gracie had released my harness from the rope, I sat down heavily and looked up at her. "My eyeball still in place?"

She squatted down in front of me and held my head in both hands to scrutinise me. "Yep, both still there. Pointing in different directions, but that'll give you a head start on all those fox-chasing twenty-year-olds." She smiled at me. "I think it's just bruised. You've already got some swelling, but if it's really tender tomorrow you better see the doctor. Your brain okay? You don't feel odd?"

I shook my head to indicate the negative, but also

to test out how it was feeling. It didn't seem to be functioning any different from normal.

"Do you know where you are and what day of the week it is?"

I answered both questions without having to think very hard and kept my head still while Gracie held a hand over each eye, checking the response of my pupils.

"They seem alright. I'll get a cloth and pour some water on it. Should be cold enough to help the swelling a bit." Gracie rummaged in her bag and retrieved a first aid kit as well as a sock, which she soaked in water from her drink bottle. "Don't worry, it's clean," she said handing it to me, then turning back to open the first aid kit. "Here." She passed me two anti-inflammatories. "Prophylactic. You might develop a stinking headache after head-butting a rock."

She gave me her bottle to wash down the pills and looked at my legs. "Congratulations, Nancy. You've achieved the status of official Cheese Grater on your first climb. Most people don't shred themselves until at least the third go, but you are way ahead of the game."

After patching my shins, we packed up and Gracie volunteered to drive me home.

Derek kept mercifully quiet during the trip and all I had to contend with was the throbbing in my face and shins.

When we parked outside the bus and she asked for the third time if I was sure I was alright, I turned to her. "Thanks for everything. See, you can be compassionate when you really have to be."

"Yeah, well, don't get used to it, old woman. You've got two days' grace, then I'm gonna be firing on all shit-flinging cylinders."

I opened the door with a groan. "I can't wait."

I TURNED up at work the next day tired, stiff and sore. Every move I made required a grunt to execute it. Luckily, Angus had me on the relatively gentle job of bagging up plants.

As was becoming normal routine, Angus would text me the day's jobs so that he could be out on the farm and not have to return to give me instruction.

When he did turn up mid-morning, he took one look at me and winced. I was sporting a striped T-shirt for a long forgotten local radio station "Radio X: Piracy on the arrrwaves" and an impressive black eye.

"What happened to you?"

"I wanted to save money on the eye patch."

He snorted, but then said, "C'mon. What happened?"

"I went rock climbing with Gracie from the café yesterday and I challenged the rockface to a fight."

"Geez, Nance, you're lucky you didn't lose your

eye." He stepped forward, holding my head in both hands and inspecting my injury with a frown.

His face was very close. My eyes were drawn to the small dimple in the middle of his bottom lip and the urge to kiss him was overwhelming, but it was outside the unsaid boundaries of our casual arrangement. I wasn't his girlfriend, so I couldn't behave like one.

I dropped my gaze, studiously ignoring the hollow at the base of his neck. "I've got a spare one," came out as a whisper.

Angus let his hands drop, but remained where he was. "I quite like you with two," he said softly. "It rather suits you." He smiled at me with a sweetness and tenderness that tightened my chest and I had to concentrate very hard to remember Hanita's warning.

I dropped down to a squat, groaning as my quads took my weight, and continued my potting task.

Angus followed and as he moved to hold open the bag I was filling with dirt, his knuckles bumped my shin.

I yelped.

Angus withdrew his hand quickly. "What'd I do?"

I rolled up my trouser legs to show him the bandages. "Gracie tells me it's called 'cheese grating' in the climbing world. Apparently, I've broken some sort of record."

Angus' eyes widened at the extent of the bandages. They ran the entire length of my shins, and fingers of black bruising stretched out from underneath them. "Nance," was the only comment he offered.

My heartbeat stumbled under the sweetness of his concern. It was so fiercely endearing that I couldn't allow myself to accept it. I said, "Look on the bright side. By the end of the week I should be a fine representation of most of the colours of the rainbow." I shrugged. "It's boring being monochrome."

Angus didn't laugh. He shook his head and reached out to roll one of my trouser legs down. "How you manage to attract mishap, I don't know, but you don't do it by halves."

I tried again to deflect his concern. "It's actually a finely-honed skill. I'm thinking of adding it to my resume, alongside tap dancing and gun running."

Angus withdrew his hands and said through a thin smile, "Shit, you can be frustrating, Nancy. You can't make a joke out of everything. This" – he gestured towards my legs – "is not remotely funny." He sighed. "You have to get better at looking after yourself, because sooner or later you're not going to come away with just grazes."

He stood up. "The house is open. Go up and have a soak in the bath. It'll ease your muscles." He walked towards the greenhouse door. "And take tomorrow off. You can work Friday instead."

· · ·

ONCE AT THE HOUSE, I made a strong cup of tea and drew a large bath. I found some Epsom salts in a cupboard and sprinkled the water liberally with them.

When I'd removed my clothes, I stood in front of the large bathroom mirror and measured the full extent of my injuries for the first time. The underside of my forearms were purple from where I'd attempted to brace myself from hitting the rock.

The graze on the shin Angus had knocked had reopened and blood seeped through the bandage in a L-shaped blot. The upper lid of my blackened eye was tight and shiny, the plum discolouration flecked with red where capillaries had broken.

Derek's words from the café reverberated in my head. *Nancy, you're a mess.*

"And that's just the outside," I said into the mirror with a wry smile.

In the space of three heartbeats, I watched a growing realisation roll across my features. The smile faded and my skin blanched, the contrast with the bruising seeming to turn my eye into the black hole of an empty socket.

Had I really just said that?

For the first time since my sessions with Lou, I was fully cognisant of the fact Derek's words were my own. I knew they were, in theory, but they were so nasty, I struggled to accept that I would say those things to myself. And yet, here I was telling myself out of my own mouth, not Derek's, that I was a fuck up.

"Oh my God," I said to my mirror self.

I would never speak to anybody else like that. Why on earth would I speak to *myself* in such a hurtful way?

I turned to the bath, easing myself into its warm depths. Propping my legs on the side so the bandages didn't get wet, I sank to the bottom and looked up at the watery ceiling.

Angus was right. I had to do better at looking after myself. I needed to control the urge to belittle. I needed to tell Insecure Nancy she was doing okay.

I sat up and drew a deep breath. "Nancy, your injuries are no reflection of what's going on in your life. You have some challenges, yes, but they are surmountable and you have the ability and strength to work through them." Squeezing my eyes shut, I repeated my words with a fierceness that would force out any doubt.

I opened my eyes and they drifted towards the mirror. I could not and would not let that happen again. I sighed. If only Derek were so easy. I'd have to work a lot harder at forcing him out.

I took a gulp of my cooling tea and my thoughts turned to Angus. His reaction to my injuries was not what I would have expected from someone with emotional disinterest. A mere friend would have found some humour in the situation, been less shocked, less upset at the extent of the damage.

It was possible I was reading into things, but I didn't think so. My attempts to divert his concern had worked to push him back, but not in the way I'd intended. If he found me frustrating, maybe he would begin to like me less. I should have been comforted, but a coolness bloomed under my ribs, despite the warmth of the water. In my mind's eye, a blonde woman with full lips and large, almond-shaped eyes waved at me and smirked.

FIFTEEN
CARBON ZERO HERO

JUNE.

As autumn moved in to winter and the snowline on the mountains crept lower, I finally got the green light from the council.

Late in the month, I had the piles approved and the floor sub-structure built. Andre was juggling my build with another job, so progress was slow even though he had another builder to assist him and me rousying four hours a day.

The slow construction gave me financial breathing space and I figured I could raise enough money and contribute enough labour to have a house by Christmas if I crossed my fingers very tight.

Angus and I made a pretty committed effort to keep each other warm as the temperatures dropped. I enforced the "no staying over rule" for both of us and the "no reading into Angus' behaviour" rule for myself. I tried not to think too hard about whether it was working or not.

The ski season started after the mountains were cocooned in an undulating mass of white and grey for a whole week. Occasionally, the strong winds would rent the top of the clouds open and the peak of Rakiariki would briefly appear as if checking on the world below.

When the swirling mantle eventually lifted overnight and the range emerged at dawn, dazzling in its nakedness, the ski reports flooded in. Two feet of snow had fallen on an already thick base and I got regular weekend work at the café and co-op again, which helped ease the financial strain on my shrinking bank account.

It was during a post-skier, mid-morning lull that I was approached by my first carpentry customer. She looked to be in her late fifties and was dressed in a heavy woollen bush-shirt, jeans and gumboots. She might have been of that hardened, high country station variety who ventured into town once a month for supplies, were it not for the soft-pink lipstick and matching nails.

She introduced herself as Penny. "I want my laundry remodelled. Not one of those kitset jobbies. I want it cottage-y, with curtains over the cupboards and a wooden bench-top, you know?"

I did.

She continued, "I saw one of your videos and was really impressed. I figured, why not give you a go?"

I stood up straighter. "You did? How did you find me on there?"

"My husband showed it to me. Found it on your Facebook page."

Inwardly, I fist-pumped. Outwardly, I said, "I'm happy my page is being discovered locally. It can be hard to get a toehold when you're new to town."

"Well, I'll be glad to vouch for you if you do a good job. When are you free?"

I arranged to visit the next Monday afternoon after I'd finished work on the farm, and once she'd left, I went over to Gracie at the coffee machine, shouted, "You little beauty!" over the hiss of the milk frother and planted a kiss on her cheek.

She made a half-hearted attempt to fend me off with a raised shoulder and an "Eww, get off", but grinned as she said, "People might get the wrong idea."

I clapped a hand on her shoulder. "After work, my friend, I am buying you a drink."

ON MONDAY AFTERNOON, at precisely a quarter past one, I knocked on Penny's front door and retreated down a step as it opened to reveal a large man with beefy forearms and a familiar waistline.

Jim. From Martin and Anoushka's party.

"Oh fuck," I said up at him.

Jim rocked back on his heels and laughed.

I had no idea of the tenor of his laughter, but it didn't matter if it was malicious or not. He was about to employ me. When I felt my face return to its normal hue, I hurried out the apology that was overdue by some months. "Jim, I am so, so sorry for my terrible behaviour at Martin and Anoushka's. It was absolutely inexcusable. And" – I looked down at my shoes, then forced my head up – "I'm sorry it's taken so long to run into you again, so I could apologise in person."

"Nancy, isn't it?" The humour hadn't left his lips.

"Yes."

"Nancy, I'm not going to give you a dressing down. You might do drunk and rude very well, but I was being – as my wife calls it – a horn-headed tease. I was asking for some prodding in another direction."

"Maybe, but not like that. I was appalling."

"Nah, you're alright. I thought it was funny after I got over the shock." He stood aside to give me admittance to a long, wide hallway. "Go on through."

I took my boots off and padded along the floorboards towards an open doorway at the end, distracted by how lightly I'd got off from my bad behaviour.

Halfway down I halted and turned to him.

"Thanks for sticking up for me on the Puke notice board. I didn't deserve that. Not from you."

"Well." He smiled at me and shoved his meaty hands in his trouser pockets. "I try not to be too small-minded all of the time." We continued down the hall and as we entered the living room he added, "And the moaning and mud-flinging that goes on on that page really gets my goat."

Penny's voice echoed down the hallway behind us. "Nancy. Hello love. He's got a lot of goat to get, so don't get him started." She patted Jim's expansive stomach on her way past. "Laundry's through here." She led me through her kitchen and into a small, tongue and groove lean-to crowded with salmon-coloured cabinetry that was swollen with age and water absorption. "It's God-awful, isn't it?" Her grimace turned into a smile as she grasped my hand. "Please make it beautiful."

THE DAY after I finished Penny's laundry and received a hug (Penny) and a handshake (Jim) of gratitude, I was approached in the potting shed by a somewhat awkward Angus.

He stood nearby, scuffing a boot on the floor and watching me seed trays. He didn't say anything.

I didn't look up from what I was doing. "Can I help you?"

"Um, I don't suppose you want to come with me to a farming dinner thing I have to attend?" He stepped up to the bench and brushed loose soil onto the floor. "I need a plus one, and seeing as you're my..."

"Yes?" I smiled into the dirt I was lightly punching with a dibble.

"...only employee, it would be only fair to ask you."

"Right." I compressed the dirt a little too hard and the plastic at the bottom of the tray crackled.

"And" – his little finger knotted around mine and he picked up my left hand and gently shook it – "I'd quite like your company."

My right hand dropped the dibble and I had to scrabble for it before it rolled off the bench.

"When is it?" I asked nonchalantly.

He released my hand. "Next Tuesday. In Wallaceton." Wallaceton was Pukeroa's closest urban centre and the place where I met with Psychologist Lou every six weeks or so.

I wanted to say something collected before accepting, like *I'll have to check my diary* or *I don't know, I've got lots of offers from other men and my week's filling up fast*, but my tongue spat out "okay" and "I'd love to" before my brain could intercept it.

"Cool." He pivoted to walk out the door, then stopped and turned around. "Oh, it's a bow tie thing. Wear your wedding dress."

. . .

WHEN ANGUS ARRIVED to pick me up for the dinner and jumped out of his ute with a grin splitting his face, I felt absurdly like we were re-enacting that scene in *Footloose* when Kevin Bacon picks up his date for the prom. Which made me wonder if I'd get another opportunity tonight to see him dance and my groin tightened and did a little dance of its own.

Angus, resplendent in black suit and bow tie, smiled up at me, one hand in a trouser pocket, one leg resting slightly forward of the other.

It took me a moment to gather the brain power to say, "Wow, look at you. You'd make a pretty decent James Bond."

Angus smiled down at his polished shoes and shifted his feet. "I bet you say that to all the men who accompany you to poncy parties."

"I might if I went to any. This is my first in a very long time."

When I wobbled on my descent from the top step in my four-inch heels, he reached up to hold my hand.

"You look out of practise. Has Puke finally squeezed the city out of you?"

"I think so. My gumboots are now my favourite shoes. If they made a dress variety, I'd probably be in them right now."

I was helped up into the cab and had the door closed for me.

"I'm very happy they don't," Angus said as he opened his door. "Not very chivalrous of me to say, but I appreciate you sacrificing your comfort this evening."

He placed a hand on my thigh and gave it a small squeeze before shifting into gear.

By the time we arrived at Wallaceton's town hall, its car park was almost full and Angus was forced to park in between a Dodge Ram and a Toyota Tacoma. I had to squeeze out the door through a twenty-centimetre gap without cleaning the dust off either vehicle with my dress.

"Sorry," Angus said, putting an arm around me and resting his hand on my hip. "I should've let you out before I parked. My head was elsewhere."

I hoped his head was in a place where I featured, and not the beautiful blonde. I needn't have worried. Two steps towards the hall and his hand had slipped down to cup my right buttock.

I moved it up to my waist. "I'm here as your employee, remember. No workplace harassment. Well, not at least until we leave the parking lot at the end of the night."

He leaned in close to my ear. "Your dress is very tight."

"And?"

"Your bum's a hand magnet in it."

"Fondle it all you want *at the end of the night*."

"Oh, I intend to. This dress and I have some unfinished business." Another couple approached from our left and Angus leaned down, lowering his voice. "I've had five months to fantasise about what I'm going to do to you in it."

A shiver ran down my spine and I stumbled on the first step up to the hall's double doors.

"Careful." His arm tightened around me. "I need you in full pliable order."

"How long is this dinner going to take?"

He grinned down at me. "We can make a quick exit if you're happy to skip dessert."

Once inside, we were directed to a table and invited to help ourselves to the wine sitting in the centre of it.

At the front of the venue, *Selwyn District Agricultural Awards* was projected onto a large screen. I looked from it to Angus and back again. "Looks like you've downplayed this whole 'farming dinner thing'."

Angus' head was bowed over the order of events card he'd picked up off his chair. "Mmm?"

"You're up for an award, aren't you?"

He didn't lift his head, but a smile played at the corners of his lips. "Nominated. I might not get anything."

"Angus, you bugger!" I poked him in the ribs. "This is huge. Why do you have to be one of those blokes? All humble and monosyllabic."

"Nominated has four syllables."

"You know what I mean. Aren't you proud to be recognised?"

"Yeah?"

"No one's going to think less of you if you tell them about it. God, rural men. If my name was on that card, I'd make sure the local paper did an article."

"We don't have a local paper."

"Well, shared on the Puke Facebook page or something." I took out my phone. "I'm going to do it now."

"No, you're bloody not."

I pulled the phone out of his reach and pretended to type as I slowly said, "Pukeroa's very own carbon zero hero." I eyed him and pushed the screen once with my thumb. "Post."

Angus stopped jostling me for the phone and said, "You're just pulling my leg." But the smile on his face told me how pleased he was that I cared enough about his achievement to go as far as trying to fool him.

ANGUS' name appeared on the screen early in the evening's proceedings alongside three other nominees, the awards for sustainability coming after those for innovation and diversification. Water and pasture management seemed to be a hot theme in the area's arid summer climate, and the amount of crossover between the innovation, diversification and sustainability sections gave me renewed confidence in the future of New Zealand's farming sector.

I reached under the table and gripped his hand as the Master of Ceremonies read out Angus' achievements in his bid to run a carbon neutral farm.

When "Angus Ross" was announced as the award's recipient, my screech, somewhat embarrassingly, pierced through the loud applause and two hundred heads swivelled in our direction. Not caring whose scrutiny we were under, I threw my arms around him and whispered into his ear, "Well done you," then pushed him off the chair. "Go get 'em tiger."

As he took the podium, my chest flooded with warmth and I fumbled for my phone when I remembered I should be taking pictures. He looked dapper and strong next to the rotund, grey-haired mayor who'd been invited to present the award, and he stood tall as he delivered his acceptance speech.

His eyes held mine at his mention of my name before they swept across the audience, leaving me tingling in the wake of his gaze.

Upon his return to the table, he sat down and

placed the award next to the table's centrepiece. Then, beaming at me, he leaned forward for a kiss.

It was slightly longer than a mere I'm-still-high-on-my-adrenaline-rush-and-I-choose-to-celebrate-by-pressing-my-lips-to-my-companion kiss. It was the type of kiss delivered to a girlfriend. I tried not to notice, but the lingering warmth of his lips after he'd withdrawn his head made it very hard not to.

THE PSYCHOLOGIST. *Session five:*

The first thing I noticed about Lou was the large diamond on her ring finger. It hadn't been there at the last session and I offered my congratulations. In all our sessions we'd naturally never ventured into her personal territory, and I wasn't expecting her to offer any glimpse into her life, but instead of stopping at a distancing, "Thank you," she added, "It's all happened very quickly, actually, but you just know when it's right."

I didn't respond, not thinking I needed to, but also because there was no way in my hit-and-miss experience of love that I could agree with her. It was, however, reassuring to know that the professional I was paying to help me iron out my kinks knew a thing or two about how a healthy relationship should look.

"How's your self-talk going?"

"Better. I'm starting to recognise when I'm negative and changing it to a self-affirmation. I feel...good about it. I guess that's the control thing, right? I've got power over the situation."

"That's *exactly* it, and it's just the direction we want you heading in." Lou fiddled with her ring as she frowned in thought. "What else is going on that you feel good about? Internally or externally?"

I told her about my first Sawcraft job.

"That's wonderful. I can see how excited you are, Nancy. The corner your business has turned has been a real boost for you. Hold onto that. Remind yourself how hard you've worked to get there and how deserving you are of it. I want you to do that every day. In fact, I'm going to give you another exercise to practise. When you first wake up in the morning and when you go to bed at night, spend a few minutes thinking through all the things going on in your life that you feel good about. Focusing on positives, like what you have under control, is a powerful device in your self-help toolbox. The better you feel about yourself, the more Derek will recede."

"Just like his hairline," I said more savagely than I intended.

Lou leaned forward in her chair slightly. "Directing negativity at Derek, jokingly or not, won't help you, Nancy. Sure, it offers some instant gratification, like a hit of sugar, but it tamps your anger down, holding it in place. You need to stop holding Derek personally responsible for the manifestation of him *you've* created."

"That reminds me of a joke. Why did Frankenstein take his monster to the psychologist? He had a screw loose."

Lou was quiet for a moment. "Do you always use humour as a deflection mechanism when you're feeling uncomfortable?"

My smile faded. "Yeah, quite often."

"You've done it every session. Do you realise that?"

I shook my head. "Doesn't surprise me, though. I think I've been doing it all my life. You're not the first person to draw attention to it."

"Next time you feel uncomfortable, take the time to pause and soak it in. Think about *why* you're feeling that way. It should encourage you to be more constructive in your reaction, because being a lovable clown might endear you to others, but it won't allow you to process things in a healthy way."

A lovable clown. How did she do that? How did she see inside my head so clearly, like she'd cracked it open, categorised and cross-referenced the contents?

I thought back to my reaction to Angus' concern over my rock climbing injuries. A lovable clown was exactly how I wanted to project myself in those moments of awkwardness. To be honest, I quite liked being one. But perhaps I needed to be more discerning about when it was appropriate to break out the red nose and juggling balls.

I sat back in the chair determined to fully open myself up to Lou. No more resistance.

AS I GOT up to leave at the end of the session, Lou stopped me. "Oh, I've been meaning to ask. Do you have a business card?"

SIXTEEN

SABRE-TOOTH COUGAR

JULY.

Once all the framing was up, I employed a roofer and within a day the house started to resemble one.

As is customary, I organised a roof shout for the workers and thought I'd combine the occasion with celebrations for my forty-first birthday, which was fast approaching. A pig would be spit-roasted, courtesy of one of Andre's hunting mates and the invitations broad enough to graciously include Stu's delightful wife.

Will and Sina and the kids came over from the city and stayed with Margot, and Hanita and Jasper hired a house for their family in Pukeroa. When they arrived, the first thing out of Hanita's mouth was not "Happy birthday", or "It's so good to see you, Nance" or even "This place is great, you did really well, you lucky thing", but, "Is Angus here, yet?"

I rolled my eyes and inwardly groaned, knowing that Angus was in for a large amount of scrutiny from several people. "No, and you are not to attempt to vet him, give him twenty questions, or make suggestive comments. He's not my boyfriend, and you are not to behave in any way that might indicate to others that we are involved."

"Well, that's no fun."

I gave her The Frown and turned to watch the children run off in the direction of the sheep paddock.

"Don't forget the sheep fence is electric, you guys," I called after them, hoping the evening would remain tear-free, but knowing some were inevitable.

"Let's play rodeos and see who can sit on the sheep the longest," I heard one of them yell.

"Oh Lord," groaned Will.

"They're safe," I laughed. "If the electric fence doesn't stop them, they'll just expend all their energy chasing the sheep."

Half an hour later, an exhilarated-looking Maia appeared, grass and manure stains down the front of her jeans. "I'm cowgirl Jody Raynes," she announced.

"Did you make that name up?" I asked her.

"Yes. 'Cos Raynes is a last name and horses have reins. It's called a pun."

I threw Sina and Will the open-mouthed 'see,

your daughter is a genius' look and Will returned it with one of acute smugness.

Sina smiled into her drink.

"That is actually an excellent cowgirl name, Maia," I said when I had recovered. "How did you get on with the sheep rodeo?"

"Well..." She took a deep breath in preparation for the forthcoming monologue. "The boys were a bit useless, but I dived on Sprout and grabbed his leg, and he dragged me for a bit, then he got away and Ben tried to stop him, but Sprout knocked him over and he got poo on his bum, which was really funny and we all laughed, but Ben cried, so I gave him a cuddle and he's alright now."

"Where is he?" asked Sina.

"Blowing bubbles in the sheep trough. There're all these squirmy things in the water. I told him they were larvae, not tadpoles, but he's trying to talk to them to see if he can turn them into frogs."

Will sighed and got up out of his chair. "I'd better rescue the larvae before he renders them deaf, or sucks in a lungful and starts burping up frogs."

Maia skipped after him. "But they're not tadpoles, Daddy!" She slipped a hand into his. "It would be funny, though, if every time he went to say something he started croaking like a frog."

"Yeah," said Will. "That would be absolutely rib-biting." We could hear Maia giggling her way down the bank towards the sheep paddock.

Will reappeared some time later and only mildly damp to watch Angus arrive, fashionably late by an hour and a half.

As he walked towards where Will, Sina, Hanita, Jasper, and I stood, the conversation immediately ceased, all five heads pivoting his way.

"That's him, isn't it?" asked Sina in a slightly awe-struck tone.

"For goodness sake, stop gawking and act natural," I hissed at the group. "And close your mouth, Hanita."

"He's gorgeous!" she purred out the side of her mouth. "His thighs fill those jeans like anacondas in a pair of socks."

I turned to her. "What on earth did you just say?"

"And such thick hair!" she continued.

Jasper self-consciously ran a hand over the bristles of his own thinning hair.

"Phwar. Even I need a bib," whispered Will.

Angus stopped just short of us and studied our group. "Am I interrupting something?"

"Only the birth of a new religion," said Jasper under his breath.

Hanita stepped forward with her hand extended. "It's alright, the interruption is absolutely welcome. You must be Angus. I'm Hanita."

"Ah," said Angus in recognition. "Hanita."

Hanita looked immediately at me. "What have you told him?"

What hadn't I told him? I'd kept Angus entertained during many a tree-planting session with stories from our mis-spent school years. I shrugged. "Everything." I flashed a grin at Angus, thinking back to Thursday when I told him how Hanita had got a week's suspension from school after she'd organised an all-girl flash mob in the rugby change room before the first XV's season final.

"Not the flash mob?"

I smirked, but said nothing.

"Great. Thanks, Nance," she said brightly and insincerely. She then addressed Angus and her tone turned defensive, "It was meant to be rousing and motivating, only I got the timing wrong and they were mostly" – she shot a sheepish look in Will's direction – "in a state of undress."

Will shuddered. "It was horrendous."

"It was awesome!" I countered. "I was pure and virginal, but that changing room had more sausage than a wurstfest. Talk about a swift and thorough education."

"Yeah, of my junk," Will added indignantly, "which you got on film, Hanita, along with everyone else's. I know you made copies before it was confiscated, because I caught Nan watching it in rapt fascination. She didn't even have the decency to be embarrassed. Thank God social media hadn't been invented back then."

"It's not too late. I think I've still got it somewhere," I said, grinning mischievously at him.

"You might be forty-one, but you are not too old to get a sound thrashing from your older brother, Nancy Robyn."

I backed out of range, putting my hands up in a kung fu fighting stance and warned, "Beware the iron octopus, brother."

When I was at a safe distance, I introduced Angus to the rest of the group then led him to the house structure to show off the latest building developments.

"You don't look anything like your brother," he said.

"Thank goodness. Will looks like Roger Ramjet – he's even got the chimple. A chin that big looks okay on a man with shoulders broad enough to offset it, but it's not so attractive on a lady. I'm too little to counter-balance it. I'd always be tripping over my face."

Angus nudged me playfully with his shoulder. "You don't need a big chin as an excuse to use your face as landing gear."

"Oh, shit. Sorry Angus, I saved you some dinner, but I just remembered I fed it to the chickens."

"I wouldn't put it past you." He watched his feet as we walked towards the house. "Sorry I was late. I wanted to be here earlier, but...other stuff came up."

"Everything okay?"

He stopped and looked up at me, his eyebrows

knitted in their customary frown and his mouth loosening to answer. Then his gaze shifted past my ear. "What are those kids doing?"

I turned. All four children took turns to roll down the hill, gathering speed until they hit a lip and were launched sideways onto a pile of pillows. There was only one place on the property that had a collection of pillows. "I'm taking those children to their mothers and stuffing them back up."

JUST AS DUSK was falling and the mountains were a dark outline against rapidly fading blue, a hand curled around my elbow and led me towards the house. Mona walked slightly ahead of me at a gentle pace but the firm grip of my arm brooked no argument. "We need to talk."

She stopped in front of the metal framing that would house the massive window in the end wall and said, "Pretty amazing view that, isn't it?"

"Yes, it is."

"And I suppose you want to keep it?" It wasn't a question, and I kept quiet. "Have they asked about easement rights, yet?"

I paused before answering, "No. They think there already are easement rights."

"Ah." She nodded. "So they haven't discovered the paperwork's missing yet."

I jerked my head back and peered at her in the

gathering dark. "What do you mean by 'missing'?"

"Exactly that, Nancy." She sniffed. "I've got my connections." Her smile in the direction of the mountains seemed to exude the smugness of assumed omnipotence. But it was dark and I could have been imagining things.

"That's...illegal." It came out almost reverently.

"Yessss. And you're welcome." She turned back to me. "Sooner or later they're going to notice and they're going to be very desperate to get you to sign that piece of paper. Don't be a fool for the elderly, Nancy. You need to steer clear of that emotive trap, because" – she looked again towards the mountains – "you've got a lot to lose." Then she stepped down into the dark and disappeared.

A whoop issued from behind me. *That was intense! She has the makings of an underworld queenpin.* Derek emerged from behind the bathroom wall. *She terrifies me.*

"Oh, don't be dramatic, Derek."

It's not me who's courting drama, Nancy. Time is ticking away. You need to make a move, because there's no running away from it, and to be perfectly honest, you've compounded things by knowingly building. Right. On. This. Spot. He jabbed his index finger downwards with each word. *That's a commitment to welcoming inevitable crisis with open arms if ever I saw one.*

I turned my back on him and held onto the metal

portal with both hands.

"You're not real. What do you know?"

I know all that you do.

I closed my eyes and concentrated on steadying my breathing. "Nancy, you have the situation under control. Jasper's working on the plans and when they're ready, you'll talk to Rob and Liz, explain everything and reach a compromise. There's no point in freaking them out about the missing document now when you've got nothing to negotiate with. You're not a bad person by withholding information. You're... You're..." I couldn't find an affirmation. The truth was I didn't know *what* I was. I hadn't done anything wrong, but as yet, I hadn't done anything right.

I walked back into the circle of chairs surrounding the fire. Liz, deep in conversation with Andre's father, reached out and brushed my arm as I walked past. I looked down and smiled at her hand, but I couldn't raise my eyes to meet hers.

Pivoting, I retraced my steps to the house frame and turned on the fairy lights I'd strung that morning. It summoned a sense of magic-ness, the ethereal glow working somewhat to buoy me out of the pit of shit-smelling doom I had been slipping towards.

As I stepped down to return to the fire, Gracie appeared and thrust a bottle of wine in my hand. "Well done for making it into another year, grey dog. At your age, I expect you treat every day as if it was your last."

"Gracie, we should all make the most of every day as if it was our last. What interesting lives we would lead if we did."

"Ew, don't get all philosophical on me. My moral compass will get disorientated. I need your abuse to keep me on an even keel."

"You don't have a moral compass. You have at best a moral obtuseness, and in your case, the emphasis is firmly on 'obtuse'."

Gracie grinned. "That's more like it." Then she introduced me to her companion, Meals, ostensibly shortened from Amelia.

"Nice to meet you, Meals. Welcome to my future home."

Her round face was full of youthful energy. "It looks cool with the fairy lights."

I agreed, and when she went off to have a better look, I asked Gracie, "Are you two...?"

"Nah, we're just friends. I've got my eye on someone, though. She's from Argentina," she said as if that explained everything.

"Argentina? Okay. All the best...scoring her?"

"Yes, 'scoring', Nancy. The lingo's still the same whether you're into taco or hot dog. You look so frightened talking to me about it. You're not going to offend me. Unless you keep treading so carefully you make me feel like I've got a terminal case of the clap instead of a different sexual orientation. Loosen up."

I rolled my head from side to side and raised my shoulders a couple of times. "Okay. I'm loosened."

"Good. Can you give me my bottle of wine back now so I can have a drink? The service is shit around here."

WHEN THE CHILDREN had finally run out of steam and been put to bed in the bus, Gracie challenged the flexible and foolhardy to The Box Game. Players competed to pick up an ever-decreasing cardboard box off the floor using only their mouths. Most people moved up to the house to take part or watch, but as I stood up to join in, Angus brushed past me.

"I need to give you your birthday present," he said into my ear. "Follow me."

Once we were outside the circle of light, he reached for my hand and led me down towards the trees. He dropped the blanket he was carrying and turned to me.

"What's my present?"

"This," he said, holding my face and pulling me in for the kind of kiss that renders everything else, even the need to breathe, insignificant.

"Wow, that's a pretty decent birthday present. All I got from my mum was an email."

He smiled against my lips. "That was just the ribbon. You still have to unwrap it." He placed my hands on his fly and helped me unzip him, then guided my hands to his erection.

My breath quickened.

"This is all yours for as long as you want or as many times as you want."

"Okay," I whispered, my voice stuck in my throat. "I think I would like you to take me up against a tree."

"Alright, then let me help you out of your trousers, my lady." He squatted down to pull my boots off, then straightened to kiss me while undoing my buckle and waistband. Running a finger lightly over my underwear, he drew lazy circles in the front, then lowered himself to help me step out of my jeans and knickers, leaning forward to briefly and tantalisingly lick my clit.

I trembled. My shivering had little to do with the cold that now eddied around my legs and everything to do with the sudden heat between them. A rush of blood met the warmth of his breath, my own coming in jagged gasps.

He stood up and sought my tongue with his while he fumbled with a condom packet and rolled on the sheath.

"This tree here?" he asked.

I nodded, not having any idea what tree it was, nor caring.

He picked me up, placed me against the bark and slowly slid inside me. "Okay?" he asked huskily. "It's not too rough on your back?"

I shook my head, finding his mouth and grabbing his buttocks to pull them in the direction of my vagina.

He started to thrust in long, slow strokes. The gentleness with which he'd set out to make love to me, despite the difficulty of the place and the position I'd chosen, sparked a warmth that travelled up my chest to nestle in my throat in a hard lump.

I seized up.

My fingers uncurled, my lips turned to rubber under his and my tongue retracted, lying prone against my upper palate.

I was bloody well going to cry.

Angus stopped and retracted his head a couple of inches. "You okay?"

I wasn't. I couldn't afford to be swept up by emotion. It wasn't part of the deal. Swallowing the lump back down, I nodded and with a tightening of my pelvic muscles, coaxed him to resume the steady rolling of his hips. I urged him to move faster and faster, my own hips rocking with a frantic and urgent energy until I came with my head thrown back against the trunk and his mouth on my neck.

"Happy birthday," he whispered.

LATE INTO THE EVENING, when the party attendees were well lubricated and the volume of conversation edged towards rowdiness, Barbara disappeared in the direction of her car and returned with a guitar in hand to initiate Act 4 of the evening: The Drunken Fireside Singalong.

Hanita, having moved from white wine, to red, and back again, out-sang everybody, her over-performing saved by her ability to hold a tune.

The guitar eventually ended up in Angus' hands. He played a set of chords in a minor key and when he began singing and I heard his voice clearly for the first time, I wasn't prepared for how lovely he would sound.

His voice was rich and melodious and he played the guitar with a graceful ease.

Halfway through the song, he looked up from the guitar and met my eyes.

A bolt of electricity surged through me and when his gaze didn't leave me, my core radiated a heat that left me sweating, despite the chill of the night air.

It wasn't just that he was singing a beautiful song that might have been for me – for my birthday, or for something with more meaning – it was also knowing that everybody else was watching this moment between us.

When he finally dropped his eyes and I was released from his hold, I glanced at Sina. She threw me an expression that betrayed a mix of emotions, one of which I didn't want to see.

Pity.

I knew what she was thinking: *How can you not fall for this man?*

I looked down into my glass, gave it a swirl, then upended it, draining it in one large mouthful. From across the fire, Derek winked at me.

When the guitar eventually fell silent and conversations gathered momentum again, Hanita unsteadily stood up from her chair. She rapped a fingernail on the side of her glass, but her attempt to gain attention failed amid the hubbub of conversation. "Hey! HEY! I've got something to say, so shut the fuck up everyone." She paused, waiting for quiet. "Thank you. Right. I've known Nancy longer than any of you buggers." She waved her glass in the air, her index finger pointing accusingly around the circle.

Someone cleared their throat.

"Except Will." Pausing to take a sip of her drink, she caught Margot's eye over the top of her glass. "And Margot." She raised her glass to Margot, slopping out some of the contents and soaking her sleeve. "So, apart from Will and Margot, I know Nancy the most and the best, and I'll tell you one thing. You can take it or leave it, I don't give a shit, but Nancy Myers has always been there for me. She held my hair back when I made actual boats out of Josh-up-himself-Peterson's Polo Ralph Lauren boat shoes by vomiting in them. And they weren't very boat-like, were they, you smarmy twat?" Hanita raged at an imaginary Josh.

"Not chunder-tight or puke-proof. It turns out they couldn't even float when Nancy threw them in the neighbours' pool to hide the carrot-laced evidence. Hah!"

She punched the air with her drinks hand, losing half the contents and sending up a jet of flame from the fire. Her eyes searched the group for me, even though I hadn't moved from her side in over an hour. "Nancy-Pants, you are a true friend, and I love you, the muppet that you are, and I always will. So, happy forty-first birthday. You are now officially a sabre-tooth cougar."

"Nita," Jasper said warningly.

"What? I didn't say anything about her shagging Angus." Hanita, realisation trickling through the alcoholic fog in her brain, looked around at the crowd. "Oops."

I threw a look in Angus' direction, but he appeared more amused than concerned by any tarnishing of his reputation.

Liz and Rob studiously peered into their drinks, and Martin and Anoushka exchanged knowing looks.

Gracie said, "Nancy, you dirty dawg. Respect."

Margot let out a series of cackles. "Remind me to invite you to my next big birthday celebration, Hanita. That was some class-A entertainment. You can be Mistress of Ceremonies."

SEVENTEEN
SLEEPLESS IN PUKEROA

THE FOLLOWING week turned bitterly cold and I began to hear rustling in parts of the bus as mice from the surrounding countryside sought shelter and warmth.

When I found droppings on top of the plates in the cupboard, I lost all tolerance and complained at length about it to Angus during one of our coffee breaks.

He leant me some mouse traps and advised that peanut butter was the crack cocaine of the rodent party scene.

When I got home, I dutifully laced the traps with the organic peanut butter I had swapped my first-born child for, set them in places most likely to see mice traffic, and waited.

Nothing happened.

Each night, I heard tell-tale rustling and scratching from several points in the bus, but not the happy snap of a trap.

Angus assured me that the naturally wary mice would eventually take the bait, I just had to be patient.

One morning, I turned up to work bleary-eyed and grumpy. Angus took one look at me and said with gentlemanly tact, "You look rubbish. You feeling okay?"

"I'm fine, I just didn't get much sleep last night, no thanks to you." I tried to stare him down, but tripped over a tower of empty plant pots, scattering them across the floor and somewhat ruining the intended effect.

Angus laughed at me, which only served to enrage me more and I kicked several pots in his direction.

He laughed harder, easily deflecting them and asked how my current state of sleep deprivation could possibly be his responsibility. "I mean, a sleepless night due to me is definitely possible. I'm still hoping on winning that bet, but I'd actually have to be present."

I ignored his quip. "It's because your bloody mouse traps aren't doing their job and I woke up during the night with a mouse straddling my face. I was on my side and it had both front paws planted on my temple. I didn't know if it was intending to run off with my eyeball or make love to my nostril."

Angus let out another burst of laughter.

"Fortunately, I disturbed it before I could find out. Unfortunately, the episode freaked me out so much that sleep was very elusive for the next few hours. I was in such a blissful, deep sleep when my alarm went off..." I rounded on Angus. "Your traps are shit and you owe me half a night's sleep!"

Still laughing, Angus pulled me into a hug. "I'll happily put you to bed early tonight if you like. In the meantime, can I make you a very strong coffee?"

I nodded against his chest.

"After work we'll go around to yours and see what you're doing wrong with the traps."

I gasped, pulling out of the hug to loudly give him another think, when I saw the grin on his face. "You're going to wind me up all morning, aren't you? Don't you have to go and neuter some sheep or something?"

"Nope. I've just decided I'm having a plant day today. You are such great sport. Anyone ever tell you that?"

"Yes. Quite recently as it happens," I said sulkily. "Alright, game on – last plant jockey standing. But just to warn you, I fire with deadly aim when I shoot from the hip, cowboy."

I stalked over to the barn to put the jug on for coffee and felt something hit me in the back of the head.

I turned.

Angus blew smoke from his finger gun. "You gotta be quicker than that, Calamity Jane, I just blew your head off."

"What did you hit me with?" I asked, rubbing the spot where it had made contact.

"A rubber band from off the potting bench."

"Nice shot," I conceded. "Please at least allow me to knock back some caffeine to get my brain cranking over before you attempt to kill me again. I'm at a bit of a disadvantage."

"I'll give you five minutes."

As soon as I got into the shed, I filled the jug and turned it on to hide any noise I might make and went over to the animal medical cupboard.

I found a box of rubber gloves and started filling them with warm water, knotting them when they were stretched as far as I dared to fill them. Once I had fifteen ready to go, I put one in each of my jacket pockets, one in each hand, sidled up to the nearest barn door, and tentatively looked around.

A ball of dirt exploded by my head.

Angus, anticipating my duplicity had dragged a couple of hay bales just outside the greenhouse door and used it as cover as he lobbed dirt grenades at me made from the soil I had recently collected from a gully on the farm.

I knew that I wouldn't be able to throw the gloves as directly as he could throw dirt balls. They were too awkward and un-aerodynamic. My best chance was to lob them high so that they landed on him from above.

I feinted, drawing his fire, then stepped out into the open and threw my first glove. It arced high and landed harmlessly two feet behind him.

Angus looked at the mess and nodded at my choice of ammunition. "Nice! Very inventive. Though, clearly your talk of 'deadly aim' was all bluster."

I cut him off at the pass with a watery explosion on top of the hay bales. "Less talk, more fight."

I retreated to replace the two water bombs I had expended and stuffed two extra into the pockets of my jacket. Then I made a dash for the cover of the tractor, which was closer to the greenhouse than the barn. I copped a dirt ball on one of my legs and managed to goose-step out of the way of a second.

"Now you've lost one leg *and* your head. You going to have any body parts left when I've finished whopping your arse?"

I lined up my six bombs on one of the rear wheels and when I had my breath back, unleashed a blitzkrieg. Angus never had a chance. The balls of water rained down on him in quick succession, soaking his head and back.

"Warm water? Very thoughtful of you, Nance, but that won't save you from the mighty power of the posse."

I ran back towards the barn to reload, but Angus ran at an angle towards me, firing ball after ball from where he had them balanced in the crook of his arm. I took two on my right shoulder and was forced to take shelter around the side of the barn where there was no entrance to be able to access my bomb stock.

This particular wall of the barn did house a hose, however.

Angus rounded the corner, arm poised to fire another grenade, and I was ready for him.

"Dance, parrdner," I drawled, shooting water at his feet so that he was forced to an abrupt halt, then driven backwards to avoid the wild spurts from the hose. I flicked the line of water up at him to keep him moving and directed a couple of streams high enough that his shirt got wet.

"Hoh," he gasped. "Holy shit that's cold." He turned around to run away from the jet of water, but I changed direction to block off his retreat. "Okay, okay, you win."

I dowsed his shirt again for good measure.

"Stop it, Nancy!"

Only I didn't. I was having far too much fun.

Angus stopped trying to avoid the spray and stood stock still in the middle of the flow of water, his clothes getting more and more saturated.

Then he set his features to stern and started marching towards me like the Terminator.

"Angus? Angus, what are you about to do?" I backed away, the water no longer any deterrent.

He kept grimly advancing on me and in desperation I fired the water directly into his face. He didn't falter.

Eventually, I ran out of hose and was forced to drop it as I continued my retreat.

My back hit something solid. My car. I'd backed myself to a point where I had nowhere to go.

When he was two metres away and I realised I had left it too late to run, I put my hands up in the air. "Okay, I'm sorry. I didn't mean to. It was all a terrible misunderstanding. I thought you looked hot from the butt kicking you were unleashing and needed to cool down."

He lowered his head like a bull about to charge.

"Anguuuuuus?" I squealed as he lifted me up in a fireman's hold.

He walked over to the nearest paddock, stopped at the fence and dropped me into the trough on the other side.

I gasped at the shock of the cold water and looked up at him. I was met with a Cheshire Cat grin.

"Awake now?"

"You fucker."

Angus reached down, grabbed my arm and helped me out. "C'mon, let's go and warm up in the bath."

AUGUST.

Early the following month, I got my second Saw-craft job. I told myself it had only taken four and a half weeks after finishing Penny's laundry. The next job would be got in two, and after that, I'd be struggling to help out on my build, because I'd be so fabulously busy building stuff for other people.

Martin and Anoushka had acquired a large metal bath for the purposes of shared outdoor bathing away from the prying eyes of teenage children.

The design would see the bath recessed into a trapezoid cedar deck that was enclosed on three sides with trellising, the un-walled end giving the bath's occupants an expansive view of the snow-capped mountains.

It took me just over a week of part-time carpentering and the result, Anoushka said, was magazine-worthy.

It had been a while since I'd last blushed, but judging by the amount of heat the rest of my body traitorously channelled into my face, I made up for lost time. I didn't have the same confidence about the bath's ability to stand under the scrutiny of shiny home and garden magazine pictures, but I had to admit it had me salivating with envy. I couldn't help wondering where I could put one on my land.

As soon as it was finished, Anoushka and I set up

the steaming bath with candles and a couple of glasses of wine for the website photo shoot, and while we were artfully arranging the props, Martin showed up to watch proceedings with a couple of towels draped over his arm.

Once the final image had been captured, he grabbed me by the elbow and frog-marched me to the steps at the end of the deck.

"You've got ten seconds before I'm getting naked," he said, looking hungrily at his wife.

I grinned at Anoushka and gave her a wink, before needlessly instructing them to enjoy themselves and making a hasty getaway to celebrate with Angus.

He met me at the front door, picked me up and deposited me onto the couch. Hovering over me in a press-up position, he placed his hands just above my shoulders and offered a second night of sleep deprivation. He'd thought of a few ways in which we might ward off sleep, apparently. Not waiting for an answer, he slowly lowered himself down to kiss me and ran a hand up my thigh to reach around and pull my bottom towards him.

Some time later, after a rehydration stop in the kitchen and some brave but titillating experimentation with chilli chocolate sauce, we managed to make it all the way to the bedroom to continue our sleep-defying activities.

I woke up early the next morning to find myself facing him, our legs interlaced and our faces centimetres away from each other. I shifted my head back so I could see him in focus.

His mouth, relaxed in sleep, was slightly pursed, the dimple in the middle of his bottom lip more prominent. He was beautiful. Not in any obvious, chisel-jawed way, but in a way that snuck up on me and tapped me on the shoulder. And I was sure taking notice now.

The surprise of it constricted my throat and I had to think through the mechanics of breathing to make my lungs work again.

I attempted to move my hand to stroke his face and couldn't. He was holding it.

It was then, with a surge of elation that threatened to burst out of my chest, that it all became very clear.

Just as quickly, the elation fizzed into a heat that washed over me and I shivered in its wake.

I couldn't get enough air. I had to leave. Fast.

I ripped my hand out from his and untangled my legs with a clack of ankle bones, waking Angus, before rolling off the bed and falling onto my knees.

"What's going on?" Under the sleep-edged confusion was unease.

"I have to go." It was no answer, but the raggedness of my words delivered between sips of air said enough. I pushed myself up off the floor and ran out the door.

"Nancy!" Angus' feet thudded on the floorboards, his footsteps echoing down the hallway behind me.

I scanned the living room. My clothes had been casually discarded during the previous evening's activities and I needed to find them quickly. Heading for the couch, I skidded on the woollen rug, crashing into the coffee table and sending a pile of books cascading onto the floor.

At my feet, half under the couch, were my jeans and bra. I gathered them up, but couldn't see the rest of last night's outfit.

"Nancy?" Angus stood in the doorway, arms loose, frown deep.

I pulled cushions off the couch, tossing them across the room. "Where the fuck are my fucking undies?" My pitch rose with each word so that my voice cracked on the final one.

As I began to work on the seating cushions, I was clasped by the shoulders and turned roughly to face Angus' chest. He ducked his head to meet my eyes.

"Stop. Take a deep breath and tell me what's going on."

The lump in my throat blocked my windpipe and I had to swallow twice to make enough room for air to pass through. "I..." Even if I did know how to answer him, the words wouldn't come. I didn't want to make a declaration and I definitely didn't want to make a fool of myself. My heart beat so furiously it felt as though it was trying to fight its way out of my chest.

"You don't get to do this to me," came out in a rush before I could stop it.

"I'm not doing anything to you." His voice was gentle, but the rapidity with which his gaze ping-ponged between my eyes told me how worried he was. "Nance, what have I done?"

"Everything. You've done everything and un-done me," was not what I said, even though the words gathered on my tongue. Instead, I gulped at the air and whispered, "This is not what I wanted. I didn't want..." I didn't finish the sentence. I didn't need to. With an unfolding of the creases between his brows, Angus let his understanding known.

His hands dropped from my shoulders and as they fell a roar rose in my ears.

I didn't wait to hear what he had to say about it. I surrendered the search, bolting for the front door and hobbling naked across the gravel to my car.

There was no crunching of footsteps behind me, no shouted, "Wait!", and my hands shook so badly that I dropped my key twice trying to fit it into the door lock.

When I finally made the safety of the driver's seat, I turned the ignition and accelerated down the driveway towards home.

EIGHTEEN

THE LOT PLOT

"IT'S OVER," was the first thing I said to Hanita when I got home from working at the café.

"What? Why?"

"I broke the cardinal rule."

"You stayed over?"

"He had me ecstatically taking the Lord's name in vain 'til two in the morning, and then I fell asleep. I didn't mean to. And now Eros has punished me with the curse of eternal longing."

"Shit. Shit and arse." Hanita was silent for a moment. "What are you going to do?"

"I'm thinking of moving towns."

"Yep, that is by far and away the best way to deal with it. Give up all you've achieved, your land, your house, your new friends..."

I started to cry.

"Oh, my lovely. I'm so, so sorry. Do you want me to drive over and take a sledgehammer to his perfect kneecaps?"

I laughed through my tears. "No, it's not his fault. He was perfectly upfront with me. It's all my own stupid doing. I find the most inappropriately suited man in the room and I'm instantly sucked into his orbit."

"Nance..."

"He doesn't even deserve my bloody love. I'm so angry about it, Hanita. I'm angry with both of us. I can't believe I've done it again and I can't believe I've fallen for someone who would never truly appreciate my place in a relationship."

"You don't know that. You don't know the circumstances of his relationship or his break up. I'll tell you one thing, I couldn't stand Derek. I didn't like the man from the moment I met him. I like Angus though, and I don't think you should tarnish him with the same brush."

"It doesn't matter. Whether he deserves my judgement or not, I've still managed to board the train to One-Way Love Land." I blew my nose. "It's a bloody shit destination. How the hell am I going to face him on Monday?"

"Do you have to see him to get your work done?"

"No. Sometimes he just texts me his instructions."

"Okay, ask him to do that. I'm sure he'd understand."

. . .

AS IT TURNED OUT, I didn't need to ask. Over the next few days, Angus texted me his work directives each night for the following day. I didn't see him at all.

When I'd turned up on Monday, my washed and neatly folded clothes sat on top of my forgotten shoes on the potting bench.

I heard him come and go from the work sheds every so often, but I was far too anxious to go and see him, and he made no attempt to come and see me.

It was very difficult not to jump to the conclusion that his deliberate distancing was the result of feeling awkward around me now, because he simply did not care for me. If he did, surely he would have come and talked to me about what had happened the other morning.

ON THURSDAY, as I was making my way over to my car to drive home, his footsteps sounded behind me.

"Nance."

I stopped, took a deep breath to steady myself, then turned to face him. He looked awful. His eyes were ringed with dark shadows and his shoulders and neck hunched ever so slightly forward. I had to fight the urge to embrace him and tell him the lie that it was alright, that I was here.

"Can we...?" He faltered, then began again. "I don't really want to have this conversation standing here. Come over to the house and I'll make you a cuppa."

I nodded, a chill spreading through my stomach. It was obvious that our conversation wouldn't involve words such as "blind fool" or "undying love". Something much more difficult was on the table.

He turned without another word, walked over to his bike and drove off towards the house.

When I got to the villa the door was open and I entered without knocking. I took a seat on a bar stool in the kitchen and sat looking at my hands while he wordlessly made the tea.

He turned and placed a mug in front of me. His eyes were red-rimmed and watery from the effort of holding in emotion.

I picked up my cup and blew across the top of the tea to keep my chin steady.

"Nance, I am so sorry that you're hurting because of the stupid mess I'm in. I didn't want things to get this far."

"You were clear from the beginning about your expectations, Angus."

"No, I've been selfish. You've been a lovely distraction from things, but..."

I'd braced myself for this "but" that if I were completely honest with myself, I didn't want to come. The shitty I-don't-feel-that-way-about-you "but".

"We've been spending a lot of time together and it's understandable that feelings have developed beyond initial attraction. We probably shouldn't have started anything at all because we were working together and I am as much to blame on that."

"Okay," I said, unsure of where he was heading.

"I feel terrible. I feel like I've been using you for relief from my shit and our," he paused, searching for a word, "liaising has got out of hand."

"Angus, I don't know what you're trying to tell me."

He let out a deep sigh. "As of Monday, things have really ramped up with my ex's claim and if we can't reach an agreement then it will go to court. She's not budging from claiming half of what's mine and I can't allow her to have it, Nance. I can't afford to buy out my brother and my sister *and* someone else. The possibility of selling up is starting to look very real."

"No. Surely it won't come to that."

"Well, if it does, Mum and Dad lose their home, too. That's the really shitty thing about all this. It doesn't just affect me." He picked up his cup and put it down again, untouched. He added quietly, "She's gunning for the subdivision, too. Says it was her idea and she got the process started. She wants her share of it. And she *can* make a claim on it since it currently sits on land I own."

"But...that's unethical. Isn't it?"

He shook his head. "Part of me can understand her claim on my portion of the farm, but there's nothing about this next move that makes any sense to me. It's so low."

"Maybe..." I fiddled with the handle of my cup. "Maybe she's pulling out the big guns to force your hand on settling her original claim?"

"Hell of a way to do it. I don't like being backed into corners. Desperation tends to turn things very ugly." He wiped an imaginary crumb from the bench. "Look, Nance, I've been wanting to talk to you about the other morning and by the time I faced up to how I felt about it, I'd heard from my cousin and now I am... all at sea." The ghost of a smile, tight and sad, flickered across his face. "The timing is appalling."

I sat mutely, not sure how to respond, but alert to the sudden amplification of the pulsing of my blood.

"When this is...over – whatever 'over' will look like – can we revisit the other morning? See if we can have a conversation about it instead of you running out the door?"

I looked down into my cup and said into the cooling tea, "I don't know."

"Nance," Angus whispered, "please give me a better answer than that."

I lifted my head and met his eyes. "This is hard to say and it's probably not going to be easy to hear, but...I can't respect you if you don't recognise the worth of a partnership. You were with her for eleven years. No matter what shit she's trying to pull now, you need to acknowledge her contribution to your life together on this farm."

He started to speak, but I cut him off. "I know that's going to be challenging, not just financially but to your family's relationship with this land, but that's" – I shrugged and looked back down into my cup – "how I feel."

Angus was quiet for some time. "Okay. Thanks for being honest."

I nodded slowly then looked back up at him. My voice cracked as I said, "I guess this is goodbye?"

He breathed out slowly. "Yeah."

I rapidly blinked my understanding. "You asked me here to let me go."

"I think that's better for both of us." He paused. "It's really hard having you here with everything that's going on."

Nodding, I said, "I guess we both need some space."

"I can pay you out for the next two weeks, but I think today should be your last day."

I stood up from my stool and took a deep breath, exhaling slowly. When I shifted my eyes from the floor to meet Angus', a single tear tracked down his left cheek. I turned and walked out the door before I could do anything that would make the farewell harder.

Derek was waiting for me in the passenger seat of my car. He watched me climb in and collapse onto the steering wheel, my arms draped across its top. I shuddered with a suppressed sob.

Oh, for goodness sake, let it out Nancy. No one has ever been rewarded for being an emotional martyr.

I allowed the sob to roll up my stomach and into my throat. It escaped, deep and sharp, into the dash.

That was some fine work in there, drawing a line and standing your ground. You haven't got a lot to show for it, though, have you? All that wasted time and energy, loving two men in the extraordinary space of a single year. And yet, you're still alone.

I whimpered, then gave in and let my pent-up grief and remorse run its course. When I had cried myself dry, I sat upright and wiped my face on my sleeve. I was alone.

MY WEEK WENT from scrabbling for a handhold on the cliff's edge to landing on my back at rock bottom.

I ran out of money.

I had enough to pay Andre for the current week's work and that was it. I had known it was coming and Andre had been warned, but when the time came to pull the pin after all that had gone on in the last couple of days, it felt like the knock-out punch at the end of a twelve-round bout.

I delivered the news to Andre with a quaver in my voice and what I hoped looked like a wry smile. I really didn't want to cry.

He wasn't fooled. His brows met and he stretched a hand towards me.

I stepped out of reach and held up a finger. "Don't do or say anything nice."

After a moment, he dropped his hand and shrugged. "Shit happens."

I smiled my gratitude. "It sure does."

"Well, on the plus side, there's nothing left you need a qualified builder for."

"Shame about needing a qualified sparky and plumber."

Andre put his hands in his pockets and rocked back on his heels. "I know a few. I'll ask around. See if we can at least get them to drop their mark-up on materials."

"Thanks, Andre."

We both looked up at the house, silently surveying it.

From the outside it looked complete. On the inside, it was still all ribs and bones. At the rate I was bringing in money, I'd be celebrating my sixth decade before I could call it home. Sure, I could beg some free labour from friends, but there'd be no working bees if I couldn't pay for any materials.

I'd tried hard to kick-start my business, but funny Facebook posts and hard-to-find YouTube videos clearly weren't enough to persuade Pukeroa-ites that a female carpenter was just as good as a male one. I needed to do something bold.

Right now, though, I couldn't find the energy to search for a starting point. What I wanted to do was bury my head under my pillow and wallow in grief and pity for as long as I could stand my stench. Or until I ran out of Michael Fassbender movies.

I didn't have time to do either. That afternoon I got an email from Jasper.

LIZ AND ROB'S cottage kitchen-cum-dining room smelled of freshly baked scones and sweet peas. The pale yellow walls and wooden furniture made the room seem at once airy and cosy, and I could see why they were so happy here.

We chatted politely and when my eye wasn't drawn to a photo of a twenty-something Angus on the dresser, it was searching out the window in the ridiculous hope that I would spot him on the surrounding farmland.

Eventually Liz asked, "You have something you want to discuss with us?"

I refocused my attention inside, swallowed my mouthful of scone and took a deep breath. "I've been in touch with my lawyer. There's no paperwork on file regarding the agreement to the easement. It's obviously been...misplaced somewhere along the line."

Rob and Liz exchanged worried looks.

"Don't worry, though. I'm happy to renegotiate it with you."

Rob said, "We'd better check with our lawyer first. It might just be your copy that's missing."

I dropped my eyes to my plate and rolled a crumb backwards and forwards. "Yeees, that could be the case, but I'd like you to consider what I'm about to propose anyway."

I looked up, clasping my hands together. "As you are probably aware, Lot 4 blocks my view of the mountains."

Rob nodded. "Yeah, bit of a bugger."

Liz straightened her back. "You're not suggesting we drop it?"

"No, no. I wouldn't demand that of you. But that view is very important to me. It's been, I don't know, kind of healing, if that makes any sense, and I don't want to lose it."

My hope that they'd be receptive, and my anxiety that they wouldn't, forced the rest of my words to tumble out. "I've had some plans designed for a house that could be constructed in a way that doesn't have much impact on my view. It's an earth sheltered home, built into the hillside. Here."

I took the plans out of my bag and smoothed

them out on the table. "It uses passive-energy design principles, so it doesn't require any heating or cooling. The roof-line is flush with the crest of the hill and it's narrow and long with windows right along the front to get as much sunlight, and view, as possible. It's still big. There's four bedrooms and two bathrooms in there, so there's no compromise on space."

I paused to give them enough time to scrutinise the plans and after a moment, said, "I would have discussed this with you sooner, but the architect had to do a lot of research into this type of house design. All you need to do is have the lot covenanted so that the plans or a similar design is a condition of sale."

The analogue clock on the stove ticked six times before Liz raised her head. "Nancy, honey, I'm sorry the subdivision is disruptive to you, but Lot 4 is the prime lot. Its value is much higher than the other ones. I don't think we can put any conditions on its sale in the current market."

I slumped back in my chair. "Will you at least think about it?" My added "please" had the grace to sound wheedling, which at least made my desperation clear.

Once again, a look was exchanged and I understood the meaning packed into that single, fleeting glance. *If we find the paperwork, we don't have to do anything.*

For the first time I admitted to myself that I was grateful for Mona's interference.

WORD HAD GOT out that my build was on hold and Anoushka turned up one evening toting a bottle of wine and offering her help when I was in a financial position to ask for it.

We sat inside the house on camp chairs in the fading light, watching the sky behind the mountains slowly change from pink to orange and she said, "I saw the seeming ease with which you did the outdoor bath and I want to be that woman. The one who redefines her role in the household. I'll happily give you as much help as you need if it means I learn to be handy, because I don't want to be reliant on anybody else to get things done any more. I never do" – she raised her index fingers to make air quotes – "'man jobs' because Martin looks after them."

She pointed to her chest. "*I* want to be able to do them. I want to be capable of doing anything I want." She swirled her wine and before I could offer an encouraging comment, she continued with renewed ferocity. "You know, I'm bloody sick of hearing men stroke each other's testosterone with comments like, 'you've got an enormous pair of hairy gonads' and then hear the same thing said about women who are gutsy. I want 'you've got a big, hairy, luscious vagina' to be the best compliment you can give."

I spat my wine back into my glass and laughed up at the ceiling. Anoushka considered me for a moment then moved her face close to mine, narrowing her eyes. "Times are about to change." She raised her glass to clink it with mine.

ANOUSHKA'S GENDER rant was exactly the spark I needed to start thinking "bold" in order to get Sawcraft from limping at the back of the field to Usain Bolt-sprinting gold, *and* provide a welcome distraction from life post-Angus.

I knew exactly what I needed to do. Run a free handywomen's workshop.

After a planning meeting with Anoushka, I arranged with Barbara to run it at the café, so I could do an introduction that covered the basics in a place that was not only familiar, but which might encourage some walk ins. We felt sure that the combination of coffee, cake and screw drivers would be a fairly effective draw, if just for curiosity's sake.

Anoushka rang women she thought might be interested and I advertised with "Brought to you by Sawcraft" flyers throughout town and, with the workshop's not-for-profit status, through the Pukeroa Noticeboard on Facebook. Attendees were instructed to raid whatever they were interested in learning to use from their garages and sheds.

The post on social media elicited such a large response that I felt certain the number that showed up would be beyond what I could effectively tutor. So, I roped Stu in to be my lovely assistant.

Stu took his role promoting the art of handiness very seriously. I wore my "I turn wood into things. What's your superpower?" T-shirt to the workshop and Stu turned up in one saying, "Education is important, but woodworking is importanter".

We congratulated each other on our choice of tutoring attire and decided that between us we would inspire the most splinter-phobic student to want to become a hammer and nail expert.

Twenty-one women showed up – several more than I expected.

While coffees were consumed, Stu and I explained all the tools the students would find most useful and for what types of jobs, then we went outside behind the café for the practical application.

We went through hammering technique, de-nailing, and nail punching. We discussed the merits of the different types of screw heads, and using butterfly and expansion anchors to secure things to hollow walls. We demonstrated how to set up a drill and use the different settings.

Stu was in his element. He'd clipped on a tool belt before the women arrived and when I teased him about wearing it for aesthetic effect rather than for any practical benefit, given what we'd planned to deliver, he grinned back at me. "I don't get a lot of attention from women anymore. I'm milking this for all it's worth." And he proved to be an excellent assistant, demonstrating what I was discussing with, thanks to Anoushka's encouragement, comedic flourish and rushing to assist women in need with only a mild swagger.

When we came to the part of the workshop where the drills were to be used, Stu clapped his hands and rubbed them together eagerly. "Remember ladies, this is your most powerful tool." He tapped the side of his head. "Use it wisely and you can accomplish anything."

Hedging my bets that what he'd said was more profound than it was cheesy, I thanked him for his sagaciousness and asked if the women were ready for some power tooling.

The cheer was deafening.

Over the buzz of twenty-one drills, Stu shouted, "Would you listen to that sound? Music to my ears, ladies." Then he produced a couple of ear plugs and inserted them. "I love it even more when it doesn't inflame my tinnitus."

Laughter echoed around the group.

The women proceeded to experimentally drill into their pieces of wood, getting a feel for the resistance, the pressure they needed to apply.

"Aaaaaah," Stu said, sniffing the air and closing his eyes. "There's nothing like the smell of hot wood."

I nodded solemnly. "Especially after some solid drilling."

Anoushka looked up from her work table and threw back her head in laughter.

Stu looked at us for a moment, then held up a finger and wagged it. "Don't you ruin this beautiful and simple pleasure. If I start thinking of cocks next time I'm sawing wood, I'll never forgive you."

NINETEEN
RETURN OF THE SABRE-TOOTH

THE PSYCHOLOGIST. *Session six:*

When Lou asked about my progress, I was prepared with my answer. Since I'd determined in the last session to become a model patient, I'd set aside time each day to reflect on the patterns of my behaviour, independent of my start and end of day affirmations.

I had an exact mental map of my progress and I told her so.

"It's been an interesting month. I've had some big challenges and a couple of things that I'm hopeful will create some positive change. I've had one lapse, only one, and it was a bad one, but I've been working hard to make sure it doesn't happen again. I feel like Derek's presence is waning."

"Excellent, Nancy. Let's see if we can put it to the

test. What's the thing that gives you the most strength right now in terms of self-empowerment?"

I didn't have to think hard. "My business. I ran a handiwomen's workshop in Puke and it was a huge success. Not just in turn out, but I've got three jobs off the back of it and the hits on my website have gone up three hundred percent, so I'm pretty sure there'll be more jobs. I feel like I've finally earned the respect of the locals."

"And how do you feel when you think about that achievement?"

"Euphoric. I've been on a high since and it's been a really helpful tool. I've been focusing on it when other emotions threaten to take over."

Lou smiled. "Do you realise how much strength that takes, not only to comprehend that capturing that feeling can be an aid, but in using it *successfully* as an aid? You've come a long way since our first session, Nancy. I hope you're proud of yourself, because I am."

I was. I was incredibly proud of myself, at my mental discipline, at the place I'd worked hard to end up. A place where I liked myself.

"Now, let's go back to our second session. I want to repeat an exercise. Close your eyes and hold those two words in your hands again. Dominated. Inadequate. Feel the weight of them now. What do they look like?"

I couldn't see them, but they were still there.

They danced lightly on my palm, the faint tickling a gentle but insistent reminder of their presence.

I had taken control of my relationship with Angus, I had, hopefully, been an agent of change in the subdivision, I had started working on a plan to get the house project moving again, and my business was up and running.

Those words seemed foreign to me now. Their dance was like a moth uselessly throwing itself at the window, and I knew that the night wasn't far from ending and I could sweep the little carcasses away. I opened my eyes and smiled at Lou.

When she told me I didn't need to book another session, but was welcome back if things relapsed, it wasn't unexpected. But when she asked me to pop around to her house to measure up for a quote for a new kitchen, I was surprised, until I remembered she'd asked for my card after the last session.

I, of course, said yes.

LOU'S HOUSE was 1950s ex-State – great bones, but small living areas. A wall had been removed between the kitchen and the living room to create an open plan area, but apart from that, renovations hadn't gone much further than ripping up the carpets to polish the hardwood floors.

"It's a big project," she said as she took me on the short tour around the living space. "But we'll get there slowly. The bathroom needs doing and we'd really like to put in French doors off the lounge and have them open onto a deck. It would be great to have an en suite, too, at some stage."

"You've chosen a good investment. This'll make a very comfortable home when you're done with it."

"I hope so. It needs to be if it's going to be our family home." She pivoted on the balls of her feet to face the kitchen. "So, you can see it's pretty inadequate."

The walls were dominated by cupboards that were so deep as to leave little room for working on the bench tops underneath. It was dark with only a single light source in the centre of the room and one small window above the sink. The benches lined all three walls leaving a large, empty central space.

It wasn't a kitchen I'd enjoy cooking in very much. "Have you thought about what you want?"

Lou talked me through their plans, which involved significantly less over-bench storage, a central workstation, space for a dishwasher and a built-in fridge, and a wide sink area underneath a larger bi-folding window, which they'd install at a later date.

I made a note of her descriptions and hastily sketched a plan for her approval.

"We really like the look of Meranti Ply. I want a blonde kitchen with the laminated layers on show."

"Meranti? You do know it's one of the most expensive types of ply?"

"Yes, but I want the kitchen to look right. I don't want to regret using an inferior product further down the track."

"Okay, your call. And do you want me to quote for kitchen removal as well?" I asked, reaching for my tape measure.

"No, I think we can manage that. I'm very much looking forward to taking to it with a sledgehammer."

"There's nothing wrong with this kitchen, Lou. Someone might be looking for just this style for a retro kitchen. The wood will most likely be rimu, so it'd be beautiful if it was exposed."

"No, sledgehammer it is. I have some frustration I'd like to work off."

SEPTEMBER.

For the first time since I'd moved to the land, I received a call from Hanita. It was so unusual, I was immediately alarmed and dropped the phone in my haste to answer.

I just managed to make contact with it before it hit the ground and I had to juggle it from hand to hand before I got a firm grip.

"Nita, you okay?"

"No, I'm not fucking okay. Oh my God, I can't believe it."

"Believe what? What's going on?"

"I've been sperminated."

"You've been what?"

"I've gone and got myself pregnant again. That's what's going on."

"Oh, thank Christ. I thought it was a real crisis like Jack losing your one-fifth carat diamond stud up his nose again."

"It *is* a real crisis!" Hanita wailed. "I don't even know how it happened."

"You didn't work it out the first two times?"

"No, I mean I can't remember when we last had sex. Maybe he stealth bombed me in the middle of the night."

"Ah, I'm pretty sure you'd notice any midnight salami smuggling, Hanita. How pregnant are you?"

"Very, judging by the speed with which the line appeared. I'd only squeezed one drop out and the red line blinded me with its brilliance." She gasped. "Oh shit."

"What?"

"I've just had a flash back." She groaned and her voice became muffled as if the phone was pressed to her chest.

"Tell me!"

When she came back on the line her voice carried a mixture of embarrassment and resignation. "I jumped him after your birthday party. I thought I'd try tapping into my inner sabre-tooth cougar and once I went on the prowl he never stood a chance.

Apparently, I'm quite good at role playing." She was quiet for a couple of seconds. "I've been wondering what those scratches on his buttocks were from."

"So, you're a couple of months."

"Must be. God, I thought it would be impossible at our age. My ovaries must surely be desiccated husks by now and his sperm wouldn't be able to find the exit without the help of strip lighting and a laminated evacuation plan. You know what they call women of my age at the hospital? Geriatric mothers. Geriatric, Nance! It's a complete bloody disaster."

"Look on the bright side. If this child turns out to be difficult, you can always remind him or her about the rather playful circumstances in which they were conceived. Threaten to show them the photos."

"What photos?"

"The imaginary ones that will be excellent blackmail material."

ANGUS and I had not spoken to or seen each other for nearly a month. After seeing him almost every day and being on such familiar terms that I knew how the skin on his inner thigh tasted from that under his ear, it was an adjustment that felt violent in its totality. And my want did not lessen the more the period of absence lengthened.

I did my best to shift the energy I produced

mourning for him into moving the house project forward. I found a company that flicked off excess materials from the many houses being rebuilt in Christchurch after the earthquake and sourced near new insulation and gib offcuts for a fraction of their worth. On the back of my new jobs, Margot leant me the couple of thousand to do the preliminary wiring and plumbing and Anoushka proved good on her word. It took us ten evenings to insulate and gib the entire house.

Before the month was out, two significant things happened: I got enough carpentry work that I gave my notice at the café. And I moved into the house.

One significant thing did not: Liz and Rob were quiet as the grave.

WITH MY WEEKENDS back and the loan of a paint gun to turn the walls and ceilings a crisp white, the house was finished enough that I could at least sleep in it. The bathroom and kitchen would have to wait until the numbers in my bank account thickened to more than three digits.

I arranged for my stored furniture to be delivered and set up a make-shift kitchen so that I didn't have to trek to the bus to prepare food. When everything was in place, I spent a long time moving between each living space and breathing it in. The house was designed so that the mountains could be seen out the enormous end window from every room bar the bathroom.

Today, bands of rain drifted across the foothills, their northerly path broken by thin shafts of sunlight, and I had a feeling that despite the ominousness of Liz and Rob's silence, all would be well.

THE DAY after I moved in, Gracie, who had taken to calling me various derivatives of "grey dog", turned up on my doorstep.

"Hey, Big G, you easing into retirement alright from the fast-paced demands of the café floor? I hear there's a risk of old people who suddenly find themselves with nothing to do sliding into incontinent prunedom."

"Gracie, good to see your mouth's still running faster than your brain. Though that wouldn't be difficult. You're hardly the V8 of intellectualism."

"Ooooh, that was a good one. Very cutting. I'm gonna put that in my humiliation ammo stock for my rock climbing boot camp. So, I heard you moved out of the bus." She stuck her head in the door and squinted, putting her hand up above her eyes as if shielding them from a bright light. "Geez, Nancy, you don't want to be surprised by the approaching white light when you die in here or something?" She wrinkled her nose as she swivelled her head from side to side. "It's a bit psychiatric ward."

"It's called creating the illusion of space. Light colours make rooms seem bigger."

"And creepier."

"Would you like a tour?"

"No, I can see it all from here. Bloody hell it's small." She frowned. "Ah, I think you forgot the kitchen. Bit of an oversight there, G-Dog. I'd be worried if I were you. It's a bit of a flashing neon sign that the dementia's setting in."

I made a point of sighing. "I'm guessing this isn't a friendly, 'just popping in' visit. Is there something in my possession that you are desirous of?"

"Your bus."

"You're not having my bus, Gracie."

"I don't want you to give me your bus, G." She rolled her eyes. "I want you to let it out to me. I want to be your tenant."

I was quiet for a moment. "Why do you want to rent my bus?"

"Okay, so I'm the oldest of five children and I'm like an adult now, but I'm still treated like a child, which *sucks*. And my brothers and sisters are so suffocating, you know? I want to live like a proper adult. Have my own place and start to live my life." She pointed to her chest. "*My* life. I'm tired of being seen as just one of a gaggle of yapping children. I want out."

"Alright," I said, surprising myself with the speed at which I reached my decision. "You can rent the bus, but there are two conditions. The bus stays here. You rent it from my land, and under no circumstances is it driven anywhere."

"That's cool."

"And second, no parties. More than three people is a party and if I count a number higher than that I will turn the hose on you all and, believe me, I'm a very good shot. Got it?"

"God, you're such a killjoy, Nancy. When can I move in?"

GRACIE AND I, our rough banter a front to the fact we did actually quite like each other, managed a fairly easy co-existence. I helped her transition into the responsible world of an independent adult, negotiating the tricky terrain of bill payments, clothes washing and healthy food choices.

Gracie turned out to have a flair for cooking and was happy to share meals with me as long as I was happy to consume her culinary experiments.

The first night she moved in, I volunteered Skye's latest message before she went through the usual awkwardness of finding a casual way to ask:

There was a keen girl from afar
Who cycled on rough Irish tar
Until the rain came down

> *And wearing a frown*
> *Said, "That'll teach you to not go by car."*

Yep, the glorious weather has ended with a hiss and a roar. I'm drying out in a hostel in Limerick after a few days of wind and rain – my tent and I definitely need some space from each other. It's quite an expensive hostel, but I get my own room and a continental breakfast, so to put it another way, it's a very cheap B&B with cooking facilities. Score! Since I last wrote you I have cycled around the ring of Kerry and into lake-land Killarney, which is so like New Zealand I could cry (apart from the huge, white, aggressive swans. Whenever I look at them I can't help imagining how good they'd taste roasted. I think it's because it's illegal here to kill them, and as every teenager knows, prohibition is the most effective way to induce temptation). I have cycled much of the Dingle (cool name) Peninsula, which is seafood country. I have had more fish and mussels than in my entire life – my iron levels must be soaring. I've biked over the highest, longest, hottest, and bloody monotonous-est mountain pass in the Northern hemisphere and received numerous toots of pity (I'd like to think of admiration) and waves of encouragement. Coming down the other side was well worth it though – my breakneck speed (I was going much faster than the cars) was my biggest thrill since discovering the joys of brown soda bread (so yum!). Notice that I have also discovered the joys of parenthesis. How many sets of brackets do you need in one WhatsApp message?

Love Skye Xx

P.S. Have you finished the house yet? I'll be home soon (ish) – man, talk about a bracket party – and I want to be able to lie in your loft and look at the Southern Cross through the skylight. Who would have thought I would miss constellations!

Gracie exhaled as if she'd been holding her breath throughout the whole message. "So, she's coming back soon?"

"Sounds like it. I can't imagine I'll be priority one, two or three, though. She's got two families – her mum's and her dad's – to welcome her back and a depleted bank account to recover."

Gracie nodded nonchalantly.

"I don't s'pose you want to see the photos, though?"

She moved around the dining table so fast her chair toppled over backwards.

I laughed. "You could have just reached over the table, Gracie."

TWENTY
STALEMATE

OCTOBER.

"Sorry it's taken so long to give you an answer, Nancy. Things are quite complicated at the moment between managing the subdivision consent and... other family matters."

Liz sat opposite me at my kitchen table, a mug nestled between her palms.

I nodded. "That's okay. I understand the pressure you're all under." I bit my tongue to keep from asking about Angus. My thoughts turned to him so frequently that I imagined him flinching at the force of them. I had never worried over someone as much as I did him.

"Our real estate agent has advised us not to put any covenants on the lots as it makes them less desirable..."

My parts moved independently of each other. My mouth said, "Ah," my stomach rushed to meet the floor, and my mind was adrift, rocking on violent swells somewhere just above our heads.

"...and we've debated long and hard over it, but we tend to agree with him. I'm sorry, love. I know how important this view is to you, but the way things are looking at the moment, we just can't afford to jeopardise that sale."

My brain re-entered my body and shifted its focus to Lot 4 and then the mountains behind it. It was a glorious morning and Rakiariki sat enigmatically behind a veil of blue mist.

"Do you need a new agreement?" I asked without taking my eyes off the peak.

"It seems the paperwork did a comprehensive vanishing act." Liz sighed. "It hasn't eased our stress levels, I can tell you." She rummaged in her bag and produced a set of papers with "sign here" tabs protruding from them. "Our lawyer sent through a new one."

The pile swam in and out of focus and I couldn't bring myself to say anything in response.

In my peripheral vision, a translucent figure wavered, desperate for solidity. I wasn't going to give it to him. I wasn't even going to acknowledge him. Instead, I addressed myself. *Nancy, this is a disappointment, and you've got a hard decision to make, but you are in control of the situation. You've been handed control.* It wasn't at all comforting. I'd just ring-circled in red ink the fact that I had all the power.

Derek stayed mute, but his smirk burnt into me. "Nancy?"

I stood up, suddenly wanting to be alone. "I'll get them back to you soon," I said as I slid the door open for her.

It was going to take all of my strength to kick Derek out for good.

What had Lou said? "There is one thing you have absolute power over. You can control your negative thoughts about yourself. You can control Derek."

It was time.

His arse was mine, and I had something going for me that should hand it to me on a platter.

THE WONDERFUL THING about a business taking off is not only the money, or professional respect, but the intoxicating sense that you are a badass, capable of anything.

I had more work than I ever hoped for, my busy schedule stretched further by requests for work in Wallaceton.

There was one job I was particularly proud of.

Over the last month and between other jobs, I had been working on transforming the rear of the café into an al fresco dining area. The ski season had died down enough that decommissioning the back of the building wasn't too disruptive and I worked alongside Andre on the structural features, doing the landscaping and crafting the furniture myself.

Wooden French doors opened out onto a pergola-covered patio that housed five tables, and a sandpit sat nestled into a small lawn. Raised beds bordered the entire area, and herbs and vegetables were already planted, ready to service the kitchen.

The evening of the extension's opening, Barbara decorated the garden and pergola with candles in jars and paper lanterns. It looked magical.

I arrived late due to the demands of my work schedule and bumped into Angus as he exited the café's front door.

"Nancy!" He took a step backwards towards the doorway as my stomach unhinged itself and tried to beat its way out of my body.

"You going already?"

"It's hard for me to find the motivation and energy to make small talk these days." His jersey hung off a new sharpness in his shoulders and a line was starting to work its way into the skin between his eyebrows.

I wanted to kiss it away.

"I thought I'd pop my head in and make an appearance, and I was, of course, very keen to see the fruits of your labour." He smiled. "It looks really great, Nance."

I smiled back at him. "It does, doesn't it?"

"I told you you had marvel-worthy facets." He put his hands in his jeans pockets and shuffled from one foot to the other as if trying to keep warm. "How's the business going?"

"Really well. I've got a waiting list a month long."

His lips pinched together and he said, "I'm really proud of you."

I broke eye contact and looked down at my feet. Then I reached out to stroke the back of his hand.

He pulled it out of his pocket, turning it over to grab onto mine. "I really miss you," he whispered towards our enclosed fingers.

I squeezed his hand and looked up at him.

He held my gaze for a moment, then leaned forward, his eyes on my lips just as somebody exited the café directly behind us.

Whoever it was shouted, "Hey, nice job, Nancy. It looks bloody brilliant," as they walked away in the opposite direction to where we were standing.

"Thanks," I called back, still looking at Angus, who had straightened as soon as the door opened.

He brushed his thumb over the back of my hand, then let it drop. Very softly, he said, "See you," and left me watching him depart.

I walked around the block to gather myself before I had to put on a public face, then entered the café to a loud hubbub of conversation emanating through the French doors.

Barbara laughed with a young woman then

waved as she caught sight of me. She was dressed in a flowing pink and green silk dress and glitter decorated her forehead and cheekbones. The tiny reflections shimmered and sparkled in the candlelight when she turned her head.

I picked up a glass of sparkling wine from a table and sought out Martin and Anoushka, who were standing on the other side of the young woman.

Barbara put an arm around me as I walked past her. "Here she is – the lady of the hour. Kia ora e hoa," she said in greeting as she kissed me on the cheek. "Your vision for this place was absolutely spot on. Everybody's waxing lyrical about it."

"Yeah, Nancy, it is so, so great!" said a mildly tipsy Anoushka.

Martin added, "*So* great she's at a loss for adjectives."

"Adverbs." I smiled, thinking of Angus and his mysterious passion for the English language.

"Barbs, darling," a familiar voice called above the noise of the gathering. Every smile froze and our eyes darted between each other, but no one found inspiration to stage a collective rescue.

Mona sidled up to Barbara and put an arm through hers. "Nancy," she addressed me with a wink before pulling Barbara away. "I'm loving what you've done here. It's wonderfully shabby-chic."

"Don't call me Barbs, Mona," Barbara said in a resigned tone. "And perhaps 'rustic' is the word you're looking for, not" – she wrinkled her nose – "shabby-chic," the last word uttered as if she'd just swallowed a cup of cold bile.

Mona guided Barbara in a slow perambulation of the garden, and the rest of us relaxed with guilty relief.

A large hand was placed on my shoulder and I looked up into Andre's grimly-set face. "You just missed Angus."

"No, I, ah, bumped into him on his way out."

"He's looking terrible, isn't he?" said Anoushka. "The stress is really taking its toll. I'm so worried about him."

"No, it's not good. Not good at all," added Martin. "And the bugger about it is that we have to sit here and watch it happen to him."

"It'll work out," said Niamh. "I have this sense that it's going to be okay. We should all have faith in the greater power of the multiverse."

"In the what?" I asked.

"Multiverse. It says right here." She held up the bottle she was drinking from. It read *Dr Fuller's Karmic Kombucha*. The label encompassed the entire bottle and was crammed with lines of tiny writing.

"It's true." She continued reading, "*The cosmos is a reflection of ourselves and only a child of the infinite can manifest the power of the totality.*"

"It does not say that." I grabbed the bottle from

Niamh and studied the minute writing. "It does." I held the bottle away from me then brought it close again, as if expecting the words to have reconfigured into sentences I could understand. *"We are all pilgrims of potentiality,"* I slowly read. "Is this for real?" I handed the bottle back. "Where'd you get it?"

"Next to the glasses of bubbly."

Martin chortled. "That is the profoundest sounding bullshit I've ever heard. Hey *Barbs*," he shouted above the hubbub. She disengaged herself from Mona and sashayed between people to rejoin us. "Where'd you source this?"

"It's a hoot, isn't it? I figured customers might like to enjoy sharing new age enlightenment rather than ignoring each other in favour of their phones."

Andre's smile broadened into a full-throated laugh.

"Huh," I said. "You have an interesting brain, Barbara."

Martin gave Niamh a nudge. "Do it. Share some more of your wisdom."

"I'm not some show-pony you guys. I don't perform on command. I am," she read from the label, *"an osmotic wanderer on the vector towards circuitous self-actualisation."*

THERE WAS one thing my Sawcraft success couldn't help me with. My grief for the mountains was total. It sat outside myself, nestled at the base of my neck. There was nothing I could censure myself for, nothing for Derek to raise an eyebrow over. I'd done the best I could.

As the days of procrastinating about signing the paperwork mounted, I took to spending every evening nursing a beer in front of my lounge window, watching the sun set behind the mountains. Each night, my chin sat a little closer to my chest.

It was Stu, bless him, who unwittingly helped lighten the load, albeit briefly, and gave me the strength to do what I needed to. He turned up after I had just returned home from a job, towing a high-sided trailer. "I have something I think you'll like," he said.

"It's not a pig, is it? Gracie's been begging me for one ever since she moved into the bus. Make great house pets she reckons, though how she expects to accommodate one in there, I have no idea."

"It's much better than a pig. Have a look."

I peered over the side of the trailer and saw a cream-coloured, claw-footed bath. "Stu! You can't give that to me. That has to be worth several hundred."

"I can, Nancy, and I will. I have a mate with an old farmhouse he's doing up. He didn't want it. Thought of you straight away."

I blinked rapidly. "I don't know what to say."

"Well, well. No need to get emotional," he said, looking thoroughly pleased that I was. "Where'd you like it?"

We positioned the bath on a gently sloping area to the right of the house, where the view of the mountains was uninterrupted by trees. I had to dig out a small section to get the bath level and, as soon as it was right, I thanked Stu profusely, promising as many beers as would fit in the cab of his ute.

As the bath filled with the hose, I collected my three-burner gas stove and cylinder to heat the water.

Gracie arrived home not long after I'd set everything up and peered over the edge of the deck. "Score, G-Dog."

"Not bad, huh? You want to join me in breaking it in?"

"You'll be wearing togs, right? I'm not too keen on having an eyeful of vaginasaur."

"Yes, Gracie, I'll wear togs," I answered in the voice of the long-suffering. "Shall we bring down a tray of wine and nibbles?"

"Does a one-legged duck swim in circles?"

Gracie was already in the bath when I arrived, tray in hand. I shucked off my dressing gown and could feel Gracie's eyes scrutinising me as I gingerly stepped into the bath. "What?"

"You've got an alright body. For an old lady.

Though you might want to shave your bikini line more often."

"Did I tell you I'm just getting over a stubborn case of school sores? I expect the scabs will soften in the warm water and fall off."

She grinned at me. "Mmmm, barnacle soup."

We clinked glasses.

"This place is turning into a pretty decent set-up, Grey. I might never leave at this rate. Even if you sell up, I could be one of the chattels – I come with the house."

"Well," I said, looking over towards Angus' farm, "I have no plans as yet to sell, but we'll see."

Gracie sipped her wine. "So, what are the rules around use of the bath?"

"What do you mean?"

"If I want to conduct some lesbionage, how will you respect my privacy?"

"Uh, hello!" I answered, pointing up at the large lounge window above us. "There's no privacy. How will *you* respect my need not to ever see you..." I waved my hand around in the air.

"Clam wrestling?"

"Precisely."

She shrugged. "I'll just have to get my timing right." Then she added, "Said no man ever."

"Gracie, my girl, you have no idea what you're talking about."

TWENTY-ONE
CHECKMATE

IT TOOK me just over a week to create and install Lou and Ethan's new kitchen.

When I came back to take photos of the job once the other tradies had done their work, Ethan answered the door. He was an exceptionally tall man with fair hair and a beguiling set of dimples.

I was immediately beguiled.

After I was ushered in, named a master craftswoman and had my camera unpacked for me, he leaned up against one of the kitchen worktops and crossed his ankles. "Would you like these long beauties in your shot? I make a very good kitchen model. I could put my apron on and stir something over the stove."

I smiled up at him. "I think there's more than enough blonde in the kitchen already."

"You're right. I'll just blend into the background. It'll look like the pot's stirring itself."

This time I laughed and the dimples deepened in response.

"Okay. Shoot away. Can I at least arrange the lighting concept for you?" He busied himself turning on the new directional lights above the benches. "Is that good?"

I took photos. He decanted Central Otago pinot noir into two glasses.

The sound of the back door being unlocked accompanied the clink of our toast, and Lou entered the kitchen. "Hi Nancy. Looks like you've already finished?"

"With some help from her lovely assistant." Ethan moved to retrieve another wine glass from the cupboard. "We were just celebrating a job well done."

"And so we should." Lou reached to take the offered glass. "I love it, Nancy. It's even better than I'd envisaged. It's completely transformed the space."

It was an excellent complement. One that would look very good in a written testimonial.

"Makes me impatient to get the other projects rolling, though."

I knew that feeling. I also had the benefit of experience to temper it. "Believe me, being forced to take your time in creating your house exactly how you want it gives you the luxury of careful decision-making. And plenty of time to change your mind."

"Maybe we shouldn't wait too long, then," Ethan said. "I find with Lou a quick decision's a good decision."

"Hey, I'm not that indecisive," Lou argued.

"It took you twelve test pots to find the right colour for the kitchen walls."

"Says the man who tried on three shirts this morning before choosing the first one you put on." She moved to stroke his arm, then turned to me. "Oh, did my payment for the invoice go through okay?"

"Yep, cleared this morning."

"Great." She took a sip, working the wine around her mouth before swallowing. "So, there's something rather delicate I've been wanting to discuss with you."

Ethan shifted away from the island and resumed his original position next to the sink.

I put my glass down on the island's countertop. "Oh?"

"Yeah. I've been put in a difficult situation over an investment I'm involved in and I need your help."

I stood up a little straighter. "How do you mean?"

"Well, I'm party to a land development project that I've recently discovered is next to your property and it appears some very crucial paperwork is missing, a document that –"

I held up my hand. "Wait, Lou, please stop."

"Please, just hear –"

I shushed her and put my hands to my cheeks. "I

need to unscramble the shit storm in my brain that's fighting to make its way to my tongue."

Lou opened her mouth and closed it again.

Could this really be happening? Could my psychologist, the woman with whom I'd shared my darkest thoughts also be the person who stood between me and Angus? I had the curious sensation of my brain revolving on an axis between my ears then swinging back and forward until it settled into place.

I'd never mentioned his name when we'd discussed him during my sessions. If I had, there's no way I'd be in the awkward predicament I now found myself in.

I placed both hands on the island to steady myself and took a deep breath. "So, you're Angus' ex."

Lou looked over at Ethan, then back at me. "Right. You know him, then?"

"Of course I do, he's my neighbour."

"Yes, sorry." She frowned and shook her head. "It makes complete sense you would."

"And your...investment, I'm assuming, is the subdivision of four lots adjacent to my property?"

"Yes."

"Right." I nodded. "And you need access via an easement near my northern boundary?"

Lou paused. "You're across all this, then?"

I sighed. "Yes, Lou, as it highly affects me, I am aware of the plans."

"Of course." She swirled her wine around her

glass. "Are you aware an easement was agreed to by the previous owner?"

"Yes."

"Well, the document has done a vanishing act."

I placed my thumbs against my eye sockets for two beats then looked back at her. "I'm aware of that, but how are you?"

Again, Lou shifted her eyes over to Ethan. "I know someone at FVU Group, the firm putting the consent together. They told me."

I let another sigh escape. The level of bureaucratic espionage around the subdivision might have been, if it had affected anybody other than me, on the entertaining side of alarming. "How long have you known?"

"A couple or so weeks."

"Before you employed me?"

Lou didn't say anything. Ethan turned to wash his glass in the sink.

"Oh, God, Lou, don't do this. Don't make a mockery of the sexual revolution. I've been championing your claim on the farm, your right to your share, but not this. Did you think you could use securing my signature as leverage on getting a portion of the subdivision profits?"

"The project has stalled or is about to. Someone needs to regain control of it."

"It's not your place to do that," I said as gently as I could.

Lou set down her wine glass with a loud clink. "That subdivision was my idea. I found the company they contracted with."

"But Angus won't see the profits. It all goes to Rob and Liz to support them in their retirement."

"Look, Nancy, I don't expect you to understand, but I really want you to try. I gave that man eleven years of my life and came out the other end of it at the age of thirty-three with nothing. No assets, no home, no kids, not even a fucking divorce because he wasn't interested in marriage. I felt so robbed. Do you have any idea what that feels like?"

"Yes, actually, I think I do, and I absolutely agree Angus should compensate you, but not his parents. They have nothing to do with the grievance you feel over the end of your relationship and they shouldn't be punished for it."

I pushed my untouched glass across the island and made my way towards the door. Before I stepped over the threshold, I turned. "Look, Lou, please know that I am incredibly grateful for all your help with sorting the mess in here" – I pointed to my head – "but this line should never have been crossed. I'm not interested in scratching your back."

When I got into the driver's seat, I sat still, feeling into the shadowed corners of my mind. If there was an opportunity for Derek to make his disapproving presence known, offer a snide comment, it was now.

Somehow, I'd managed to get myself entangled in

yet another complication in an already messy situation. But there was no "somehow" in how I extracted myself from it.

I probed further.

There was nothing. Not even a whisper, or the flick of lucent hair.

"Goodbye, Derek," I said quietly.

That felt good.

I shouted it into the fabric-covered ceiling and added a "Fuck yeah!" for good measure.

The woman in the rear-view mirror smiled at me. She seemed whole. No parts competed for attention.

"Hello, Nancy, you arse-kicker."

LOU'S GAME-PLAYING did nothing to change things. The die was already cast and I invited Liz and Rob around to take receipt of the papers and discuss the next steps.

The day before they were due to visit, I sat in my customary position in the lounge, my beer slowly warming in my hand.

The crunch of tyres sounded on the gravel outside. Gracie was due home from a day of climbing, but I didn't have the energy to get up and greet her. I was slumped so low in the chair, my chin was propped on my chest.

A rap on the glass jerked me out of my musings.

"Angus!" I scrambled to get up out of my chair and open the door. "Sorry, I wasn't expecting you."

"Can I join you?" He held out a six-pack of beer, then spied mine, said, "Ah," and lowered his hand again.

"Of course you can." I fetched him a chair and he set it up facing the mountains but angled towards mine.

He cracked a beer and sat staring down at it. When he eventually raised his eyes and offered a small smile, a fire blossomed in my chest and fizzled on that tiny word that has so much power in triggering the steam roller of inevitability – "So."

"So," I echoed, "you're a day early."

"I'm not here to collect, I'm here to plead my parents' case. They're...very worried."

"I know what the field of play is. It's done." I gestured towards the pile of paper on the coffee table.

Angus picked them up and thumbed through the sheets. "But they're unsigned."

I was quiet. The mountains were heart-achingly beautiful in the pink light of the dying sun.

"Nancy?"

"You know what drew me here? What made me want this land so badly that I was willing to sacrifice the life I had led up to now?"

"I'm guessing the mountains."

When I spoke again it was through the thickness of the lump of lead sitting painfully in my throat.

"That's right. They've made me so happy, Angus. You're asking me to give them up when I've only just found them."

"Look, the mountains are big. You'll still be able to see...parts of them."

I sniffed wetly. "I can't do it. I can't sign that paper."

Angus shifted forward in his seat and grabbed my hands. "Nance, look at me. Without the subdivision we are royally screwed because of Lou's claim. Regardless of whether she wins a portion of the subdivision's profits, I need to borrow money off Mum and Dad to pay her out and that money is sitting right over there." He pointed towards the lot.

I gently removed my hands from his grasp. "Those mountains are the steadiest thing I have in my life. They will always be there for me, they will always be my anchor stone. They're more reliable than my parents, the often fickle lifespan of my pets, my financial security, even you, Angus."

He sat back abruptly in his seat. "So, you're going to hold us to ransom?"

"If I don't say 'no', you'll be holding *me* to ransom."

Angus stood up and walked towards the door. Halfway across the room he stopped, turned and walked back towards me. "Who's Derek?"

"What?"

"You told him to fuck off that night of Martin and

Anoushka's party, just before you got out of my car. Who is he?" he asked, his words sharp with anger.

I eyed him for several seconds before replying. "He's my ex. He dumped me for a woman fifteen years my junior."

Angus didn't respond.

"So," I turned back towards the mountains.

"Shit. I'm sorry, Nance, that's tough."

I shrugged. "It is what it is."

"Why did you tell him to fuck off?"

"He turns up from time to time." I swivelled around to face him again and tapped the side of my head. "Tells me what a shit job I'm making of my life."

Angus' face moved through incredulity, to mortification, and settled into a carefully composed expressionlessness. "I take it he's here somewhere, then?"

The silence that followed stretched for several seconds.

Angus couldn't know the degree to which Derek had played upon my insecurities. He couldn't know how hard I'd worked to overcome my disabling self-doubts. So he couldn't know how nasty his barb, thrown thoughtlessly in anger, was. But I couldn't forgive him. Not in that moment.

I turned my back on him and faced Rakiariki as if to say *See? More reliable than you.*

The door closed softly behind me.

•   •   •

IT WAS as I lay in bed rehashing my encounter with Angus for the thirtieth time that I remembered what he'd said about needing the money from the subdivision.

He'd decided he was going to pay Lou out.

WHEN ALL THE BLOSSOMS DISAPPEARED, it was clear the warmer weather intended to arrive with a full fanfare. A large tropical front swept across the island and Pukeroa was subjected to a series of fierce electrical storms.

Gracie was off on a week-long adventure holiday, and I stood in the lounge on the first evening of turbulent weather, watching the bus rock violently in the gale-force winds. I imagined she wouldn't have slept easy cocooned in a giant electrical conductor, but I hoped that wherever she was, she was alright.

On the second evening, I ventured out in the dark to check the bus for leaks and was startled as something large shot past me and up into the bus as I opened the door.

I stumbled back onto the grass and when my heart returned to a normal rate, slowly climbed the steps.

The high-pitched whimpering of a dog emanated from somewhere in the kitchen and when I stepped into the main light of the bus, I could see it had its head buried within the tiny pantry, its body still exposed on the floor.

"Tess?"

She didn't move. Her fur stood up in wet clumps and her hind quarters trembled.

"Tess, that's not a very good hiding place. I can still see most of you."

The bus was illuminated by a flash of white light and a deafening boom echoed across the valley.

With a clattering of empty cans from the recycling bin, Tess forced her whole body into the pantry and whined even louder.

"Alright, girl, if that's where you want to be." I closed the pantry door to make it dark and snug and after hovering a shaking finger over my phone for several seconds, made a call.

It took him until my third call to answer.

"You okay?" I could barely hear him over the wind at his end of the line.

"I'm fine. You missing a dog?"

"I'm out looking for her now. She's with you?"

"Turned up terrified a few minutes ago."

"I'm on my way." He hung up.

In the few days since I handed over the unsigned papers, I lived and worked in a feverish state. I hummed with nervous energy and kept my phone in my pocket, expecting Liz and Rob to call at any moment, wanting to negotiate. Yet, I'd heard nothing. And the wait fed the fever.

I didn't want to scupper their project and ruin their future. Or Angus'. I wanted to come to an agreement that might allow us all to be happy. Or mostly happy. The thought that they might not want to have anything to do with me after we'd reached a compromise, was something I was willing to risk.

Angus was another matter entirely. I could live with Liz and Rob's resentment. I couldn't live with his. After he had taken the papers and left, it took me an hour of absorbing the calm of the mountains to forgive his unkindness.

His careful exit told me his immediate regret. And I couldn't help but think it was generous of him after my Derek revelation.

I knew how it sounded. He was now likely congratulating himself on having had a lucky escape.

I guessed I had twenty minutes before he turned up, and my innards knotted and swirled as I paced the narrow floor. The minutes stretched into days before the headlights of his ute swung up the driveway.

I opened the door before he knocked.

He raised his eyes from under the hood of his raincoat and said "Hey," so quietly that I could only tell what he said from the shape his mouth made. His gaze didn't make it past the top button of my shirt.

"Hey. Come in." I stood back to admit him.

"No, I...I'd better not." He looked past me up into the bus. "Tess?"

"For goodness sake, Angus," I said as gently as I

could over the noise of the storm, "it's pelting down and the dog won't move without you doing some exceptional coaxing wizardry. Come in."

He stepped up into the bus and silently removed his coat, shaking it out over the steps and draping it over the handrail.

We stood still, me looking at him, him looking at the floor, any words we might have wanted to say stoppered in our throats.

It was Angus who spoke first.

"So, where's the dog?" He peered around the bus. "What's she hiding under?"

"She's in here." I walked to the pantry and opened the door. Tess looked miserably out at us and the end of her tail moved with the slightest of wags.

"Hey, girl," Angus crooned as he crouched down to her. "You came all this way to hide from the big angry dog in the sky? You could have hidden in my pantry. It's a lot closer." He grabbed Tess' collar and dragged her out. "Come on," he urged as he stood up.

Tess simply looked up at him.

"Alright, my big, hairy, smelly baby. Let's do this the easy way." He picked her up and carried her towards the door. When he set her down to put his coat on, I put my hand on his arm.

He flinched as if I'd given him a shock.

"I don't want to make things impossible. I want to keep talking."

Angus finally met my eye. "Dad's angina's so bad

they've bumped him up the waiting list for surgery. Mum's beside herself. It's a heavy gun you're holding to their heads, Nancy."

He picked up Tess and left.

I sat on the top step of the bus' entrance for a long time, replaying those three sentences over and over in my head. Of course, there was only one course of action I could possibly take. Once again, Angus had undone me.

I drove over to Liz and Rob's the following day and signed the papers.

TWENTY-TWO
WOCKA WOCKA

SEVERAL EVENINGS later when I returned home from work, I opened my front door to find Gracie sitting in my lounge playing with a ginger kitten.

"What's that?" I asked, instantly regretting the stupidity of the question.

Gracie attempted a backwards somersault with her eyeballs. "It's a unicorn. I bought it as a hood ornament for your glitter mobile."

I sat down beside her. "You know, all your eye rolling's going to loosen the optic nerve. Be careful you don't lose your eyeballs somewhere in your head next time you express your disdain."

Gracie's eyes quivered in her attempt not to roll them. She clucked her tongue instead. "That guy, the one whose sausage you were saucing, dropped it off. He said it was a house-warming present."

My stomach lurched in several directions. "He came here?"

"Yeah, about an hour ago."

"And he brought me a kitten?" I suddenly felt very hot behind my eyeballs. I held the kitten up to my face and said, "Hello little guy, nice to meet you."

He mewed in reply.

"How do you know it's a boy?"

"Most gingers are boys for some reason." The kitten yawned and rapidly blinked its eyes.

Gracie said, "Oh my God, he's super cute."

I clutched him to my chest and turned abruptly to Gracie. "Did he say anything else?"

"No, his vocabulary's pretty limited. He tends to favour 'meow' above any other word."

It was my turn to roll my eyes. "Did *Angus* say anything else?"

"He just said to tell you that the kitten was a house-warming present, that he got it from someone-or-other in Puke and that there was food in the box for it. Then he left."

I gazed in the direction of Angus' farm. "I told him ages ago that I wanted another cat after my last one died, but that I was waiting until I was living in the house."

Gracie shrugged her shoulders. "Yeah, he's totally in love with you, G-Dog."

A flame of hope blazed in my chest and extinguished itself as I snorted. "I seriously doubt that after all that's gone on. This is probably a reward for having done the right thing."

Gracie was quiet for a moment, before saying, "Man, you guys totally need to sort your shit out."

"Yeah? You *totally* need the help of a thesaurus. You're beginning to sound like a generic teenager. Expand your rhetorical horizons, Gracie." It sounded unkind, and I silently cursed myself for taking out my confusion and frustration on her.

Gracie, as usual, took it in her stride. "You are like literally right. I will totes do that, right after you and your toy-boy stop torturing each other with your emotional stupidity. Forshizzle," she added as an afterthought.

I named the kitten Fozzie.

NOVEMBER.

It took two weeks after I'd signed the papers for the subdivision adverts to appear in the window of the general store, "subject to title". It took another week for the first SOLD to be stickered across the front of one of the lots.

I avoided town as much as I could. I even considered putting a conditional offer on Lot 4, but I knew that its position devalued my land so much that even with a finished house to sweeten the sale, I'd be left with no capital to build anything after I'd bought it.

I distracted myself by focusing on two projects: getting to know the newest member of my family and finishing the house.

Fozzie was a furry ball of playful delight. He scampered and skidded across the varnished plywood floors with such incredible bursts of energy that he'd quickly tire himself out and have to sleep off his escapades wherever he fell. Quite often, that meant being draped awkwardly over furniture, inside shoes, or, if I was sitting on the couch, around my neck. I was completely smitten.

The night of Fozzie's arrival I had texted Angus: I love him. Thank you.

I received a smiley cat emoji in return.

My new cash reserves allowed me to finish the deck and the bathroom, and get the kitchen underway. The costs weren't too high thanks to my ability to sniff out salvaged material and undertake all the labour myself. It was the purchasing of the appliances and the subsequent electrical and plumbing bills that brought my bank account to its knees. Again.

I was, however, able to find incredibly inventive ways to serve two-minute noodles in a desperate bid to cut expenditure.

Gracie and I had got into the habit of taking turns cooking for each other so that making dinner was a job that only had to be conducted every second day.

I called her to dinner, and as she sat down at the table, she asked what I had made.

"Chicken Noodle Broth Sans Pollo."

"Oooh, fancy." She took a sip, then looked up at me suspiciously. "It's just broth and two-minute noodles, isn't it?"

"But very special broth. If you slurp it all down, you'll find pea surprise on the bottom."

"Ah, I'm not sure a sinking pea is a good pea, G."

"I only had the dehydrated variety."

Gracie took another cautious sip. "Did you use Vegemite for stock?"

"I might have."

"Hmm. It's actually quite good. I commend you on your resourcefulness."

"Thank you. I did consider flavouring it with kitten food, given that I spend twice as much on Fozzie's food than I do on mine, but it just didn't smell appetising enough."

"You didn't!" Gracie looked at me incredulously. "You know what? I actually wouldn't put it past you. What other gems have you been sneaking in? I've noticed a high ratio of rat traps at the moment and that herb you seasoned Monday's noodle-de-jour with looked suspiciously like grass."

"One of your assumptions is correct. I'll leave it up to you to decide which."

Gracie sighed and looked at me pityingly. "G-dog, would you like an advance on next week's rent?"

"No, I'll be fine. I'm expecting some money to clear tomorrow and then I'll buy some decent food that covers all the important food groups."

"Like chocolate."

"Definitely like chocolate. Aaaaar!" I picked my right foot up off the floor with a struggling Fozzie dangling from my sock by his front claws and most of his needle baby teeth. I plucked him off by the scruff of the neck and held him up in front of me so I could shake a finger at him.

He took a swipe at the offending digit.

"How do you fancy kitten noodle soup tomorrow night?"

Gracie considered my proposition. "He looks a bit scrawny, but at his age the meat should be very tender. I'm game."

"You hear that, Fozzie? Dinner's on you tomorrow. Any last requests? What's that?" I held him up to my ear. "You want to see what Gracie's toes taste like? I wouldn't bother, Foz. Hers have all rotten and fallen off due to podiatric abuse. But I hear her ankles are particularly flavoursome." I put Fozzie back under the table.

Gracie drew her legs up onto her chair. "No, you don't, you very cute but very evil spawn of Satan." She looked back at me. "I hear declawing and de-toothing is a thing. You should consider it, Grey."

"No thanks. I find my teeth are quite useful for propping up my cheeks."

Gracie responded with a cutting eye roll.

"Yes!" I crowed. "I got you to roll your eyes in less than five minutes of talking to me. That's ten dollars you owe me." I looked under the table at Fozzie who was wrapped around one of the legs of Gracie's chair, biting it and kicking it with his back legs so that he was propelled around it.

"Foz, you're off the hook. Dinner's on Gracie tomorrow night." I looked back at her and grinned hungrily. "I think fish and chips are in order."

TWENTY-THREE
TECHNICOLOUR YAWN

THE NEWS that Lou had dropped her claim on the subdivision and she and Angus had finally reached settlement should have been something that had me sliding over the bonnet of my car in my haste to get behind the wheel to drive to his farm. Especially given his request to revisit the more permanent idea of him and me when "all this" was over, and given the fact that I was still in love with him.

However, since I received the news via a phone call from Andre while I watched diggers strip away soil for the new access way, I wasn't inclined to do anything but raid Margot's liquor cabinet.

I packed two bags for me and one for Fozzie, gave instructions to Gracie on chicken and sheep care and moved in to Margot's spare room. I had no intention of watching the progress of the diggers. The amount of glass I'd squeezed into the house design ensured I'd have a fairly spectacular view from every room of their earth-gobbling advance towards Lot 4.

Margot humoured my need to flee, but reminded me in characteristic bluntness that I couldn't hide from it forever.

Hanita, loyal to a fault, invited me to run away to her house. "You can hold my hair back while I barf up the dry crackers I ate three minutes beforehand, even though I'm in my second trimester now. How am I still being punished for one wayward night of wild and moderately violent passion? I'm miserable."

I made a noise I hoped sounded sympathetic.

"I tell you what, I'm bloody well going to get my own back. I'm going to name this child Porcelain Stir-Fry."

"What if it's a boy?"

"Then I'll call it Rainbow Yodel."

"Does Jasper get an input?"

"No, he had more than enough input when he depth charged me."

"Look, as much as I'd love to come over there to mop your brow, I can't abandon my clients. And any-way, I need the money. I just have to...paint my win-dows or something."

"You could always hang curtains. Pretty radical, but —"

"Lot 3's sold," I blurted. "That's two of the four gone."

"Oh honey. I don't know what to say to make it easier. The ones that have sold will be the cheaper lots. Hopefully Lot 4's priced beyond any sane person's budget."

I appreciated her effort, but she was right. There was nothing that could be said that would give me comfort.

A rumbling gurgle issued from my phone's speaker and Hanita said thickly, "Ah, Nance, I have to go." The call ended.

AFTER TWO WEEKS OF AVOIDANCE, I couldn't ignore the shuddering advance of the diggers any longer. And besides, I missed my sheep and the antics of the chickens. The drive home was slow. If my car could have dragged its wheels, it would have, and as I neared my property, I kept my eyes studiously on the road. I wanted that comforting hit of home before I had to face reality.

There was a car in the driveway I didn't recognise. I parked and walked around it, peering inside, but was none the wiser. It was old and battered and looked like it would shed its metal shell with one good shake on Pukeroa's many gravel roads.

"Hello?" I called out. Footsteps clumped on the deck and I turned to see a very brown Skye walking towards me from around the back of the house.

"Hey, Aunty Nan," she called as I shrieked, "Skye!" and leapt two feet into the air.

She jumped down from the deck and embraced me in a tight hug.

"My gorgeous, gorgeous girl. When did you get back into the country?"

"Last week."

"And you didn't tell me?"

"I wanted to surprise you."

She sure as hell had, but it was a pretty fucking wonderful one. "It's so good to see you. I was beginning to forget what you looked like." I gave her another hug, then held her at arm's length so I could take her in all over again. "You are going to be wonderful medicine."

"For what?"

I put an arm around her shoulders and steered her towards the steps to the front door. "Come and see my lovely house."

While we toured the property, I filled her in on the subdivision problem. Not that I needed to give any detail. It was laid out clearly before us. The diggers were gone. The gravel driveways to Lots 1 and 2 disappeared courteously behind hills, and those of Lots 3 and 4 were neatly gravelled to their respective build sites.

Skye surveyed the elevation of Lot 4. "I can see what you mean. It's going to completely ruin your view. It's too late to do anything about it?"

"Nope. I can sell."

"Oh."

"Once the house is signed off and I have my Code of Compliance, I can put it on the market. I've already rung the council to book in the building inspector."

"But Aunty Nan..." Skye's heart-shaped face creased in concern.

I didn't want her to worry about me. It wasn't her job. "How about we plan for a party? A house cooling. I never had the warming kind when I moved in, but I'd like to celebrate my short relationship with it before I move on. What do you think?"

Skye smiled and nodded, but her eyes still looked troubled.

"Hey, think of this as my practise house. The next one will be even better." I put an arm around her. "Come on, let me introduce you to my woolly babies."

WE HAD JUST STARTED to get dinner together when Gracie skipped in the open door without knocking. "Whose hunk a junk is that in the driveway?" Then she laid eyes on Skye. "Oh." She stood still, looking at her and nodding.

I suppose I shouldn't have been surprised at Gracie's immobilisation at the sight of my niece, given her interest in Skye's messages, but I'd never seen her at a loss for words before. It would have been amusing if it hadn't created a rather delicate atmosphere that I felt I should probably be respectful of.

"Ah, Gracie, this is Skye. I believe you've met briefly once before."

They "hi"-ed each other and Gracie remained motionless in the doorway, her eyes large and glued to mine.

"Come in. Have a seat," I said, and Gracie did, picking up a sleeping Fozzie en route, putting him on her lap and concentrating on stroking his fur in long, deliberate movements.

"Skye just got back into the country last week."

"Oh." Gracie's eyes flicked briefly towards Skye. "Cool," she added into Fozzie's fur.

"You'll be staying for dinner?"

"Huh?" she asked, looking at me like I'd spoken to her in another language.

"I'll take that as a 'yes'."

Thankfully, Skye stepped into Gracie's breach and began asking her questions about herself, which are the easiest kinds of questions to answer, so Gracie performed moderately well. It allowed her to relax and it wasn't long before Gracie and Skye were discussing plans to go rock climbing.

"You guys go, by all means, but just remember you have an elderly aunt who also needs your attention."

"You could come with us, Aunty Nan."

Gracie's shoulders sagged.

"No, for two reasons. One, I don't want to cramp you young things' style, and two, I'm an appallingly bad rock climber, aren't I, Gracie? I would embarrass you, let alone myself."

"Yeah, she's more like a wall donkey than a wall monkey. We'd have to pad her in bubble wrap before we sent her up."

I laughed wryly. "Can you imagine how devastating that would be for the serenity of that place? With my ability to scrape more skin off than a chemical peel clinic, I'd sound like a bunch of fire crackers going off. No, you two go and enjoy yourselves. Just remember me when you get back."

"You've got the shower and the better kitchen, Grey. We won't be forgetting you in a hurry when we come back tired, smelly and hungry."

"I'll accept that meagre ration. I might have to take what I can get."

DECEMBER.

Skye decided to stay and help me get the house ready for sale. Whether it had more to do with spending time with her doting aunt, or more to do with her new-found friendship with Gracie, didn't bother me in the least.

I put her to work painting the exterior of the house while I was away carpentering, and, concerned that The Yam might put people off, she offered to paint that as well.

As the week wore on, Skye tended to disappear across to the bus in the later part of the evenings before coming back to sleep in my loft.

I let them be. Whatever was unfolding was their business. I could see they were both happy.

THE DAY LOT 2 SOLD, I received a text from Angus: **How's Derek?**

It was three weeks since he'd settled with Lou, three weeks since he was in a position to revisit the morning I fled his bed, and this was the first I'd heard from him.

It was possible he'd changed his mind.

It was also possible he was very conscious of timing. That to pursue anything, now that I'd decided to cut and run because of decisions made by his family, might not be well received.

I wanted to reassure him that I understood. But my abject disappointment at the way things had turned out prevented me.

I texted back: **The D bag is gone. Lou helped me.**

I waited several minutes for a response. I wasn't surprised. I wanted Angus to know I wasn't a cray cray. That I'd got help. But learning I'd got it from his ex-partner would, I imagined, require some processing.

Angus: You call him The D bag? :D

Me: Fuckface was already taken by Hanitas ex

Me: Sorry officer *Hanita's*

Angus: I should think so ;) I'm glad you're being kinder to yourself. You deserve to be.

ON THE MORNING of the house cooling, I woke early and watched the mountains shuck the shadows of night and emerge golden in the soft light of dawn.

A movement in the bus caught my eye. The door opened and Skye descended the steps. She walked carefully across the gravel, tip-toed over the deck and slowly slid the door open.

"It's alright, I'm awake."

"Oh. Morning Aunty Nan." When she looked across at me, her face bathed in the brilliance of the new day, she looked heart-achingly beautiful – so young and full of expectation of what life has yet to offer. And love. Her face was full of love. The energy of it radiated from her and I greeted it with joy for her and sadness for myself.

She climbed in bed next to me and tucked herself under my chin, reaching across to stroke Fozzie who was stretched along my other side.

I gasped. "Your feet are freezing!"

She chuckled and I stroked her hair back from

her forehead, kissing it softly. "You look very happy, my love."

She was quiet for a moment. "Is this what it's like? Like, you can't contain it. Like, it wants to burst out of your chest and you have to fight to keep it in."

I sighed. "That's what it's like. It's an interesting beast – wondrous and perplexing and totally overwhelming."

"It's kind of scary."

"That it is, my love. It's always hard to lose control, and emotions can be the most difficult part of us to let go of. And make sense of."

We watched the snow on the peaks gradually change from gold to blue-white under the rising sun.

"Are you going to sort things with Angus?"

I exhaled slowly. "Gracie told you, I suppose."

She nodded against my chest.

"I don't know. Part of me wants to, but I'd have to work through the resentment I have at being put in a situation where I'm giving up my home. It's not an ideal emotion to have hanging over a new relationship."

"Will he be here tonight?"

"He said he would."

"You might know what you want when you see him."

"I might. Let's hope it's the same thing as him."

TWENTY-FOUR
THE ELUSIVE STOCKMAN

THAT AFTERNOON, Skye and I busied ourselves cleaning the house, clearing cobwebs from the exterior, tidying the vegetation around the deck and preparing food.

Even when everything was organised, I found I couldn't stay still and arranged and re-arranged the deck furniture until there was nothing left to fuss over.

Out of desperation, I grabbed my ladder and climbed onto the roof to clear out the gutters, knowing that it was highly unlikely that a) any detritus would have accumulated yet and b) the guests would be interested in inspecting the state of them. The view, however, was spectacular.

I called Skye to come and join me.

She came out of the house, looked up at me and laughed. "What on earth are you doing up there?"

"Well, I have, to coin Margot, an arse-load of nervous energy at the moment and it occurred to me that this would be an excellent way to relieve some of it. Grab a couple of glasses of wine and pass them up. We can watch the clouds chase each other over the mountains."

Gracie arrived home from work shortly afterwards and joined us sitting precariously on the steep pitch of the roof surveying the new, more extensive view.

The three of us were still up there when the first of the guests arrived.

Margot got out of her car, spotted us and said, "Oooh, that's a jolly good idea. Let me make myself a G and T and I'll come and join you."

"Ah, I think it's time we came down, Margot," I called to her. "I'd probably be a better host at ground level, considering that's where all the guests will be."

"Don't you patronise an old woman. I've climbed many a thing in my time – Ben Nevis, the flagpole outside the parliament buildings during the Vietnam War, and Roger Moore."

"You shagged Roger Moore?"

"I had a bloody good time with some famous cleft-chinned actor. It could have been Roger Moore."

I laughed and shook my head. "Look, I'm sure you're very capable, Margot, but I'm going to put the ladder away anyway. I think it's safer for everybody, not just you."

I received a tut in reply and she disappeared into the house to make her drink.

Andre, Niamh and Terence arrived soon after with Andre's parents in the car behind. They would stay to enjoy the gathering for as long as Terence could manage, then take him back to theirs for the night, leaving Andre and Niamh to enjoy the rest of the party.

Martin and Anoushka turned up with their sons, and Barbara and her new boyfriend, Matiu, joined us a little later. She gave me a kōwhai seedling for my next home. "Help you establish roots. Find a place you feel you belong and plant it. Nothing will shift you."

Stu and Mona arrived with a carved wooden cow standing upright in a pair of gumboots.

"These are really on-trend at the moment," Mona said as she handed it over. "You can get a matching set of three in different sizes, so I've included the card of the shop I bought it from if you want to go back and get the rest."

"Thanks. You really didn't need to get me a gift." I hoped my smile came across as less of a grimace.

"Of course, I did, babe. A going away present. It's what you do." She leaned over and lowered her voice. "Deserting and leaving us in the shit. *Thank you,* Nancy."

I closed my eyes in mock-graciousness and said, "Mona, you are *so* welcome," and turned my back on her to place the cow on the centre of the outdoor table. It would be its first and last showing. I wondered how I could smuggle it back into her car before she left.

Still there was no Angus.

When Liz and Rob showed up, they asked if they could speak to me in private.

There was nowhere nearby that would allow us to talk in seclusion apart from the bus, so I led the way and invited them to sit at the small table, not caring whether Gracie had left the bus tidy or not. I didn't need or want an awkward conversation about how they felt they had pushed me out and were sorry I'd made the decision to go.

But that wasn't what they'd come to say.

Rob cleared his throat. "Lot 4's sold."

I shouldn't have cared now that I'd decided to move on, but the news bought home with finality all I was giving up – a new start in a place I'd loved and worked hard to make mine. I buried my head in my hands and let my tears spill into them.

"Nancy," Liz's warm hand rested on my shoulder. "Honey, it's good news. There's more to tell. We covenanted it."

I looked up. "You did?"

"We did. The buyer has to use your house design. The first three lots sold so much quicker than we ever expected. Whether it's the start of a trend to leave the city once insurance claims have been settled, I don't know, but it's put us in a position to make demands of whoever wanted it."

Rob said, "As title's yet to be granted, we could make that change."

Liz reached out and held my hand. "Don't sell. We want you to be happy here." She gripped my hand more firmly and gave it a small shake. "Please be our neighbour."

I RAPPED a spoon on my glass and when I'd got everyone's attention, said, "I've just heard some very good news and now I'd like to give you all some."

At the back of the small gathering, Skye's eyes shone with expectation.

"I've decided that this is a house warming party after all."

Gracie whooped and in the clamour of following comments I struggled to raise my voice enough to explain.

Anoushka pulled me into the first of a succession of hugs.

Once glasses had been clinked and the excitement had settled, I went inside to retrieve more canapés.

When I turned around, plate in each hand, there he was.

Angus stood in the doorway, a smile tugging at the edges of his mouth, his two top buttons undone.

"Sorry I'm late."

I couldn't have replied if I'd tried. A tingling emanating from my stomach vibrated through my body and rooted me to the spot.

From behind me, Skye's offer to take the plates outside pulled my attention, and when I looked from her back to where Angus stood, he was leaving, having been called away by Andre to admire something about the house's exterior.

He cast an apologetic glance over his shoulder before he disappeared around the side of the house.

Rob came to stand in the spot Angus had just vacated. "How those sheep getting on?"

"Ah." I had to prise my brain from Angus before I could compute his question. "Good. They're not trying to escape now they're shorn and don't have a protective layer between their skin and the electric fence."

Martin said, "You should put a studded collar on each of them, so when they try to push through the fence, they're forced to have another think."

I smiled at the image. "Nice idea. I'm not sure sheep would make very good punks, though."

"I don't know. Joey *Ramo*ne could be a good name for a sheep with punk tendencies."

"Ew, that is one lame-arse dad joke," said Martin's teenage son, Lucas, coming up behind him and giving him a push with his shoulder. "You're such an embarrassment. Can I have a beer?"

"How old are you?"

"Aw, Dad, are we going to do this again?"

"Yes, until you remember that the legal age for drinking is eighteen, we're going to run through this script for another – how many years?"

"Twenty at this rate," Lucas replied sulkily. He turned on his heel. "I'll go ask Mum."

"He won't get very far with her, but this is all just a farce, really. Inevitably, the boys will end up stealing some bottles when no one's looking. We'll know because they'll both have mysteriously disappeared. I've brought my spotlight so I can hunt them down and peel them off the grass when we're ready to go."

Angus came back into view and was grabbed by Anoushka for a hug of greeting. He looked at me over her shoulder before his attention was forced back to her, his eyes flicking back to me while they talked.

The timer on the oven went off and I turned around to pull out its contents and plate them up.

When I brought them outside, Angus had vanished again. I turned in a circle and spotted him walking back from his ute with a bottle of sparkling wine in his hand. He cleared the steps up to the deck in a single leap and presented me with the wine.

"Hey," he smiled. "I hear you're sticking around. I brought this along just in case."

I opened my mouth and was stopped before I could form any word by a panicked, "Nancy, something's burning!" Handing Angus back his wine, I rushed inside to find smoke issuing from the oven.

I opened the door and stood back to wait for the worst of it to clear. One of the spring rolls had rolled off the tray and was being char-grilled on the element I had forgotten to turn off. Swearing, I removed the offending food item, turned the extractor fan on to max and flapped around a tea towel in the vague direction of the closest window.

When order was restored, I went in desperate search of my wine glass and the love of my life.

The glass proved easier to locate.

I asked Niamh if she had seen Angus and was directed to the side of the deck. I peered over the metre or so drop to see a stooped-over Angus being led by a gabbling Terence towards something of acute nearly-three-year-old interest.

As they passed me, Angus reached up and gently squeezed my calf before disappearing around the deck's corner.

I issued my seventh sigh of the evening.

By the time Angus and I were in close quarters again, our urgency to communicate had increased somewhat. He stood very close to me, his body blocking any would-be conversationalists. "I really want to talk to you. Alone."

Behind him, Margot attempted to climb the near

vertical ladder up to the loft with a drink in one hand and a smoked fish vol-au-vent in the other.

"Oh Lord," I muttered and brushed past him to stand beneath her with my arms held up in preparation for imminent disaster. "Margot, it might be easier with full use of your fingers. Pass your drink and the vol-au-vent to me. You can have them when you come down."

"How about I pass them to you, you hold them while I climb the ladder, then you pass them back up to me. Then I can enjoy looking down on you all while quaffing caviar."

"It's just fish."

"Close enough."

"Are you drunk?"

"Quite possibly, my girl."

I sighed. "Okay, that's fine. Just please, please be careful."

By the time Margot had positioned herself and received her food and wine back, Angus had been drawn into conversation with Martin.

I silently wished everyone but the two of us would spontaneously combust.

MONA AND STU had to head away early to another function, and when they had gone an impromptu game of target practice broke out. With the cow.

The ammunition of choice was olive pits, provided by the spittoon next to the olive bowl. The game rapidly progressed in difficulty to a moving target. Martin dropped below the deck, balancing the cow on his head so that it appeared to move of its own accord from one side of the deck to the other.

When the olives were exhausted and an empty beer bottle was thrown, knocking the cow off Martin's head to the response of wild cheers, someone grabbed my hand and pulled me in the opposite direction of the group.

Angus led me down the driveway towards his ute and invited me inside.

As soon as the doors were closed, he locked them and sighed. "No more bloody interruptions. I'm not unlocking this door for anybody."

I sat mutely looking at him, my breathing loud as if I'd run the distance between my house and his truck.

He gazed back at me, his frown fading and the corners of his mouth twitching as if trying to decide if a smile was what I needed. Finally, he let out an expulsion of air. "Well, hell of a last few months."

I agreed.

"I don't ever want to ride that rollercoaster again."

"No, the view from the top was nice while it lasted, but the rest of the ride was a bit shit."

He took my hands and moved his thumbs over the back of them. "So" – that tiny but potent word –

"remember how I asked if there was a possibility we could revisit that morning you ran away from my bed, once my...complications were resolved?"

The squeal of my inner fox lowered to a full-throated roar. "Yes."

"And remember how you said you didn't know, because I was a chauvinistic dinosaur?"

"I'm not sure I put it quite like that, but, yes, I remember."

"Well, there's something I've been desperately wanting to find out for the last couple of weeks. Do you know now?"

I didn't hesitate. "Yes."

"And?"

"And," I took a deep breath. "I think you know why I ran away that morning." I moved my eyes from our hands to his face, "I realised I was in love with you. And I freaked out. It wasn't what I wanted. But I want it now, Angus, I really do."

Angus considered me for a moment then broke into a wide smile. The kind that creases your cheeks all the way to your ears.

He reached out to pull me forward into a soft kiss. "Well, that's a relief, Nancy-pants," he whispered into my lips. "Because..." He kissed me again, then moved back to look me in the eyes. "I love you, too. You disappearing off that morning gave me a hell of a fright. It forced me to confront stuff that had been developing for some time that I'd been trying not to pay attention to. Attempting to make things simpler by not having you around only made it more obvious how deep my feelings for you were. But I'm glad you made me work for it. It made me a better person."

"You were already a good person. How much did you have to do with getting that covenant placed?"

Angus' mouth twitched again. "I might have done some loud reminding as soon as Lot 3 sold."

"See? Not too far from perfect." I grabbed his collar and pulled him into a kiss that left us gasping for air.

"So," I said, lacing my fingers with his. "Are you like my boyfriend or something?"

"Good idea. Let's formalise things so there's no more confusion." He looked at me with an acute level of sincerity. "Nancy Myers, will you forego predating on other young men and do me the honour of being *my* silver fox?"

"Yes, Angus, I will. As long as you promise to wear shorts for the rest of your life."

"Even when I'm eighty and my knee skin is slapping against my ankles?"

I pressed my forehead against his. "Especially when your knee skin is slapping against your ankles."

Angus sat back. "Of course, it's not a real relationship until we've declared it on Facebook."

"Oh shit, I didn't bring my phone with me."

"Ah well, we'll just have to live in social media

sin." He leaned forward to deliver another soft-lipped kiss.

WHEN WE EVENTUALLY ARRIVED BACK AT the house, hand in hand, the cow had somehow managed to set itself on fire and several people were roasting marshmallows off it.

I groaned. "Where did the marshmallows come from?"

Gracie answered through a mouthful of molten mallow. "I had a bag in the bus. Seemed a fitting end to such a tragic ornament."

"Why am I not surprised you're the ring leader, Gracie?"

Inside the house, Margot was fast asleep in the loft, and Martin, Niamh and Barbara were playing Jenga with the leftover finger food.

I turned to Angus. "Shall we stage an escape?"

He grinned and nodded.

"Skye," I called on my way past the flaming cow, "you're in charge. Make sure the house doesn't burn down and that Fozzie's okay. Margot's on your bed, so use mine if you want."

"Where are you two going?" Gracie called back. "Oh!" She elbowed Skye. "Nice work, G Dog. Take your time. Skye and I can manage the property for the next week or so."

"I'll be seeing you tomorrow, Gracie. And my house better be in one piece."

WHEN I WOKE up the next morning to find Angus watching me, and that rush of emotion flooded my chest, I knew that when I reached out to run a hand down his cheek, there would be no surprises and no disappointments.

"Do you think, Angus Russell Stockman, you can have a girlfriend who wants to remain on the other side of the fence?"

"Nance, it would be a huge bloody relief."

And this time, when I found my hand enclosed in his, I stayed right where I was.

THANKS FOR TAKING THE TIME
TO READ MY BOOK

My books are a complete labour of love, so I hope you enjoyed it. Please consider reviewing *The Year of the Fox* (it only needs to be a line or two). As an independent author, reviews help support my work by allowing more readers to discover me, which means I can produce more great novels for you to read. If you're not sure where to post a review, try the Goodreads website or your favourite online bookstore.

THE YEAR OF THE FOX BONUS CHAPTER

Join my Readers' Group monthly newsletter and get an **exclusive bonus chapter**, *THE JUMP: a Margot's Bucket List Adventure.*

Join Nancy, Margot and Gracie on their latest

mad-cap adventure by using this link: https://Book Hip.com/MVVFMQ

Already a member of my Readers' Group? No worries - you can still get the bonus chapter by using the above link.

You can unsubscribe at any time.

ACKNOWLEDGMENTS

A big thanks first and foremost to Dave Hill and family for encouraging me to write these stories down. This book would not exist without your emphatic suggestion that I record my tales for others to enjoy. Thanks to my first listeners, who gave me the confidence to keep going with the project: the Richards family, Epoña Keller, and Mum and Dad, my biggest fans.

Thank you to my beautiful cousin, Marisa Crockford, for her legal advice (which I took some fictional liberties with). You are one foxy 40-year-old. I owe thanks to Valerie Lubrick for imparting her knowledge of rock climbing with enthusiasm and artistic flair. Thanks Sarah Johnson and Amy Andrews for making me a better writer, and thanks to my editor, Sara Johnson, for your enthusiasm about my work.

My brothers, Mathew and Steven, helped me brainstorm (with much hilarity) titles for the book when I was at a complete loss. *Fence and Fencibility, Fresh Pastures – Dirty Knickers,* and *Country Pork* were high on the list of "most amusing, but least appropriate" titles. Both my brothers are older than me.

To various family members, friends, chickens, sheep and manta rays for directly and indirectly providing the odd bit of book material – your contributions have been very valuable.

ABOUT THE AUTHOR

Merren Tait writes quirky and irreverent romantic comedy about empowered women, and her books have earned a reputation for living up to the laugh-out-loud promise of the genre. *The Year of the Fox*, her first novel, has been optioned for television.

Merren has lived a series of bookish lives. Her first incarnation was as a book-hungry child, then as a mildly pretentious English literature student. Her third life saw her teaching English to somewhat-willing high school students, and her fourth, sharing her love of books as a librarian. Now she has been reincarnated as a fiction creator.

She is of Scottish, Ngāti Apa ki te Rā Tō, English,

Irish and German extraction and attributes her cross-cultural comedic flair to the enthusiastic inter-breeding of her ancestors.

Merren lives in a small house on a large piece of land near Raglan, New Zealand, where she dreams up fabulous names for her chickens, like Princess Layer.

www.ingramcontent.com/pod-product-compliance
Lightning Source LLC
Chambersburg PA
CBHW030827110726
47900CB00006B/1779